MURDER AT LOUGHFARRAIG HOUSE

Alex Cardo

Contents

01. Mustelus 5

02. Loughfarraig House 9

03. Dinner 14

04. A Scheme 20

05. Christmas Day 24

06. The Body In The Lake 28

07. The Storm 35

08. Sirens 38

09. Muldoon Arrives 42

10. The Solicitor's Office 48

11. Interviews 52

12. A Surprise 55

13. The Letter 59

14. The Fixer 62

15. The American 70

16. The Will 75

17. Emma's Story 79

18. The Billiard Room 85

19. Victims 92

20. The Journalist 98

21. Scandal? 106

22. Disappearance and Collapse 112

23. Back in Briarstown 119

24. Unanswered Questions 122

25. Body on the Beach 134

26. Not So Solid Alibis! 140

27. "Te Amo" And The Vicissitudes Of Man 145

28. 12th January... 149

29. A Break In The Case. 155

30. Sociopathy 163

31. The Keyring 170

32. Winnie Pours Tea 175

33. Miguel..180

34. Sustenance 186

35. Where Can It Be? 191

36. New Beginnings 196

37. The Second Article...................................... 201

38. An Unforeseen Development 204

39. A Close Call 210

40. The Doctor And The Mystery........................... 217

41. Liaisons 221

42. Revelations 228

43. News From Bogota...................................... 238

44. An Engagement 242

45. The Letter.. 247

46. Untangling The Web 250

47. Proteus 263

CHAPTER 01

MUSTELUS

In early December, Donal Hawke arrived at the office of Kelly and Son, Solicitors, in Galway City. When he arrived into the front office, Miss Henry was sitting at her desk, typing a letter. She is a slim young woman of about thirty, who wears glasses and her hair tied back in a neat bun. She is dressed in a navy pencil skirt, white blouse and navy jacket with a gold lapel pin as usual. She looks up from her typewriter as the door opens, sees the client enter the room and stands up to greet him.

"Good morning, Mr. Hawke," she says in a chirpy voice.

"Good morning, Miss Henry," replies Donal Hawke.

"Please go into the office. Mr. Kelly is expecting you."

Donal Hawke is a very tall, towering man in his mid seventies. He has a shock of unruly blond hair, and always has a scowl on his face. His thick, shaggy eyebrows make his small eyes look menacing. He is somewhat overweight, and walks in a lumbering fashion, which makes him appear even more threatening. Some have even likened his gait to that of an alpha gorilla, aggressively patrolling his territory.

Donal Hawke is obviously a man who likes to be in charge. He walks towards the office, does not knock, and walks straight into the room.

"Lovely to see you, Mr. Hawke, please take a seat," said Jonathan Kelly from behind an oak desk.

"What the hell are you doing here? I was supposed to meet your father," replied Donal Hawke.

"He is indisposed at the moment and asked me to take the meeting."

"Indisposed?" said Hawke, raising his voice slightly. "This isn't good enough, What's wrong with him?"

"He has a stomach bug and just couldn't get out of bed this morning," replied Kelly, more meekly. " I'm sure I can help you."

"Maybe you could get the ball rolling, I suppose."

Donal Hawke sat down on the comfortable armchair in front of the desk, while Jonathan Kelly sat behind the desk, feeling a little chastised and not quite as sure of himself.

"Your father has been my solicitor here in Galway for forty years. My will is here in the office. I intend making changes to my will and also to the way my businesses are managed."

Jonathan sat quietly in the chair.

"Well, young man, start taking notes."

Jonathan looked across the desk at this beady eyed, bullying man. "He always was the same," he thought to himself. Donal Hawke and his father Jonathan Senior had been friends for years. The children were always wary of this big brute. Jonathan had been in boarding school with the Hawke boys and he had remained friends with David, the eldest boy.

"Concentrate, Jonathan," barked Hawke.

Jonathan straightened in his chair and felt as if he were back in the Principal's office receiving an admonishment for some infraction of a school rule.

"I know that you're still hanging out with my useless son David, but keep in mind that you're my solicitor and I don't need to tell you that not a word of this is to get back to my family."

"That goes without saying, Mr. Hawke," replied Jonathan.

"OK then," said Hawke. "I need this office to draw up several documents for my perusal and signature. When you do your homework, you will realise that I have total control over every element of my portfolio. My offspring at the moment are in charge of various arms of the business, but I can revoke that whenever I want to. I also want to change my will. I am fed up with my family leeching off me. Some of my businesses are loosing money because of their ineptitude. My ex-wife is still hanging around and managing to get through her very generous settlement and allowance with alacrity. The present Mrs. Hawke also has expensive tastes. Your father will know what to do."

"My father wanted me to ask you about the other business – you know – the illegitimate child in England. He would like to know if you wish to continue to contest the veracity of the claim, or make a settlement?"

"I've had private detectives looking into it – I may wish to change my will in the child's favour."

"You'd want to be very careful there, Mr. Hawke. Why were you only contacted recently, after so many years? I don't think David and the others will be pleased with this development either."

"Listen, laddie, you do your job. I don't want your opinion – I didn't ask for it. I built up my portfolio from scratch. I'll do what I want with it. I'll leave it to whomsoever I wish."

"I just think as your solicitor, it behoves me...."

"It behoves you, – my foot – I've known you all your life – I've no more respect for you than I have for my own offspring. Let me make this very clear. You are not my solicitor. Your father is the only person in this office who represents me. So your father will handle this. You have my instructions. Kindly pass them on to him. I hope he's better soon."

"Would you like me to make an appointment to see him next week, Mr. Hawke?"

"Not possible, I'm afraid. I'm away in London and then in New York. I will make an appointment for the 8th January. I will only see your father on that date."

"Are your family to be made aware of the impending changes?" asked Kelly.

"Firstly, as I've already made clear, you are to say nothing to my son, David. I intend taking the whole family away, for ten days over the Christmas. I will break the good news to them over the holidays."

Jonathan Kelly noticed a slight grin on the normally grumpy face of Donal Hawke.

"That's it then Jonathan," added Hawke as he lifted his heavy frame up from the chair, straightened his jacket and proffered his hand to Jonathan Kelly. Both men shook hands and Donal Hawke left the room, leaving Kelly somewhat shocked at what he had just heard.

Jonathan and David were very good friends. Boarding school had been very tough on both of them. Neither of the boys were any good at rugby so they didn't really fit in. Neither had been academically gifted either, so life was not pleasant in an all-boys, rugby school where many of the students were destined for great things. However, they found each other, and despite many scrapes and visits to the Principal's office, and threats of expulsion, they managed to last the five years. After many repeat exams, Jonathan finally passed his law exams, and went into his father's practice. University was not for David, so he went straight into the Hawke empire. In the intervening years, they were travelling buddies – horse racing, dog racing, Vegas, the best restaurants and hotels. They both married ladies who would be deemed "high maintenance" and so they continued to enjoy the high life.

Jonathan stood behind his desk, contemplating what he should do. He knew that David's life would be ruined if his father cut him off. He also didn't believe that some illegitimate child should swoop in and get a share of millions. He obviously wasn't a great fan of solicitor client confidentiality. He picked up the receiver and dialled a number he knew by heart.

"David, it's Jonathan."

CHAPTER 02

LOUGHFARRAIG HOUSE

"Hurry up children, we really need to get on the road, there's a likelihood of snow today."

The three teenagers, Alice, Maeve and Max de Bruin were busy packing their cases for the ten day Christmas holiday in the west of Ireland.

"Nearly ready Mam," answered Alice, the eldest of the three.

"Where's Dad?" asked Max, as he carried his belongings down the hallway and towards the front door.

"He's over with the Brownes, just delivering Zeus and Cleopatra."

Zeus and Cleopatra were their two beloved Bernese mountain dogs. They were going to spend the next ten days with the Browne family, who were the immediate neighbours of the de Bruin's. They lived in the Old Rectory, which was a beautiful red bricked, two storey house that dated back to the nineteenth century. The two families always looked after each other's ponies, horses, dogs and cats during holidays.

Monique de Bruin looked out the front window, hoping to see her husband Alex walking down the avenue towards the house. Snow flakes were beginning to fall. He reached the front door of The Lodge which Monique threw open.

"We really need to get a move on Alex," said Monique.

Ten minutes later the family were driving out the gate and waving goodbye to Briarstown, looking forward to their holidays at Loughfarraig House in Mayo.

The children were very excited as they were very much anticipating a wonderful holiday with their friends, the Kings.

The de Bruins and Kings were great friends since their time living in army quarters in the Curragh Camp. Colonel Robert King was still a serving officer and had just returned from a deployment to the Middle East. Commandant de Bruin had retired from the army a few years previously and was now working with his wife, mostly from his beautiful house in Briarstown in North Kildare.

"Look Dad, you can see our old house," said Max excitedly, as they passed through the Curragh Plains.

The snow had turned to sleet, so Monique was hopeful that the journey would be uneventful. After Monasterevan, Alex turned right towards Portarlington. The road was dangerous and winding, and the landscape became bleaker as they travelled west. They had left the rich, green pastures of Kildare and were moving steadily into boggier terrain. The three children were quietly reading their books en route. Alice's English teacher had given the class a Christmas assignment. They were all to read "To Kill a Mockingbird" over the Christmas holidays. Monique always loved that book since she had read it herself as a teenager. Following discussions with Alice about it's contents, Maeve and Max also wanted to read it. So, two more copies were purchased and now, on their way to the west, the three teenagers were engrossed in Harper Lee's wonderful masterpiece. Monique had promised that, once the book was read by all, she would rent out the film version, starring Gregory Peck as Atticus Finch. She had purchased a VCR player a few years previously and it was still going strong.

The journey from Briarstown to Loughfarraig House took four hours usually, but today because of the weather, it would take longer.

Finally they reached Castlebar and then on towards Westport. As they passed through Westport, the children knew that they were nearly at their destination. They put down their books and with heart in mouth, began staring out the windows. Alex took a road that the children said leads nowhere except to their beloved Loughfarraig House. The car trundled along for five miles into the wilderness. Then suddenly, they spied the two white pillars. They drove between the pillars and down the long, winding avenue. Some of the Copper Beech still held onto their brown leaves. The Rhodedendron bushes still looked lush. On the right hand side they passed the vegetable garden and the little woodland. Then they saw, coming into view, the beautiful fresh water lake with it's tiny jetty. On the shore beside the lake sat small rowing boats, upside down because of the rain. In the woods by the lake, the trees are devoid of leaves and their skeletal branches rise beseechingly and imploringly towards the sky, like strange creatures from the Netherworld of Hades in Homer's Iliad.

"Dad, Dad, do you think we'll be allowed to take the boats out on the lake?" Max asked, interrupting their quiet thoughts.

"I don't see why not," answered Alexander, "As long as the lake is fairly calm, and you wear your lifejackets."

The sleet had now turned to rain. The windscreen wipers move from side to side as the raindrops pitter-patter on the windscreen.

The old house comes into view, this old, long, grey house covered in ivy with all it's history.

"Wow. it never changes," said Maeve. "It's like we've gone back in history."

Alexander parked the car opposite the house. They all sat quietly for a few minutes contemplating the great beauty and solitude of Loughfarraig House, which had been destroyed and rebuilt, burned to the ground during the War of Independence, and like a Phoenix rose again out of the ashes.

The family usually went for a stroll to see the magnificent Atlantic Ocean, where every time they stood in awe at it's strength and beauty. But today, the rain was still falling heavily and the wind was picking up.

"We'll go straight into the hotel," said Monique. "When it clears up a bit, we can go down to the sea."

"When are the others arriving?" asked Max.

"They'll be a few hours behind us. Robert had to go into the Curragh for a few hours this morning. Be patient, Max, we have ten days here. We are so lucky."

"As long as Dad doesn't have a murder to solve again!" laughed Maeve.

"It's not a laughing matter," interjected Monique.

"It's like he's a murder magnet," joked Max. "Even when we leave the country, something happens."

"Let's hope that we have an uneventful ten days of fun and relaxation," said Monique.

"OK, we are going to just run into the house. We'll take in our bags later when the rain eases," suggested Alex.

The whole family jumped out of the car and managed to get to the front door without getting drenched. Alexander opened the big wooden door with the brass latch. This led to the porch with it's umbrella stand and brass coat hooks. They enter the lobby from the porch, which is really a large sitting room with an old wooden oak polished floor with colourful rugs beside the two fireplaces – one on either side. The old stone fireplaces have a wooden mantelpiece with red brick surround. Atop the mantlepieces hung green garlands with white lights, cones and robins and gold painted leaves, and in the hearths the turf fire warmed the room, the flames dancing and sparkling. The smell of smouldering peat wafted through the air. Straight in front of the entrance was the wooden staircase and underneath it a Christmas tree dressed in white twinkling lights, red baubles and ribbons with a spider web of gauze enveloping it to give it an air of ghostliness.

The red and white Christmas stockings hung on either end of the mantlepieces, waiting for Santa to fill them with goodies. Green wreaths hung on every door, a magnificent garland with red berries and pine cones was wrapped around the banister of the wooden staircase, leading to the bedrooms.

Greeting the guests as they entered Loughfarraig house was a punch bowl of mulled wine for the adults and a bowl of fruit punch for the children.

Alex and the children sat down on the comfortable armchairs in front of the turf fire, while Monique walked up to the reception to check in. Their rooms were not yet ready and the Kings had not yet arrived.

"Take a seat Mrs. de Bruin and the waiter will serve afternoon tea by the fire," said the young lady with long brown hair and mellow Mayo accent. Five minutes later the young waiter appeared with their tea and freshly baked scones and local jams and honey. They were all sipping their punch when afternoon tea was served.

"I haven't seen you here before," said Monique.

"No, I arrived in September from Colombia. I worked in Spain for a year before here. My name is Juan."

"I hope you are enjoying Ireland Juan," said Monique.

"Yes, everyone is very kind to me here. I miss my home sometimes, especially my girlfriend. I am saving my money so that she can come here too."

"I hope that it all works out for you," said Alex.

A half an hour later, having finished their afternoon tea, the family wrapped up well and walked to the back of the house towards the sea. It had stopped raining, but it was still very blustery. They stood in awe looking out at the powerful Atlantic. The waves were magnificent, breaking on the shore. The cold wind stung their faces. They turned left and walked onto the golf course. There had been some damage to it during the last storm. Three boulders had been flung onto the edge of the course by powerful waves.

"How puny we all are in the face of nature," thought Monique.

Suddenly Max noticed the Kings walking towards them.

"They're here," he shouted excitedly as he ran to greet them.

The two families waved at each other.

They all embraced and headed back to the warmth of the turf fires.

"Your rooms are all ready," said Jenny from reception and handed Monique all the keys with wooden rings engraved with the room numbers.

"Can the boys have one room and the girls the other?" asked Max.

"I don't see why not," answered Monique.

The five teenagers were delighted.

"I think we should all breakfast together and then you kids are free to have lunch together, and perhaps dine together in the evening at six thirty. That will give you the rest of the evenings to hang out and play games in the Rec room."

"That's a great idea Mam," answered Alice.

Twenty minutes later everyone had unpacked and were settled in their rooms, looking forward to a wonderful Christmas.

CHAPTER 03

DINNER

"How was your deployment this time Robert?" asked Alexander as he poured wine at dinner.

"Thankfully, there were no major incidents – it was all rather smooth. Everyone got home in one piece," replied Robert.

"You'll have to tell us about your experience in Switzerland," said Alison. "We really haven't had time to have a good catch up since we got back from the Middle East."

"Well, as you've probably heard it was a bit of a disaster," replied Monique.

"Do tell all," retorted Alison.

"During the murder case at Briarstown, which you know was eventually solved by Alexander and Inspector Muldoon, with a great deal of help from you Robert, and our next door neighbour Damien, we received an invitation to visit my Aunt Amelie in Montana Crans in Switzerland. She had given us a choice to either visit that summer or at Christmas. As Alex did not know when the murders would be solved, we decided on Christmas. We also thought that it would be a wonderful opportunity for the children to go skiing. As you know she was a very wealthy widow and a really horribly selfish, manipulating person. We are also very grateful that you looked after our place for the first week, before you had to leave for the Middle East."

"It was our pleasure," replied Robert. "It was wonderful that Damien Browne took over from us when you were delayed and we had to leave."

"Please continue," urged Alison.

"The first few days in Switzerland were quite wonderful, The children went skiing for hours each day. Amelie was in quite good form for a change. Her long suffering companion was as patient as ever. As you know Amelie was a dreadful snob, and married her two daughters off to two minor Italian aristocrats. The two daughters and their husbands arrived unexpectedly on the 27th December. Amelie's mood changed for the worse and the tension rose. Trying to make polite conversation at the dinner table was painful. We started looking forward to going home and even the children could sense that there was something up. As you know, we were due to fly home on the thirtieth. On the night of the 29th Aunt Amelie died. Her companion found her the next morning, dead in the bed. The doctor was called, who became suspicious as she had been in rude health. He contacted the Swiss police who arrived to question everyone. She had been poisoned. Needless to say we were all suspects. It was very difficult dealing with the Swiss police. They seemed to be more suspicious of us because we were from Ireland. They showed a lot of deference of course to the two Italian aristocrats and my cousins as they have Swiss citizenship. They were downright rude to us and dismissed Alex's offer of help. I even explained to them in French about his intelligence work in the past and his experience with helping the Irish police. It looked to us as if they really wanted to pin this on Alex. We were asked to remain in the chalet with the others. That's when we contacted Damien Browne to ask him to look after the horses and dogs in Briarstown. We knew that you would have to leave, and prepare for deployment on the 31st.

Of course Alex wasn't just going to wait around and be a scapegoat, so he contacted his army pals in France and the Gendarmes, with whom he had worked while he himself was in France. They were quite marvellous. They knew that neither of us had committed the murder, so then it was either the companion, one of the other servants, one of the daughters or one of the Italian husbands. Two days later they contacted Alex with lots of information about her will, everyone's financial status. Of course Amelie had left nearly all her wealth to her two daughters with provision for her companion and other servants. Low and behold, but one of the husbands was in great financial trouble. He had debts in several countries. Interpol was now involved and when all this new information reached the Swiss police, they began to change tack and investigate properly. Their attitude towards Alex changed and they even asked for his assistance.

It appears that Aunt Amelie had become aware of her son-in-law's financial troubles. She was none too pleased, and had made up her mind to cut him off.

We had witnessed an altercation between them on the evening of the 27th. Perhaps he had asked her for money and she had refused him – that we'll probably never know. Seemingly he poisoned her hot chocolate which she drank every night before retiring."

"These things keep happening to you," interjected Alison.

"Hopefully not during these holidays," added Monique. "Although Max made the comment in the car that Alex was a murder magnet."

The four friends laughed, raised their wine glasses and toasted to an uneventful few days.

Fifteen minutes later, as the two couples were enjoying their main courses, a great kerfuffle was in motion at the entrance to the dining room. The maitre d' rushed over to the entrance. Several waiters headed to the long table to the right of the dining room. It was obvious to the other diners that some V.I.P. was present.

The maitre d', menus and wine lists in hand, showed a party of eight people to the long table. The group was headed by a very tall, severe looking man in his seventies, behind him was a blond woman in her early forties. There were three other couples, a teenager and a woman in her seventies, carrying a large gin and tonic, who looked slightly worse for wear and somewhat unsteady on her feet.

The maitre d' organised his staff with great aplomb. The man in charge took his seat at the top of the table. The waiters dutifully held back the chairs so that the ladies could take their places. The woman in her seventies took her seat at the opposite end of the long table.

The blond lady sat beside the man in charge. The other diners had watched the spectacle with interest but were trying to remain discreet. The new arrivals perused the menus and wine lists in silence. Suddenly one of the other men at the table clicked his fingers at one of the waiters. This did not go unnoticed in the room.

"How rude," said Alison. "Who on earth are they?"

"I don't know," answered Monique. "Despite all their apparent wealth and status, there seems to be an obvious lack of manners."

"Manners maketh man," interjected Alison.

The two couples observed the party, where everyone was dressed in extremely expensive attire and the ladies were "dripping" in gold and diamonds.

"I know who they are," said Alexander suddenly. The other three looked at him in anticipation. Alexander took another bite of his salmon and had a sip of wine.

"Don't keep us in suspense," said Monique.

"The head honcho is Donal Hawke, the CEO of Mustelus Developments. It's an extremely powerful and successful company – worth millions. He's one of the wealthiest men in the world. I read an article about him in a magazine about a month ago, but he had been in the media before that."

"How did he make his money?" asked Alison.

"He's originally from Galway somewhere, but emigrated to England in the early 50's. Rumour has it that he was dodgy from the beginning. He was involved with gangsters in the East End of London and got his start-up money from some of them. He started, as a lot of Irish did, on the building sites, got his injection of cash, became a developer and it just got bigger and bigger from there. He now has a huge development company, a chain of hotels, and a portfolio of rental accommodation. He has interests in Ireland, America and Britain. His eldest son David looks after the British side of things, the youngest son Jack, the American interests and the only daughter Joanne, the Irish businesses.

The lady at the end of the table is his first wife, Winnie. They were married in the 40's before he ever went to London. She is the mother of his three children. He divorced her two years ago to marry his second wife Natalia – that's the blond lady sitting beside him."

"That's a strange kind of set-up – to have your two wives at the same table, celebrating Christmas together – must make for very stressful conversations," added Alison.

They all took a sneaky look at the elderly lady at the end of the table, sipping copious amounts of both gin and wine. She really didn't come across as a happy camper.

The teenage boy who looked about fourteen was sulkily playing with his soup. There certainly didn't seem to be much sign of a convivial conversation at the table.

"So, you said that he was in the media before, what was that all about?" asked Monique.

"Well, Donal Hawke has a lot of rental accommodation. Unfortunately, it appears that he is a slum landlord. There was a dreadful accident somewhere in Birmingham, in one of his block of flats. A young child was killed when the balcony gave way. Hawke was being sued for negligence. There were also other cases of tenants suing him for various reasons – he doesn't appear to maintain the properties correctly but charges exorbitant rents. He has these type of properties in Dublin, Galway and Limerick as well."

"That's dreadful! I wonder will he ever get his comeuppance?" added Monique.

"Some of these types who run roughshod over everyone seem to be able to get away with anything. They have no moral compass, and just don't have any empathy for others," said Robert.

"A bit like your first case, Alexander, with Inspector Muldoon," interjected Monique.

"Yes, but there was a comeuppance in that case," said Alison.

"Indeed, but the innocent also suffered," continued Robert.

The two couples sat silently for a few moments, thinking of the awful occurrences in Briarstown, – that beautiful tranquil townland in North Kildare, where the de Bruins live with their dogs and horses – now nearly two years ago.

"Let's not dwell on those sad times now," said Monique. "It's Christmas and we have so much to look forward to in this beautiful place."

"Yes, indeed," answered Alison. "The children have settled in well. Ellen told me that they had a lovely dinner. They are down in the Rec room. They are all looking forward to taking the ponies for a ride along the beach tomorrow. They are determined to go hail, rain or snow."

There was a bit of commotion at the long table as the first Mrs. Hawke spilled her wine all over the white linen table cloth. One of the waitresses rushed over to try to clean up the mess. She dabbed at the spilled wine and quickly put another cloth over the offending stain. Mr. Donal Hawke glared menacingly down the table at the inebriated Winnie Hawke. She didn't seem to care or notice, and ordered another gin and tonic. The teenager looked sullenly down at his dessert and then pushed it away. It seemed as if he were about to ask for permission to leave the table, but then looked at his grandfather's face and thought better of it.

As the de Bruins and Kings finished their dessert course, the waitress who had tried to salvage the spilled wine situation came over to their table to ask if there was anything else they needed. All the staff wore name tags and Monique noticed that the girls name was Emma.

"Thanks for everything, Emma, you've had a busy night, you must be tired," said Monique.

"Not too bad Mam, my shift is nearly over." The young waitress spoke with a London accent.

"What brings you to the wilds of Mayo?" continued Monique.

"I just wanted to get out of London. I have a friend who lives not far from here and she told me about the job. I really like it here."

"Well, thanks again for everything," added Monique.

The two couples made their way from the dining room to the long room where they sat in front of a welcoming turf fire sipping port and brandy.

The Hawke family were still in the dining room.

CHAPTER 04

A SCHEME

"Your mother has turned into a total lush, David. She was completely twisted tonight. I lost count of the number of G+Ts she had, not to mention all the wine," said Emily Hawke, as she stood in front of the mirror in their bedroom. She unclasped her gold and diamond necklace before placing it on the dressing table together with her matching earrings.

"I don't know what we are going to do about her – she really lets the side down," continued Emily as she opened the button of her sleek Versace dress and threw her high heeled Gucci shoes in a corner.

"We have a lot more to worry about than mother's propensity to consume copious amounts of alcohol, my dear," said David as he undid his tie.

"What on earth are you talking about?" asked Emily.

"My father called into his solicitors in Galway at the beginning of the month – you know Kelly and Son. Jonathan Kelly Senior has been his friend and solicitor for years."

"Oh, your friend's father! Your partner in crime's father!" interjected Emily.

"Yes, that Jonathan. You know very well who I'm talking about, Emily. Fortunately Jonathan Senior was ill that morning and Jonathan Junior – my friend – took the meeting. He said that Dad was very annoyed to see him but nonetheless told him why he was there. Seemingly Dad wants to make big changes to his will and also to our businesses. You do know Emily, that Dad has complete control over all the company. He allows me to run the English side of things, but if he feels like it, he can take it all away from us, with the stroke of a pen. Jack and Joanne are in the same boat."

"That's ridiculous," said Emily. "Everything in England is supposed to be ours. And you do work so hard, darling – that is when you're not galavanting with Jonathan Kelly to your casinos, night clubs, horse racing, card games. Have I left anything out?"

"Don't be so damn smart, Emily. You're going to be very badly affected by any changes as well. Where do you think your designer clothes, shoes and handbags come from. How could we possibly afford our flat in Mayfair or the country house in Kent, or boarding school for Toby, if Dad decides to cut us off – even if he only decides to cut back on what we have?"

Emily sat down on the side of the bed and looked disbelievingly at David.

"Do the others know?"

"I telephoned both of them after I found out, but we haven't had a chance to sit down face to face to discuss it. Jack was in America and Joanne was in France. She only got back to Ireland a few days ago."

"Does Jonathan Kelly have any idea about the changes he wants to make?" asked Emily.

"Jonathan believes that they could be quite drastic, as Dad referred to us all as leeches. He intimated that he was fed up of the whole lot of us."

"What are we going to do?"

"There's more good news. There appears to be an illegitimate child in the wings – not a child as such but an eighteen year old girl in London."

"You can't be serious!"

"Yes, I am, my dear. Jonathan said that Dad received a letter about six months ago from this person. He put a private detective on the case in London. The solicitors thought that he would keep fighting it, and that she would eventually give up and just go away. But at the latest meeting he seems to have changed his mind, for whatever reason and intends to do right by her and make some sort of provision for her."

"She's probably scamming him – looking for a payout. What on earth is he thinking of? You'll have to talk him around."

"I'm not supposed to know about any of this. Jonathan is his solicitor – you know the concept – solicitor client privilege. A client's solicitor has a legal duty not to disclose any legally privileged communications to anyone. Jonathan did say that Dad intended to tell us all about his plans during these holidays. So, none of us can say anything until he decides to give us the news."

"Has he made any changes yet?"

"No. He's going back to their office on the 8th of January, where he will only meet Jonathan Senior to make the changes. He insisted that he would only meet with him. It appears that Dad dislikes and distrusts my good friend Jonathan as much as ever."

"With good cause it seems," smirked Emily. "We'll have to meet up with Jack and Joanne as soon as possible. We could suggest an early walk on the beach. Natalia, we know won't join us, and your mother will be hungover. Ring their rooms now and organise it for before breakfast tomorrow. I wonder will Jack bring Ava with him? – can't see her being much use to us – she's such a churchmouse. I'm sure Joanne won't involve Francois as nobody knows if he's a permanent fixture yet."

"Did you notice that Ava looked paler than usual at dinner and hardly touched her food?"

"Can't say I did," replied Emily. "She always looks anemic. Maybe she's pregnant after all these years!"

"Well, if she is, that might be helpful to us, as it might throw a spanner in the works for Dad's plans."

David did as he was instructed and called all the rooms. As expected only Jack and Joanne agreed to the early walk on the beach. Jack informed his brother that Ava wasn't feeling very well and would probably be resting the next morning.

The following morning at seven o'clock the three Hawke siblings and Emily met up at the front door of Loughfarraig House as planned. Donal Hawke always insisted on having breakfast at 8.30, so they didn't have a great deal of time to hatch a plan.

"Before we talk about Dad, I need to tell you something. Ava is pregnant. It's early days – she's only three months and she has been very ill. I don't know how she got through dinner last night without having to get sick."

"Congratulations Jack!" said all three.

"That's wonderful news," added Emily.

"Yes," replied Jack. "We had just about given up. So, fingers crossed for us."

"Did you tell Ava about Dad's plans for us?" asked David.

"I told her after you phoned me. I thought she had a right to know. She was very upset. She thinks it's really unfair. We've worked very hard in America for the company."

"Francois doesn't know anything," added Joanne. "I really don't know about a future with him, so we'll leave him out of any of our schemes."

The four walked to the back of the house and down onto the beach. The waves were crashing against the shore. It was still quite dark and the mountains cast shadows on the water.

"What do you think of the latest twist in the saga? – you know the illegitimate English "daughter," asked Emily, as she tightened her coat around her against the wind.

"I'm very surprised that he's not fighting it," said Joanne. "It's not a bit like him to want to do the right thing."

"Agreed," said David. "And I certainly don't want to share what we have with her."

"We may have nothing to share – he may want to cut us off completely," said Jack.

"He hasn't told us anything yet," continued David, "and according to Jonathan, we have until the 8th January to change his mind."

"Maybe Ava being pregnant might soften him a bit," added Jack.

"Let's hope something happens," concluded Emily.

CHAPTER 05

CHRISTMAS DAY

At nine o'clock on Christmas morning, twenty of the forty guests staying at Loughfarraig House assembled in the front sitting room in their swimming gear, bath robes wrapped tightly around them and flip flops for the customary Christmas morning dip in the sea behind the house.

Everyone was chatting and waiting in anticipation of the run down the beach, and splash into the ice cold ocean, led by Mr. and Mrs. Moore, the proprietors of the house.

All the de Bruins and Kings were there. The teenagers were gathered together in one corner of the room discussing whatever games they had been playing in the rec room the evening before. Toby Hawke had joined them. He was looking less sullen this morning as he joined in animated conversation with the others.

"Good morning everyone and Happy Christmas to one and all," said Gerald Moore, as he and his wife joined the party. "Are we all ready? Let's go."

The congregation followed the Moores out of the front door, where they were met with a chilly breeze coming in from the ocean. They all shivered slightly and picked up the pace, making their way onto the beach, where they removed their bathrobes and flip flops and ran towards the sea. There were screams and screeches when the bodies hit the icy water, especially from the teenagers and some of the ladies, but their bodies soon adjusted to the temperature. They all swam about splashing and sploshing around in the waves. The House staff were waiting with warm towels as they emerged from the water. All the guests donned their bath robes once more, ran quickly back to the warmth of the sitting room, where piping hot punch was proffered. They all eagerly took the warm glasses into their cold hands.

"That was invigorating," said Alison. "I've never done a Christmas sea swim before. The body adjusts surprisingly quickly to the temperature. Although five or ten minutes is enough."

"I've only done it once before, but I don't remember it being that icy," answered Monique.

"Character building, Mam, as you would say," interjected Maeve, as all the youngsters laughed. They continued to sip the warm, comforting punch.

"There was no sign of any of the Hawke family except for Toby," said Alison.

"Don't look now, but I've just seen the sons, their wives and the daughter huddled together in the card room," uttered Alexander. The others shuffled around discreetly until they were able to get a view of the card room. There was obviously something amiss, as the conversation looked very serious indeed, animated but hushed. They certainly didn't want anyone to overhear them.

"I wonder what's going on there?" whispered Alison.

"God only knows," replied Robert. "There are always squabbles in powerful rich families like the Hawkes."

"No sign of Donal Hawke or either of the two wives," added Alexander.

"I'd say the first Mrs. Hawke is still recovering – that poor woman has a major drink problem – I really don't know how she manages to consume so much alcohol," continued Alison.

"Breakfast is at eleven," interjected Monique. "We'd all better have our showers before we catch cold. Children, off with you! We'll meet back here at precisely five to eleven."

An hour and fifteen minutes later, the two families made their way to the large round table in the dining room to have breakfast. They noticed that the Hawkes were seated at their usual long table on the right of the room.

As they took their seats, the teenagers waved across at Toby. He waved back and smiled. His mother and father appeared quite surprised, looked over towards the two families and nodded.

"There's a special breakfast this morning," said Alison. "One can have smoked salmon and scrambled eggs or cold meat and cheese, or any mixture you want. What a treat!"

"Did you see the wonderful display of scones and brown bread, cakes, mince pies, and all sorts of marmalades and jams?" added Monique. "Just as well, there's no lunch today. This will certainly keep us going until Christmas dinner."

"It will be very interesting to see what the Hawke ladies will be wearing tonight," said Monique, as she applied her makeup in front of the dressing table mirror. I'm sure it will be designer from head to toe."

"I have no idea about ladies' designer outfits, but you don't look half bad yourself," laughed Alexander as he fidgeted with his bow tie.

"Let me do that for you," said Monique. She walked over to her husband and carefully adjusted the tie. She kissed him on the cheek, then returned to the dressing table to add the finishing touches.

Christmas dinner was a formal affair – the ladies in their long evening dresses and the men in their tuxedos. Colonel Robert King wore his army dress uniform. The teenagers were also dressed formally. The three girls were delighted to show off their new dresses which had been purchased especially for this occasion. The boys were less keen to don suits and bow ties. At precisely seven thirty, the dinner gong was sounded, and Mr. and Mrs. Moore led all the guests into the dining room. The tables were splendidly dressed with the usual white linen and silver cutlery. There was a beautiful vase of Christmas themed flowers in the centre, a party hat and crackers placed beside each setting. In the corner, beside a Christmas tree sat a beautiful young girl with long red hair playing her harp.

The Hawkes were the last to be seated as they were five minutes late. Donal Hawke made his usual lumbering entrance, followed by the rest of his family. Monique had been right, the ladies were attired in the latest designer dresses. Their jewellery was even more ostentatious than before.

A delicious, traditional Christmas dinner was served to all. The local piper heralded the entrance of the flaming pudding. Everyone clapped as the pudding was placed in front of Mr. and Mrs. Moore at the top table.

"That's a real army tradition," whispered Alison.

"Yes, I think Moore himself might have some army connections. I'll certainly ask him when I get the chance," answered Robert.

As the guests ate their dessert course, Gerald Moore made a short speech, thanking his guests for having chosen Loughfarraig House for their Christmas celebrations and wishing them good tidings, peace and happiness for the new year.

"What a wonderful day this has been!" said Alison. "Everything was just perfect."

"I agree completely," added Monique. "What did you think, children?"

"Absolutely wonderful," concurred Maeve and immediately the other children agreed.

"May we be excused please?" asked Maeve. "We would like to go to the rec room. They are going to show the "Indiana Jones" film. Toby is joining us as well."

"Of course you may. Have a lovely evening. We are retiring to the Long Room for a few drinks. Don't think we'll stay up too late tonight. It's been a very tiring but wonderful day."

"I'd like to take a stroll outside, if you don't mind," said Robert.

"I'll join you," said Alexander.

The two friends made their way out of the House and over towards the lake. There was no wind and the water of the lake was completely still.

"It's eerily quiet," said Robert. "It really feels like the calm before the storm. There's no wind and very little movement in the sea. I can barely hear the waves."

"Was there any mention of a storm?" asked Alexander.

"I don't think so, but we were all so busy today. I didn't listen to a news at all."

They stood in the silence. The ducks and swans had found shelter for the night. The branches of the trees in the forest seemed motionless.

Suddenly another group of guests emerged from the house laughing and chattering, their voices echoing in the void. Alexander and Robert returned to the Long Room to join the ladies for a drink still wondering if there was a storm brewing.

CHAPTER 06

THE BODY IN
THE LAKE

On St. Stephen's Day at 8.15am, there was a knock on Monique and Alexander's bedroom door.

"Mam, we are all going down to the stables," said Max. "Just letting you know. The others are downstairs waiting for me. Robert and Alison know about it already. Toby is coming with us as well."

"Are you riding out on the beach?" asked Alexander.

"Yes, just for an hour," answered Max.

"You know the rules, stay together, make sure the leather gear is in good nick. Is Toby a proficient horseman?"

"He says he it. We'll soon know. We won't take any chances. Should be back by ten o'clock."

"Enjoy yourselves," added Monique.

Alexander looked out the window. "The weather is still very calm. There isn't any breeze at all. It's very strange. Can you turn on the radio, just to see if there's bad weather expected."

Monique switched on the radio on the side table. They listened to "Call Me" by Blondie before the news headlines and weather.

"There is a weather warning for the West of Ireland. The storm has changed course, and will now make land at around midday today. The areas worst affected will be Galway, Mayo and Donegal."

"You were right darling, there is a storm coming. No panic though. The kids will be back way before it lands."

Alexander picked up the receiver of the phone beside the bed and dialled 032.

"Hello!, Alison King speaking."

"Morning Alison, Alexander here – just letting you know that there's a storm on it's way. Won't arrive until about midday, so no need to worry about the children. They'll be back around ten o'clock. Do you fancy going down for breakfast now and let the kids have theirs when they get back?"

"Good idea, Alex, we'll see you downstairs in about ten minutes."

Fifteen minutes later, the two couples were sitting at a window table in the dining room.

"Hope the storm isn't too bad," said Monique.

"I was chatting to Gerald Moore at the reception area. They are well used to storms here. This one is a bit of a surprise though. It was meant to miss Ireland altogether, but then changed course. They have a large back-up generator, so the lights won't go out," continued Alexander.

They had just finished their breakfast and were sipping their coffee, when they noticed a huge commotion. There were staff running all over the place. They could see the lake from their window seat. One of the waiters had his arm around one of the waitresses who was sobbing. He was leading her back towards the front door. Gerald Moore appeared and ran down towards the lake.

Their breakfast waitress Emma came over to clear some of the dishes and cutlery. Her eyes were red and she looked very upset.

"Are you OK, Emma?" asked Monique.

"It's awful – they found a body in the lake. Two of the waiters went out for a cigarette, and there was this body floating on the lake. They ran back into the kitchen to tell Chef. Chef told Mr. Moore. He rang the police, I think. I have to get back to the kitchen."

Emma carried the tray back into the kitchen. The four friends sat in silence for a few moments.

"Robert and I will go down to the lake to see if we can be of any assistance. Will you ladies go down to the stables to meet the kids when they get back from their ride and make sure that they go nowhere near the lake," suggested Alexander.

"Good idea," said Alison.

The two ladies went to their rooms to get their coats, hats and gloves, and then made their way down to the stables where they waited patiently for their children to return.

Ten minutes later, they noticed the six riders on their ponies trotting towards the stable area. The children all waved at the adults, surprised to see them there.

"What are you two doing here?" asked Maeve, as they all dismounted, loosened and removed the saddles and led the ponies back into their individual stables.

"Finish what you're doing and we'll explain," said Alison.

The children removed the bridle and bit carefully from each of the ponies and carried them into the tack room.

"Well explain!" said Max playfully, as they all emerged through the door of the tack room.

"There has been some sort of accident down by the lake. We are not sure of all the details as yet," said Alison.

"Did someone fall in?" asked Ellen.

"We have no idea, as yet," replied Monique. "We would like you all to go back to your rooms, have your showers and avoid the lake area. Take Toby back to his parents first, of course. We'll all meet up in the rec room in forty minutes."

There were no more questions as they all walked slowly back to Loughfarraig House.

Alexander and Robert made their way to the scene of the incident. There was a crowd gathered in a circle around the body of a man. Gerald Moore looked very distraught as he stared down at the lifeless corpse.

"Well, they've trampled all over the scene," muttered Alexander.

"They certainly have," replied Robert. "Lets hope it was an accident – if it's a crime scene – well – there will be very little chance of collecting viable evidence."

Gerald Moore saw the two men approaching the scene and moved quickly towards them.

"Can we be of assistance in any way?" asked Alexander.

"It's Donal Hawke. He's dead. He drowned in the lake. I've rung 999 and explained, so they're sending the guards from Castlebar and an ambulance, but not until after the storm. I really don't know what to do. Have either of you any experience in these matters?"

"Yes, I have worked on cases before with the Gardai," replied Alexander. "Is there a doctor among our guests who could make a preliminary examination of the body?"

"Yes, John O'Neill is a retired surgeon. He is here with his wife."

"Great, first of all we need to cordon off the scene. We should restrict access to the area immediately. You will need some rope and a tarpaulin to protect the body."

Gerald Moore ordered his staff away from the lake and back to their duties. Two of the waiters were asked to locate the rope and tarpaulin. Five minutes later the area was secured.

"We need to find out if he was found in the lake or on the shore," said Alexander.

"Indeed," replied Robert.

"Mr. Moore, I need to speak to whoever found the body immediately, will you ask them to come here to us, please?"

Five minutes later John and Joe, the two waiters, were standing in front of Alexander and Robert explaining exactly what happened.

"We went out to have a cigarette before our shift. We saw someone in the lake, face down. We both jumped in and dragged him to shore. We rolled him onto his back but we knew he was dead. It was awful, his eyes were wide open and his mouth was open. There were huge gashes in his head. We knew who he was, of course, that VIP who was here with his family."

"Thanks very much lads. You can go back into the house now. Well done, for trying to save his life. The guards of course will want to speak to you when they arrive," said Alexander.

"That sounds very suspicious. If he drowned, why would there be gashes to his head? We'll have to get the retired surgeon to take a look."

"The emergency services won't arrive for hours. God only knows what will happen to the body if it's left out in the storm. I really need to phone

Inspector Muldoon to get some advice. I'll ring Naas Garda Station first and if he's not there, I'll ring his home."

Inspector John Muldoon and Commandant Alexander de Bruin had worked their first case together almost two years ago. They had become good friends during the murder investigation in Briarstown and their friendship had endured ever since.

"Inspector John Muldoon speaking, how can I help you?"

"Good morning John, it's Alexander de Bruin."

"How are you, Alex? Great to hear from you. How are you enjoying your Christmas holidays in the wilds of Mayo?"

"It was going really well until this morning, when a body was found in the lake."

"Good grief, is it suspicious?"

"Unfortunately, yes. It doesn't look like an ordinary drowning – there are gashes to his head."

"Who is the victim?"

"That will be another big headache for the authorities. It's Donal Hawke – head of Mustelus Developments. He was here with his whole family. To tell you the truth, John, he was a most unpleasant fellow, and must have had quite a number of enemies."

"I know who you're talking about. He was always very dodgy. No one really knows how he made so much money. Lots of rumours of course."

"We have a big problem here. Firstly two young lads took the body from the lake onto the shore. Then numerous people walked over the area. To cap it all, there's a storm going to arrive here in about an hours time. I've cordoned off the scene now. First of all, I think it's too late for evidence gathering around the body and secondly I don't know what will happen to the body during the storm. But I did not want to move it until I got permission. Fortunately, there's a retired surgeon staying in the House as well, so I was thinking of asking him to examine the body in situ and remove it to a safe location."

"Good thinking, Alex. Please do all you can. I give you the authority to take charge and make whatever decisions you deem necessary. I will make the appropriate phone calls to Garda Headquarters, Castlebar and Galway. You'd better get a move on and good luck."

"Mr. Moore, is there anywhere on the estate where we could keep the body?" asked Alexander de Bruin.

"There's an old ice house on the grounds that dates back to Victorian times. They used to take ice from the lake and store it there. There are steps down to it and I still keep some gas lanterns there, so we'll have no trouble getting around."

"I would like John O'Neill to examine the body in situ, and then we'll move it to the ice house before the storm hits. Colonel King and I will carry the body to the ice house, but we'll need some help. Do you think any of your staff would be up to it?"

"Yes, we have two waiters in mind – nothing ever fazes them."

"How did the family take the news?" asked Alexander.

"Surprisingly well – more curiosity than grief. I told them that you were going to be in charge of affairs until the authorities arrive after the storm. All the other guests know about it as well. News travels fast around here."

Alexander noticed a man with grey hair wearing a tweed jacket and carrying a briefcase, walking in their direction. He appeared to be about 75 years old, but extremely distinguished looking.

"How do you do, I'm John O'Neill. I hear you have a body for me to examine. Please call me John."

"How do you do, I'm Alexander de Bruin."

"Yes, I've heard all about you. Please lead on."

The three men made their way over to the body, which was covered in tarpaulin, itself held in place by rocks. Alexander noticed that the sky had become very grey and the wind had started to bluster. They hadn't much time. John O'Neill lifted the tarpaulin and perused the body. He examined the head wounds and any other parts of the body that were visible without removing the clothing.

"We are going to remove the body to the icehouse before the storm comes in," said Alexander.

"Good idea – can't examine him properly here. Is there any lighting in the icehouse?"

"Yes, there are gas lamps that give off surprisingly good light," answered Moore.

"On preliminary examination, it looks like he's been struck over the head several times. Did you take a look around already for a weapon, maybe a large branch?"

"There's nothing close to the body," answered Alexander.

He looked out over the lake, and saw two oars floating in the middle of it.

Donal Hawke's body was carried by the four men, Commandant de Bruin, Colonel King and two strongly built waiters from the lake shore to the icehouse, followed by John O'Neill and Gerald Moore. It was a difficult task as the body weighed heavily, and the terrain wasn't flat. Finally, the remains were carried down the steps and placed on a type of rock shelf. It was extremely cold underground.

"I want to examine the body more thoroughly," said John O'Neill.

"I think we should get back to the house and batten down the hatches," suggested Gerald Moore. "The body isn't going anywhere."

"Agreed," said Alexander.

CHAPTER 07

THE STORM

At 12.30pm on St. Stephen's day, Storm Debbie, as it was later called, hit the West coast of Ireland with ferocity. The winds reached seventy miles an hour and the waves lashed the shore.

Some of the guests watched the spectacle from their bedroom window. Others preferred to sit in various lounges and sitting rooms of Loughfarraig House, comforted by turf fires and the hospitality of the Moore family. The teenagers all gathered in the rec room to play cards and board games.

Alexander did not want to waste time, so asked if he could meet the Hawke family in the billiard room.

The young widow arrived into the room, looking grief stricken, dabbing her eyes with a monogrammed white linen handkerchief. The first Mrs. Hawke walked in, gin and tonic in hand. They did not sit together. Gerald Moore had organised the placement of small armchairs in the room, around and in front of the billiard table. David, Emily and young Toby arrived next and sat together. Joanne and her partner Francois sat beside Natalia and comforted her. Jack and Ava were last to take their seats.

"My name is Alexander de Bruin. Firstly, I would like to offer my sincere condolences on your very sad loss. It must be a very great shock to you all."

They all muttered something inaudible.

"Mr. Moore has told you that I will be in charge of the investigation until the relevant authorities arrive. This is Colonel Robert King who will be assisting me."

"May I also offer my condolences," said Robert King.

Some more muttering and head nodding ensued.

"At this juncture, I would like each of you to tell me when you last saw Donal Hawke? Can I start with you Toby?"

"I saw him at dinner. When it was over I went down to the rec room until about 11.30 and then went up to my room and to bed."

"Thank you, Toby. With your parent's permission you may leave. I believe the other teenagers are playing cards and board games, if you would like to join them."

"That would be great thanks. Can I leave Dad?"

"Of course you can. Off you go," said David.

"I went straight up to my room after dinner. I had a dreadful headache," interjected Natalia, still dabbing her eyes. "I took painkillers and a sleeping tablet. I didn't wake up until seven o'clock this morning. Donal wasn't in the room. When I take my sleeping tablets, I'm comatose for the night, so I don't know if Donal came into the room at all."

There was some more sniffling and tear dabbing. Francois put his arm around her shoulder comfortingly, as Joanne muttered words of solace.

"All of us went into the Long Room for after-dinner drinks," added David, "except for Natalia who went upstairs, as she said. At about ten o'clock, Dad said that he was leaving and just disappeared. We presumed that he had gone to bed. None of us saw him after that."

The others nodded in agreement. Winnie Hawke took another sip of her G and T.

"Did you all leave the Long Room together?" asked Alexander.

"We left shortly after Dad," said Jack. "Ava was very tired."

"Francois and I left about eleven thirty," interjected Joanne.

"Mother, Emily and I had another drink," added David. "Then we showed Mother to her room and went to bed ourselves at around midnight."

"Please don't read anything into my next question. It's just procedure, but can each partner alibi the other partner?"

They all nodded enthusiastically.

"Why on earth would we need an alibi? I thought he fell into the lake and drowned. He couldn't swim you know," said David in a raised voice.

"We are just keeping an open mind at this stage. We have to ask these questions," responded Alexander.

Natalia started to sob, put her head in her hands and began shaking. Winnie was looking for the waiter to order another drink. Ava turned white and ran out of the room, followed by her husband.

Alexander decided to dismiss the group before there was complete mayhem.

"Perhaps we could leave it at that for the moment," he suggested.

Joanne and Francois helped Natalia out of the room.

"Come along Mother, take my arm," said David.

Winnie took his arm and with as much dignity as she could muster, accompanied her son.

"Ava is pregnant," said Emily helpfully, addressing Alexander as she sauntered past him.

Alexander and Robert stood silently for a moment.

"Well, that was a great triumph, Alex."

They both smiled at each other.

The wind was still howling outside. Suddenly the lights flickered and went out. Thirty seconds later, they came on again.

"Electricity has gone, that's the generator kicking in," suggested Alex.

"The phone lines are gone as well. No way of contacting John Muldoon."

CHAPTER 08

SIRENS

The storm raged for nearly five hours. The electricity had gone as Alexander had thought, and the phone lines were also down.

Finally the wind subsided. Gerald Moore and a number of his staff checked the house and grounds for damage. Fortunately, there was very little damage to the house, apart from a few missing slates, which his handyman could easily fix. There were two trees down in the wood beside the lake. The sea had thrown up some small boulders onto the headland, but all in all, it could have been a lot worse. The generator had done it's job well, and the guests remained comfortable and well fed.

The teenagers found the storm very exciting. They had not witnessed such a raging, angry sea before. Toby spent his time with the other teenagers mainly in the rec room.

"How is Toby coping, Max, after his grandfather's death?" Monique had asked.

"He's perfectly fine Mam. He doesn't seem to care – none of them do. It's weird, they all seem to have hated him. To tell you the truth, I think they're glad he's dead. Toby said that he was an awful bully."

"He may be more upset than he realises," answered Monique. "Just look after him."

Alexander and Robert were strolling outside the house, near the lake. It was eerily still again. The ducks and swans were swimming near the shore.

"I wonder where they hid during the storm!" said Robert.

"I'm sure they're used to this around here," answered Alexander.

"Hello there!" a voice came from behind them. "We've survived it then!"

It was John O'Neill, the surgeon, accompanied by an elderly lady with grey hair, pinned back in a bun.

"Good morning, John," said Alexander.

"Let me introduce my wife, Helen."

"How do you do, Mrs. O'Neill," replied both men.

"Just thinking about going down to the icehouse to examine the body."

"Good idea," retorted Alexander. "We'll come with you."

"No need, my wife was a nurse, so I'd prefer if it were just the two of us, if you don't mind – I work better like that. I'll seek you out when I'm finished."

"As you wish," said Alexander

John and Helen O'Neill walked away purposefully in the direction of the icehouse. Alexander and Robert returned indoors to locate the rest of the party.

Alison and Monique were sitting in the Long Room, sipping coffee and nibbling on scones with cream and jam.

The two men sat down beside them. A waiter appeared with more coffee and cakes.

"Mrs. Moore told us that the telephone lines are still down. There are also a few trees blocking the roads, so there won't be anyone coming from Castlebar or Galway any time soon," said Monique.

"There's no way for me to contact John Muldoon at the moment. We met John O'Neill and his wife Helen outside. He has gone to the icehouse to examine the body more thoroughly. I can't see the forensic team and the Gardai being able to get through to us in the next few hours."

"Do you think there's a murderer amongst us?" asked Alison nervously.

"Unfortunately, it looks like it," Robert answered. "We'll have more information when we see John O'Neill again. Where are the children?"

"They've all gone down to check on the ponies. They said that they might ride them out if everything is OK. Toby is with them and they are happy to look after him. He doesn't appear to be particularly upset about his grandfather's death," added Monique.

"Not a very popular fellow, it seems," continued Robert.

"I can see O'Neill and his wife coming back. Let's go Robert and hear what he has for us."

The two men stood up and made their way towards the front sitting room. John O'Neill acknowledged them with a wave as they approached the couple.

"Well, what's the verdict?" asked Alexander.

"As I suspected, the man was coshed over the head with some implement – I'm thinking an oar or a branch. He was struck twice on the side of the head. If I were to guess, I'd say the first blow killed him, and the second one was just for insurance. Hard to be sure without an autopsy, but I don't think there's water in his lungs – so dead before he went into the water. There are a few scratches on his hands, arms and legs but I don't think they're defensive wounds – too slight. I'd say the man was taken by surprise and smack, wallop...."

Mrs. O'Neill was standing at her husband's side, nodding away at everything he said.

"We are very grateful for all your help," said Alexander. "When the guards arrive, I'm sure they will want to interview you, and Mrs. O'Neill."

"My pleasure – great to be back on the horse again, as they say – felt very useful today." Helen O'Neill was still nodding her head.

"I don't think I'll inform the family yet. I might leave that to the guards. I hope the phone will be back soon – really need to speak to John Muldoon."

"Lets go for a walk to clear our heads," suggested Monique. "Once the authorities arrive, we probably won't get a chance, with all the interviews, statements etc. and Alexander is going to be involved in it all again."

They donned their coats, scarves and gloves and headed for the beach. In the distance they could see a man with his three legged dog. The man had a hurley and a tennis ball. The three legged sheepdog was very quick and agile for a dog with three legs. The dog chased the ball which had been struck with the hurley into the sea, retrieved the ball, brought it back to his master who repeated the manoeuvre.

There were ripples in the soft sand, formed by the ebb and flow of the tide. They could hear the lapping of the water and intermittently the crashing of breaking waves on the shore. What a beautiful place, she thought – it's blue sky with cotton clouds, mountains on every side, mist floating on the peaks, the sun breaking through, flashes of light on the mountains, dappled with colours of brown, green and yellow.

"What's that screeching noise?" asked Alison.

"Sirens." said Robert.

CHAPTER 09

MULDOON ARRIVES

As the four friends made their way back from the beach, they saw an ambulance, two squad cars and an unmarked police car. Alexander thought he recognised the two occupants of the black Mercedes. They watched as the four vehicles drove up the long avenue, sirens blaring, towards Loughfarraig House.

Alexander and the other three reached the back of the house just as the vehicles came to a stop near the lake.

Inspector John Muldoon and Sergeant Michael Dunne alighted from the black Mercedes and looked around to try to take in their surroundings. They saw Alexander and Robert walking towards them. The men waved at each other.

"I'm very glad to see you John," said Alexander. "You too Sergeant Dunne. I'm sure you remember Robert King."

They all shook hands.

"You can't be let out at all, Alexander. Here we go again – another suspicious death in your vicinity," said Muldoon, with a wry smile.

"Will you fill me in please," continued Muldoon. "The phone lines were down, so I had no way of contacting you. I made the decision to come down myself to investigate as it sounded very suspicious. The powers that be were happy to have you on board as well, considering what a powerful man Donal Hawke was. We'll all be under a great deal of pressure and scrutiny. The Commissioner is also relieved that you are helping us out as well."

Alexander explained about the finding of the body in the lake – the suspicions regarding the injuries to the head – the good luck that there was a retired surgeon staying in the hotel.

"Where is the body now?" asked Muldoon.

"We placed it in an old icehouse on the property – it was ideal. John O'Neill, the retired surgeon, conducted a brief examination on the lake shore and then, after the storm, he did a more thorough examination together with his wife, who is a retired nurse."

"What are the preliminary findings?" asked Muldoon.

"He's convinced that it's foul play. There were two blows to the head. He believes that the first one was probably fatal, so the second one was just for good measure. O'Neill doesn't believe that there's any water in the lungs, so – dead before he went into the water."

Four men in PPE gear were instructed to locate the body in the icehouse, place it in the ambulance and head straight back to Mayo General Hospital.

"Any sign of the murder weapon?"

"Again, O'Neill believes that it could be a large branch or an oar. We didn't locate any branches with blood on them. There are oars floating in the lake, and others with the rowing boats, down by the jetty. The storm has really hampered everything. We did a thorough search but there's a woodland by the lake – there are so many places to hide a weapon. We didn't have a great deal of time with the storm threatening. We had to move very quickly."

The ambulance drove down the avenue on its way to Castlebar hospital – Donal Hawke's body in the back of it, accompanied by two men in white PPE gear.

"We still need to do a big search of the whole area," said Muldoon. "I will have to send for a large number of men. This will be worse than the search at Briarstown,"

He turned to his Sergeant.

"When the phone lines are back, will you organise a search party, Michael. You'll have to get help from Castlebar and Galway."

"Will do."

The eight young guards who had arrived in the two squad cars were instructed to secure the area – not to allow anyone in or out of the grounds. It was a vast area, so easier said than done.

Alexander, Robert and Inspector Muldoon made their way into the front sitting room of the house where they met the proprietor of the house, Gerald Moore.

"Mr. Moore, please allow me to introduce Inspector John Muldoon, from Naas Garda Station who is in charge of the case."

"How do you do, Inspector. I'm at your disposal – anything you require. By the way, will you need accommodation? If so, I only have two rooms on the top floor where the staff live. As you can imagine, we are completely full for Christmas. The rooms are very comfortable."

"That would be very helpful Mr. Moore. Sergeant Dunne and I would like to stay. Would you have another room available for interviews etc.?"

"Yes, indeed. There's a lounge, at the back of the house, that's rarely used. May I get you gentlemen some refreshments? The phones aren't working yet. I'll let you know as soon as they've repaired the connection."

"I would love some coffee, please. It's been a long trip from Kildare, although the storm wasn't at all bad around Naas. It seems to have veered north after hitting the west."

Alexander and John Muldoon sat down in front of one of the turf fires as Robert King took his leave.

"Well, tell me about the family then."

"There are two wives here. Winnie is the first Mrs. Hawke. They were divorced about three years ago to make way for the second, much younger Mrs. Natalia Hawke. The eldest son is David who is married to Emily. Their son Toby is also here – about 14 years old. He is hanging out with our youngsters. The second son is Jack, married to Ava who appears to be in the early stages of pregnancy. Finally, the only daughter Joanne who is accompanied by her French boyfriend, Francois. From what I could see, there was great tension between them all . They all sat at a long dining table. Donal Hawke obviously ruled the roost. Our children are under the impression that nobody liked the man – that he was a complete bully. The first wife, Winnie seems to have a major drink problem. The three children come across as extremely arrogant, especially the eldest David. Emily, his wife seems overbearing and haughty. Jack is quieter, as is his wife Ava – but she has been ill since she arrived. Joanne also appears proud and distasteful. I suppose they are a product of a rich powerful dynasty. There were some histrionics when I asked them for an alibi, so I had to call a halt to proceedings – as Robert said – it was a triumph! According to Max, young Toby hated his grandfather and is quite relieved that he's gone. I was thinking about how we should approach the family. We really need to split them up when interviewing them – just to avoid any more drama."

"You're right Alex. I will just introduce myself to them. Tell them that I must wait for the post mortem before I can give out any further information. I will do that after my coffee and scones."

The young waiter Juan from Colombia had just placed freshly baked scones with cream, butter and jams in front of the two men. He poured the coffee into porcelain cups, with a broad smile.

"You are looking very pleased with yourself today, Juan," said Alexander.

"Yes, Sir, I've had some good fortune."

"Good for you Juan," replied Alexander. "Use it wisely."

"I will – maybe my girlfriend will come now, from Colombia."

Juan bowed slightly, still a wide grin on his face, showing his pearly white, perfect teeth and moved towards the kitchen.

"What was that all about?" asked Muldoon.

"Monique, you know what she's like – curious about everyone's life – was chatting to him one night about Colombia and his hopes to bring his girlfriend to Ireland."

Muldoon picked up a warm scone smothered in jam and cream. "This looks delicious." Inspector Muldoon enjoyed his scones and coffee before facing into meeting the Hawke family.

John Muldoon had a brief meeting with the Hawke family to explain that Donal Hawke's death appeared suspicious but that he would know more when he received the results of the post mortem. He did not allow time for histrionics. Muldoon informed them that they would have to stay in Loughfarraig House until everything was wrapped up.

Most of the guests were booked in for eight to ten days, and despite the death, wished to stay on for the remainder of their holidays. Gerald Moore saw no problem in carrying on. All the provisions were already on site and he was willing and able to cater for the young guards who would be milling about.

Two young guards had donned life jackets and rowed out to the middle of the lake to retrieve two oars that were floating on the water. They looked somewhat awkward. Muldoon wondered as he watched them, whether they had ever been on a boat on a lake before. He hoped they could swim. Perhaps he should have asked Alexander or Colonel King to do the honours.

They arrived safely back to shore twenty minutes later. As Muldoon had suspected, there was no sign of blood or any other evidence to be seen on the oars. Nevertheless, he sent a young guard off to Castlebar with them, – maybe the oars would match the wounds.

On the morning of the 28th December, a sergeant from Castlebar arrived with the autopsy report.

Alexander and John Muldoon headed for the sitting room which they were now calling the interview room.

They both perused the report.

"No doubt so, the man was murdered as John O'Neill suspected," said Muldoon.

"Two deep wounds to the side of his head. First one, probably fatal. There was a very small amount of water in the lungs, which is confusing, as the coroner believes that he was dead when he entered the water. There are scrapes on his hands, arms and legs which are thought to be perimortem – again confusing, as if he were grabbing at branches or rocks before being hit on the head. Yet, no sign of defence wounds – just scrapes and small cuts."

"Yes, if he had been defending himself by holding up his arms, there would be severe wounds on his hands and wrists," added Alexander.

"I wonder, could he have been pushed into the water and then, as he was struggling to get out, hit twice on the side of the head," said Muldoon. "The coroner also states that the blade of the oar matches the wounds on his head. Unfortunately, any evidence has been washed away during the storm – blood, hair etc. Time to give the family the bad news."

Muldoon dialled the room number of David Hawke and asked him to assemble the family in the interview room.

Alexander and Muldoon awaited the family. On their arrival, they imparted the news as gently as possible. He asked David Hawke to remain behind as he dismissed the others.

"Mr. Hawke, I just need some information from you. Could you please tell me, who is your father's solicitor here in Ireland. I presume there are other law firms who represent the company in other jurisdictions."

"Yes, Inspector, the company, "Mustelus Developments," has representatives in America and England, but my father's solicitor in Ireland is Jonathan Kelly in Galway. I'll get you his phone number."

"Thank you for your co-operation, Mr. Hawke. We will interview each member of the family in time. May I also have his doctor's contact details?" concluded Muldoon.

"This is going to be quite a complicated business," reflected Alexander, after David Hawke had left the room. "I think the name of the company reflects the whole business. Muselus is the latin name for a smooth hound shark. I presume Hawke, when he named his company so aptly, intended from the beginning to be that shark, and so he was. I think we'll find an awful lot of shady, underhand business practices right from the origins of this company. I fear that we are going to find a plethora of skeletons in the closet."

CHAPTER 10

THE SOLICITOR'S OFFICE

Alexander and Muldoon were greeted in the front office of Kelly and Son, solicitors, in Galway City, by Miss Henry, the firm's secretary.

"Good morning gentlemen," she greeted them cheerfully. "Mr. Kelly is expecting you. Please follow me."

The two men dutifully followed the young woman into the impressive office with a beautiful oak desk. Sitting behind the desk is a distinguished, grey haired man in his seventies, wearing an expensive suit and a school tie. Standing by the desk is a much younger man, also wearing an expensive navy suit and the same school tie.

"Good morning, Jonathan Kelly and this is my son, Jonathan Junior,"

"How do you do. I'm Inspector Muldoon, and this is my associate Commandant de Bruin. As you know, we are investigating the death of your client, Donal Hawke. We've been informed by his son, David, that you are the family's long time solicitor and friend."

"I've been Donal's friend for many years. We became friends after he set up his business in London and needed a representative in Ireland. Donal was a self made man. We didn't go to the same schools, but then our sons went to the same boarding school and also became close friends."

"We noticed the school ties," interjected Alexander. "A great school by all accounts."

"I'm Jonathan Junior, David's friend," said Jonathan as he shook hands with both men.

"Please take a seat gentlemen."

The two men sat down in comfortable armchairs on the other side of the oak desk.

"We would like to know about Donal Hawke's Company and more importantly, his will," said Muldoon. "We need all the information you have, as this is now a murder inquiry."

The two Kellys looked extremely shocked. "We were informed late last night by David that he drowned," interjected Jonathan, the younger.

"Following receipt of the autopsy report, matters have changed – he was murdered."

"He made a will several years ago leaving his business affairs in America to Jack, those in England to David and those in Ireland to Joanne. His first wife Winnie is well provided for, with a substantial house in Galway and a lump sum of half a million pounds. When he re-married two years ago he inserted a codicil, leaving a lump sum of two hundred thousand to his new wife, Natalia. We had an appointment, he and I, on the 7th December. Unfortunately, I was ill, so my son took the meeting."

Muldoon and Alexander both looked in Jonathan Junior's direction.

"He wasn't very pleased to see me. Mr. Hawke always treated me like a child and preferred to deal with my father. David and I are very good friends since boarding school. He told me that he wanted to make changes to his company and his will. Although the three children are running various arms of the company, he still had complete control, and could pull the rug from under them whenever he pleased. Mr. Hawke was in dreadful humour. He also wanted to make changes to the provisions for his wives."

"There were also, other complications," interjected Senior. "A young English girl had written to him claiming to be his daughter. She's eighteen years old. She claims that she didn't know who her father was until after her mother died and read her diaries. I advised Donal to ignore it – that it was someone just looking for a pay-out. But, he put a private detective onto it, and was convinced after the investigation, that she was his daughter. Seemingly, he wanted to make some provisions for her in his will.

The second complication was the prenup that he had with his second wife. I know that this isn't legal here, but it is in America where they were married. Anything left to Natalia is in an America bank account, and linked to the prenup. You would have to contact his American lawyers for this information. If they divorced or separated or she was unfaithful – she would be cut off. Now that he is dead – she will inherit. Of course the original will now stands as he did not change it. He was meant to come back here on the 8th January to make the changes. I'm afraid the illegitimate daughter has lost out," Kelly senior said smugly.

Alexander directed the next question at Jonathon Kelly Junior. "Did the family know about these impending changes to the will?"

Jonathan blushed and averted his gaze, looking down at his shoes. "I couldn't inform them because of client confidentially, so I don't know. Perhaps he told them, himself – that was the plan after all – to take them away for Christmas and inform them."

Neither Muldoon nor Alexander believed him.

On the trip back from Galway to Loughfarraig House, both men contemplated the conversation in the solicitor's office.

"Did you believe any of that?" asked Muldoon.

"Junior is telling lies anyway. He went straight onto the phone to his good friend David Hawke as soon as the father had left the office. David probably told his siblings, so now they are all suspects, as they would have lost an awful lot if their father had changed the will."

"I wonder do the two Mrs. Hawkes know?" continued Muldoon.

"There doesn't seem to be any love lost between the current Mrs. Hawke, Natalia, and the Hawke children. Can't see much point in letting Winnie Hawke know – she probably wouldn't have been very badly affected, in any case. Her main interest seems to be where the next gin and tonic is coming from. The siblings knew that they had until the 8th January to change their father's mind. Although he didn't seem like the type of man to be swayed."

"We'll have to find out about the daughter in England. If he had changed his will, she would have profited big time. Therefore, wherever she is, she is not a likely suspect – why kill him before he changed the will?" Alexander reflected.

"I need to track down the private detective who looked into her case. The Kellys didn't give us his name. I'll ask Sergeant Dunne to find him."

The two men drove the rest of the way back to Loughfarraig House in silence, both churning around ideas in their head.

CHAPTER 11

INTERVIEWS

David and Emily Hawke entered the interview room, where Alexander and Muldoon were waiting to question them.

"Please take a seat, Mr. and Mrs. Hawke," said Muldoon.

Alexander and Muldoon were sitting behind a teak table. The couple sat opposite them.

"We have just returned from Kelly solicitors in Galway. They have informed us that your father was in the process of changing the make-up of his company and his will. This would have been signed on the 8th January, had he lived, stated Muldoon. "Did you know, David, that this was about to happen?"

"We knew nothing about that – actually I find it very hard to believe. My father was very pleased at how the company was being run. He said nothing of the sort to any of us."

"So, your very good friend Jonathan Kelly didn't even give you a hint?" asked Alexander.

"Absolutely not," proclaimed David in a very agitated tone. "He couldn't and wouldn't have – you do know about client confidentiality."

"We really object to this type of questioning," Emily interrupted. "David has lost his beloved father and I, my very dear father-in-law. We learn that he has been murdered and now you are insinuating that we had a motive. We knew absolutely nothing about a will change. We are all grieving."

"Mrs. Hawke, we have to ask these questions, – it's our job. We do not mean to offend you," said Muldoon gently.

"I also, don't think it's right that you should insinuate that Jonathon Kelly passed on confidential information to me. I hold him in the highest regard," insisted David.

"May we check your alibi," said Muldoon.

"We went upstairs together after our drinks and stayed in the room all night," Emily said.

"Thank you, that will be all for now," concluded Muldoon.

The couple stood up, looked down their very haughty noses at the two men behind the desk and left the room.

"They'll all have the same story – they knew nothing about the will change, therefore they have no motive. They will all have the same alibi – in their bedrooms all night," muttered Muldoon.

Muldoon had been correct. The other two couples had exactly the same story – no knowledge of the will change – no motive – in their bedrooms all night. Alexander and Muldoon knew that they would stick to their story. They also were convinced that they were all lying. They didn't suspect Winnie Hawke, as she didn't have the wherewithal to murder her ex-husband. Everyone in the dining room had witnessed how much she had to drink. She was barely capable of walking. She had been helped by her son to keep her balance on her way out.

None of the family disputed Natalia's story of retiring early because of a headache. Of course, she had no alibi as she was alone in the bedroom. However, she did not appear to have a clear motive, as the others would not have informed her about the intended will changes.

"Of course there's the prenup," said Alexander suddenly. "If the marriage broke up, she would get nothing."

"But, there are easier ways to kill your husband, especially a big burly man like Donal Hawke, than to lure him down to the lake and hit him over the head with an oar. I really think that that's farfetched."

"Agreed," said Alexander.

"So, Natalia went to bed straight after dinner because of a headache. The others went into the sitting room to have drinks. Donal Hawke left very soon afterwards – the others believing that he had retired to bed. Maybe he went to meet someone – but who?" wondered Muldoon.

"I don't think that they knew anyone else here. They didn't speak to anyone except the owner, Gerald Moore. They barely nodded at anyone else. If he had met someone, it was in secret. He didn't inform his family.

Of course, he doesn't seem to have told them about a lot of things," concluded Alexander.

"We are none the wiser after those interviews. The only conclusions that we can reach, is that they are all liars, covering up the fact that Jonathon Kelly spilled the beans to David."

"I wonder is it too farfetched to think that it could be someone from his past, from his dodgy business dealings. I'm sure he has a lot of enemies. He was the type of man who would run roughshod over anyone who got in his way. Then you have the lawsuits against him. He must have been hated by his tenants, being a slum landlord."

"We have a lot of work to do," said Muldoon. "Sergeant Dunne and a group of officers are interviewing the staff, to see if they noticed anything – one of them might have been out for a smoke. We can't hold the other guests here indefinitely. I know most of them are booked in until the New Year, so, we'll get to interview them little by little and then allow them to leave. How are you fixed to stay on for a few days?"

"We are not due to leave yet. If I have to stay on, Monique can take the kids home,"

"Let's hope that we can make more progress tomorrow," said Muldoon.

CHAPTER 12

A SURPRISE

John Muldoon received a very interesting phone call from Garda Headquarters regarding a solicitor's office in Galway – James Byrne and Associates. The secretary had contacted Garda Headquarters, stating that her office had new, very important information regarding Donal Hawke. The message was relayed to Inspector John Muldoon at Loughfarraig House.

Alexander and Muldoon arrived at the solicitor's office early in the morning of the 30th December. They were shown into a rather small office, – that is in comparison to the large, ostentatious offices of Jonathan Kelly. A man of about forty years stood up to greet them.

"How do you do, I'm James Byrne."

Alexander and John introduced themselves and all three shook hands.

"Please take a seat, gentlemen."

"I hear that you have some information pertaining to our murder case," said Muldoon.

"Yes, I read in the papers about the sudden death of Donal Hawke. I was very much taken aback as he had visited our offices here on the 8th December to make his will and also to make changes to how his company was run."

Alexander and Muldoon sat up very straight in their chairs to listen very attentively to what was being said.

"Donal Hawke, as you've probably gleaned from the newspaper reports has been murdered," said Muldoon. "So, please relate every detail that occurred during your meeting."

"Well, as you can imagine, I was quite surprised when he requested a consultation. I had never met the man before, nor had any dealings with his family or company. Of course, like everyone else in the country, I knew him by reputation. He arrived at precisely 9am. He had a huge presence – not just his size, but his personality. To tell you the truth, I found him to be a very unpleasant man, gruff, overbearing – verging on the despotic. He barked out orders.

I asked him why he had decided to use me as his solicitor. Everyone in our circle knew that the Kellys were his long time solicitors.

He became quite annoyed but nevertheless, forthcoming with his reply.

He stated that he no longer trusted Kelly Junior who was best buddies with his son. I pointed out to him that Junior could not impart information to Hawke's son because of client confidentiality. He sneered at this and insisted that we got down to preparing the papers.

I pointed out to him that there didn't seem much point in changing matters pertaining to the running of the company, as he had total control of it. His children were only running the different entities, at his pleasure. Nevertheless, he insisted. He intimated that time mattered. Although, he looked like a man in rude health, I wonder if he had received bad news – medically. If I may suggest that to you, contact his doctor – whose name I do not know.

Regarding the company, Jack is to receive 80% of the American business, 40% of the British business and 40% of the Irish business. He has been made President of Hawke Developments – in other words – overall boss. The eldest son David is only to receive 20% of the British business. Joanne is to receive 20% of the Irish business. The surprise element of this is that there is another daughter, Emma Jones, an eighteen year old girl from London. Mr. Hawke had only been made aware of her existence in the last year or so. He had put his private detective, Frank Smith on the case, who determined that her claim was legitimate. She is to get 20% of the American business, and 40% of the other two. This is a huge inheritance. I pointed out that his other children would not be happy. He became quite agitated, more or less told me that it was none of my business and to just do my job. However, having chastised me, he proceeded to say that David was a waste of space. He spent a fortune on wine, women, song and gambling. His wife Emily was no better and was burning through money like there was no tomorrow. He seemed to have very little time for his daughter Joanne, either. He said that she had a penchant for unsuitable men – the latest being some French fellow. He thought more highly of his son Jack and his wife, Ava. He didn't explain why he had left such a considerable part of his business to a child that he doesn't really know. I was under the impression that his private detective Frank Smith knows the whole story.

His first wife Winnie will receive the substantial home where she now resides, plus £500,000. His second wife Natalia will receive £200,000 as per their agreement – but no property. He set up a generous trust fund for his grandson Toby. He has stipulated in his will that Toby's parents cannot get their hands on it. The trust fund will be managed by Jack Hawke and ourselves. There are bequests for some of the staff. Frank Smith will receive £50,000."

Alexander and Muldoon thanked James Byrne for all the information and assistance. They left the office to make their way back to the car.

"Well, that will certainly put the cat amongst the pigeons," said Alexander as they sat into the car.

"I would really love to be there at the reading of the will," laughed Muldoon.

"We have so much to investigate," continued Alexander. "All his business dealings in Ireland and abroad, his dealings with the East End mob, any law suits against him. We really need to speak to his private investigator, Frank Smith, as soon as possible – and his doctor."

"Absolutely," answered Muldoon. "I intend to ask the Commissioner to contact Scotland Yard and the F.B.I. so that we can get a full picture of Donal Hawke and whatever investigations there may have been in Britain and America. We don't know what sort of skulduggery that he was involved in, in the past."

By the time Alexander and Muldoon had returned to Loughfarraig House, many of the interviews had been completed. All the staff had been questioned – to no avail. The guests had also been quizzed but unfortunately, there did not seem to be any witnesses to the incident. Addresses were taken and the guests were allowed to leave the premises, as they wished..

The Hawke family decided to remain at Loughfarraig House until there was some progress made with the case. Most of the other guests who had been there for Christmas left on the 31st December. A small number of new guests arrived on the 31st for the New Year celebrations.

The Kings, Monique and the children left on the 31st as well, while Alexander stayed on with Inspector Muldoon.

"I'm really sorry Monique, but I must stay on here with John to help out. I hate leaving everything to you."

"Don't worry, darling, we'll manage perfectly well. I know that you're needed here. Hopefully, you'll make progress quickly."

"I wouldn't bet on it. I have a dreadful feeling that it's going to be very complicated. Donal Hawke has led a very eventful life. It appears that he made a great many enemies. And his children seemed to have despised him, and he them."

"We had better leave, Alexander. I know you'll get to the bottom of this, as you always do. I'll ring you tonight at eight o'clock. Bye, darling."

"Have a safe drive. Take care of your mother, kids. Be good."

"No problem Dad," said Max.

"See you soon, bye!" came the chorus from the back seat.

Alexander waved his family off and watched as they drove along the avenue. He knew that they would all manage perfectly well without him and now he could concentrate on who murdered Donal Hawke.

CHAPTER 13

THE LETTER

At 7.30pm, all the guests assembled in the front lounge for pre-dinner drinks. There weren't the same number of guests for New Year's dinner, as there had been for Christmas – only 20 guests – including the nine Hawkes, Alexander and John Muldoon. After the drinks, Mr. and Mrs. Moore led the diners into the dining room.

Alexander and John sat at a corner table, where they could observe what was happening elsewhere. Their corner table, gave them a great view of the long table, where the Hawkes were seated. David Hawke sat at the top of the table, where his father had sat only a few days ago. Beside him was his wife Emily instead of Natalia, who had been moved down the pecking order. Winnie Hawke was in her usual spot at the far end, sipping her gin and tonic.

The atmosphere at the Hawke table was more relaxed than hitherto. David was still clicking his fingers at the waiters and waitresses. He had obviously taken over as head of the family. Juan, the Colombian waiter was fussing over them and smiling broadly. Emma, the English waitress, with whom Monique had been chatting, was nowhere to be seen. Perhaps it was her night off.

"David Hawke is in for a hell of a surprise when the will is read," commented Alexander.

"He sure is. He's obviously taken over already in his head. He's sitting at the top of the table, lording it over everyone. Emily Hawke is also looking suitably smug," smiled John Muldoon.

David Hawke clicked his fingers once more at Juan and ordered a bottle of the most expensive champagne. Jack Hawke looked more sombre, and his wife Ava still appeared very off colour. But, in general, one would not have been of the impression that this was a family in mourning – only having lost their father and head of the family, five days ago. If one didn't know better, one would have thought that it was a celebration.

The following morning, during breakfast, a letter arrived by courier addressed to Jack Hawke. Mr. Moore had approached the family to ask Jack to accompany him to reception where the courier would not hand over the document without Jack's signature.

David and Emily looked very surprised that it was Jack's signature that was requested and not David's. Jack returned to the table a few minutes later holding a large brown envelope. He sat down and opened the envelope. The expression on his face went from curious to surprise, to shock. He sat staring at the contents in disbelief.

Alexander and John looked on in fascination. They had a pretty good idea what was in the envelope. The Hawkes were about to find out that their lives had changed – that their futures were not as expected. The two men watched as Jack said something, inaudible from where they were sitting, that resulted in David, Emily, Joanne and Jack quickly fleeing the table and walking at pace out of the dining room, abandoning the rest of the group, who looked after them in puzzlement.

"I'd love to be a fly on the wall for that conversation," said Alexander, sipping his coffee.

"What the hell is this all about?" shouted David angrily.

"I don't know, I just got the damned letter," replied Jack.

"What does it say exactly?" asked Emily.

"It's from a solicitor's office that I've never heard of – James Byrne and Associates. Dad visited him on the 8th December and changed his will. Seemingly, I'm the executor. The solicitor wants to speak to the whole family to relate who are the beneficiaries of the will. We can either go to his office or he has volunteered to come here, if that would be more convenient for us."

"How on earth could you be the executor Jack, David is taking over," said Emily.

"I haven't the foggiest, Emily," replied Jack curtly.

"Dad obviously didn't trust your good friend Jonathan, David, and sussed what he would do – tell us about his intentions. So he went to another solicitor and made all the changes that he wanted to."

"Tell that damned solicitor to come here," ordered David, who then stormed out of the room, leaving the others flabbergasted.

"What else was in the letter, Jack?" asked Joanne.

"It says that Dad made a great deal of changes. He also made provision for this illegitimate English daughter. Her name is Emma Jones. The solicitor mentions that she will be entitled to a large share of the company. He is endeavouring to locate her. I don't have the exact details, but it sounds extremely serious.

"We are just not going to put up with this," said Emily. "We'll fight it. Why should we share anything with this Emma creature and why should you be left to run the company, when it was always meant to be David."

"What kind of fool do you think Dad was?" interrupted Joanne. "He knew exactly how David was behaving. He spent more of his time in casinos, horse tracks, golfing, the most expensive hotels and restaurants than running his part of the company. Dad wasn't any kind of fool. He knew all about David's shenanigans with Jonathan Kelly."

"Well you're no angel, Joanne," retorted Emily. "Do you really think that Donal Hawke approved of all your younger men – you changed boyfriends more often than you changed suits. He despised you for that – and that latest fellow, Francois – just a typical toy boy. What age is he? 28.?"

"Please, please, stop bickering. It's not going to do any good," said Jack in despair.

The two women took deep breaths, looked at each other and then sat down on the armchairs in front of the fire.

"We could be very badly affected by all this," said Emily. "We'll have to stick together. We can't let that little trollop take what's rightfully ours."

"Does anyone really think that whatever Dad has done legally, will not be airtight? You'll see there will be no loopholes," concluded Jack.

CHAPTER 14

THE FIXER

At two o'clock on the 1st January, Alexander and Muldoon parked their car in front of The Great Southern Hotel in Eyre Square in Galway city. There were very few people about. Most were probably recovering from the festivities of the night before.

Muldoon had received a phone call from Sergeant Dunne at eleven o'clock stating that Frank Smith was willing to meet with them at the hotel that afternoon.

This grand hotel which was originally called The Railway Hotel, was opened to the public on the 16th August 1862. Prince Louis Napoleon of France was the first royal visitor in July 1857. Many other notable and historic figures have crossed it's threshold.

Alexander and Muldoon climbed up the few steps to it's grand entrance. A beautifully attired doorman opened the oak door, and the two men entered the foyer. The hotel hadn't lost it's elegance and exquisite luxury. The furniture was opulent, the drapes were made of the most expensive fabric and the chandeliers hung majestically. They scanned the foyer – there were two elderly couples having afternoon tea by the fireplace. They walked past the reception area and turned right into an adjacent sitting room. There, they saw a man sitting alone reading the morning paper. They walked towards him. He heard them approach, put down the newspaper on the table and looked in their direction. He nodded as if to say, "you've the right man." He stood up as they reached his table, held out his hand and introduced himself.

"I'm Frank Smith – heard you wanted to have a chat."

They all shook hands. Alexander and Muldoon sat on the couch opposite. Frank Smith was a man in his seventies, dressed in an expensive grey suit and grey tie with tie pin. His white shirt was immaculate and his black shoes were shining. He was about 5 feet 8 inches in height and extremely skinny. Muldoon noticed brown nicotine marks on his fingers. His face was well worn and his hair silver grey. His eyes, which were also grey, were cold and steely. Alexander thought about how different Smith and Hawke were in appearance – little and large.

"How can I help you gentlemen?" Smith asked.

"As you know, the body of Donal Hawke was found in the lake of Loughfarraig House in Mayo on St. Stephen's day. He had been murdered," began Muldoon. "We were informed by Jonathan Kelly, his solicitor, that he had intended changing his will. He wished to make provision for an English daughter that he didn't know existed until recently. It appears that you found her and checked out her story and deemed it to be true."

"That's correct," replied Smith, taking a packet of Woodbines and a lighter from his jacket pocket.

"Anyone for a fag?"

"No thanks," replied both men.

Smith placed the cigarette in his mouth, lit it with his silver lighter and inhaled the smoke deeply into his lungs. He then beckoned to a waiter who had been hovering around.

"Double whiskey and a black coffee, please. What about you gentlemen?"

"Just coffee please," answered Alexander.

"Same here,"

"Emma Jones contacted Mr. Hawke by letter about a year ago. Donal spoke to his solicitor who advised him to ignore it – that it was probably some gold digger after his money. He spoke to me about it – it was niggling at him. So he put me on the job and off I took to London to find her. That wasn't much of a problem as we had her address – Shephard's Bush – a small bedsit. I knocked on the door, explained to her who I was and she let me in."

The waiter suddenly appeared with the coffees and whiskey. Smith drank the coffee first and then took a slug of the whiskey before continuing.

"Emma Jones' mother died about 18 months ago. She had never known who her father was. Emma went through her mother's stuff and found her diary. That's how she found out about Donal Hawke. He wasn't mentioned on her birth certificate. She showed me her mother's diary. Her mother's name was Katie Jones. I only had to read a few pages of the diary before recognising who she was. You see, I knew her. I remembered her. She worked as a hostess in a club in the East End. Donal Hawke used to frequent the "Sunflower Club". It was a way of socialising with some of his business acquaintances. I usually went with him.

Katie was serving our table one night. She seemed to be new to the job and came across as a bit shy and innocent. She was only about twenty – a very pretty little thing. Well, Donal took a shine to her and they began seeing a lot of each other. There was a huge age gap. He was mid fifties and I hadn't seen him smitten like this before – he had been married to Winnie for years. He had always been more interested in business than women. Then suddenly, she just upped and left – disappeared – nowhere to be found. That was nearly nineteen years ago. Donal hadn't heard from her at all during the intervening years. Emma said that she and her mother lived in Scotland for a long while. They moved back to London when she was twelve. Her mother worked as a chambermaid in the Regent Palace Hotel. Anytime she had asked about her father, her mother just told her that he had moved away before she was born. Emma had hoped to go to university after school but unfortunately her mother got leukemia and passed away very quickly. Amongst her mother's letters and diaries, Emma found a gold locket with a photo of a smiling Donal Hawke with her mother. Katie had always kept the box locked, so this was the first time that Emma had seen his face. Emma allowed me to take the diary and locket to show to Donal as proof of her existence. He was convinced that Emma was his daughter, the moment he laid eyes on the locket – he had given it to Katie as a present."

"How did Mr. Hawke react to the news?" Muldoon asked.

"Well at first he was very surprised – stunned really, but then became very happy about the discovery. I remember him saying to me that Katie was the only one who never asked him for anything. He still didn't understand why she just disappeared, without a word, to bring up a child on her own. I suppose we'll never know that, as Katie has taken it to the grave with her. She never married or had any more children – it was just herself and Emma. Donal Hawke was determined, from the moment he saw the locket, that he would do right by Emma."

"Did they ever meet up?" Alexander asked.

"That, I don't know. I suppose he never got around to changing his will either," said Smith.

"That's where you're wrong, Mr. Smith. He went to a different solicitor and the will was changed on the 8th December," answered Muldoon.

A wry smile appeared on the wrinkled face of Frank Smith.

"Well, well, crafty old devil. The rest of them won't like that much."

He finished his whiskey and ordered another double, lit another Woodbine and inhaled the smoke with satisfaction. Alexander and Muldoon sipped their coffee as they watched Smith stub out his cigarette butt in the Waterford glass ashtray on the mahogany table in front of them.

"I've been friends with Donal Hawke since national school. We were in first class when we hit it off. I was a small puny kid. There was this fellow always stealing my lunch. Donal came over one day and hit him a punch – that was it – friends forever."

"So you're from the same village," said Muldoon.

"We are indeed – went right through school together. We hadn't much growing up. I joined the army at sixteen, and Donal went off to London to work on the buildings. We always stayed in touch. I didn't like the army much. He started making money and so he offered me a job. I've been with him ever since. He needed someone he could really trust."

"What kind of work did you do for him?" Muldoon asked.

Alexander noticed Smith's demeanour change slightly. He sat back in his chair, crossed his arms, and then took out another cigarette and lit it.

"I did all sorts, whenever he needed help. If he was going to buy a new business or take on new investors, I'd look into them and I made sure that everything was the way it was supposed to be."

"Did you just work in England?" asked Muldoon.

"No. If he needed me in America to suss something out, I'd go there. If I was needed here in Ireland – I'd be here. I'd go wherever I was needed. He paid me very well. He always looked after me."

Smith took another slug of his whiskey followed by a few drags on his cigarette. Alexander noticed that despite all the whiskey there was absolutely no sign of Smith becoming tipsy. He was well able to hold his liquor. He was as tough as old boots.

"Did you know that Mr. Hawke had provided for you in his will?" asked Alexander.

"Yes, I knew – he told me as much. He was my family. I never married – never really was bothered about all that. Just loved my job. Think I'll retire now – don't fancy working for his children. I have a nice flat here in Galway."

"I think we'll leave it at that," said Muldoon. "Thank you very much for meeting us. You've been very helpful. I hope you accept our condolences. You've lost your very good friend. it must be very hard for you."

"Yes, thanks for that," replied Smith.

"Just one more thing. On the off chance, would you know who his doctor was?"

"He had doctors in America, England and here, but the one he trusted most was Dr. O'Brien, here, in Salthill. He's known him for years."

The three men shook hands. Alexander and Muldoon made their way into the foyer, out the main door, opened for them once more by the same doorman and down the steps towards their car as Frank Smith ordered another double whiskey and lit another cigarette.

The two men sat into the car. John Muldoon began searching for something in a bag under the back seat.

"I have a Yellow Pages here somewhere. It would be very handy if we could locate Donal Hawke's doctor. We'd be very lucky if he were at home on New Year's day and willing to see us."

John located the book and began flicking through the pages. He stopped at a page and pointed at a name.

"That must be him. There's only one Dr. O'Brien in Salthill."

Muldoon placed an envelope between the pages and closed the book.

"I'm going back into the hotel to make a phone call – let's hope he's home."

John Muldoon alighted from the car and ran up the steps of the hotel – yellow pages under his arm. The door was held open for him.

Alexander watched as he disappeared into the foyer.

Five minutes later, Muldoon returned to the car.

"Great news – he's there and he will see us in fifteen minutes."

They drove the relatively short distance from Eyre square to Salthill. There were a few people walking along the promenade in Salthill. It was quite windy so the waves were high and breaking on the sand. The walkers were wrapped up in heavy coats, hats and scarves. Muldoon turned right at the end of the promenade as he had been directed to do by the very helpful receptionist at the Great Southern. They entered a small estate with well established, large houses. They stopped at Number one, which had a very large garden, the house covered in ivy, with impressive bay windows.

Dr. O'Brien had seen them arrive and was waiting at the door to show them in. He led them into the front parlour – a very comfortable room with a large Christmas tree in a corner, and a garland hanging over the mantlepiece.

"Please take a seat gentlemen."

Alexander and John sat on the couch as the doctor took up his seat on one of the armchairs, facing the couch.

"I gather this is about Donal Hawke."

"Yes, indeed," answered Muldoon. "Please allow me to introduce Commandant de Bruin, who is assisting us with our investigation."

Both men exchanged pleasantries.

"I heard through the grapevine that he had passed away. I have no details, apart from what I've read in the papers," said the doctor.

"We must inform you that he has been murdered. As you've probably read, the body was found in the lake at Loughfarraig House on St. Stephen's Day. At first we thought that he had drowned, having fallen into the lake accidentally, but on examination, it was discovered that there were fatal wounds to his head."

"What a dreadful thing to have happened," interjected the doctor. "I suppose I can speak freely about his health as it's a murder."

"Yes you can. I can assure you of that," added Muldoon.

"Donal Hawke had been my patient for over thirty years. I know that he also saw doctors in America and England, as he spent so much time abroad, but he tended to come back to me for a general check-up about once a year. Last August he made an appointment to see me. He told me that he had pains in his back and abdomen and was feeling generally very lethargic. Lethargy wasn't something that befell Donal. He was a man with great stores of energy. He was always on the go – wheeling and dealing. To cut a long story short – I had very bad news to impart to him. There was nothing to be done, apart from getting his medication right, so that he would feel more comfortable. His illness was terminal."

"How long had you given him?" asked Alexander.

"Twelve months – give or take a few weeks," answered the doctor. "He told me that he had no intention of telling his family, until near the end. Donal wanted to put everything in order. So, as far as I am aware, I am the only person who knew that his end was nigh. We had arranged for a medical team to look after him at his home in Mayo when the time came. So at best he had about 8 months left. Fortunately, the medication was doing a very good job and he wasn't suffering with a lot of pain."

"I think that gives us all the information we need," said Muldoon. "Thank you so much for seeing us on such short notice and on New Year's day. We are very grateful to you."

The three men said their goodbyes. Alexander and Muldoon returned to the car.

"That's a bit of a shock," said Alexander. "Donal Hawke certainly didn't look like a man who had only a few months to live. So, it would appear that he was going to tell his family over the Christmas holidays, that he was going to make changes to his will and business. He was also going to inform them about the existence of his long lost daughter, and his provision for her in his will. It seems that he never got around to any of this before he was murdered."

"We are also fairly certain that David Hawke's good friend Jonathan Kelly informed him about the impending changes and most likely the other family members knew about it as well. They thought that they had a number of weeks to change his mind, before he returned to Jonathan Kelly, solicitor, in January. Unbeknown to them, he had already made the changes at the offices of James Byrne and Associates, being rightly suspicious that Jonathan Kelly junior would inform his good friend David about his plans."

"No one in that family will ever admit to us that they knew about Donal Hawke's intentions," added Alexander. "First of all Jonathan Kelly would be struck off for breaking client confidentiality and secondly it would give them all a very strong motive for the murder."

"We have to find the daughter, Emma Jones. I will ask Sergeant Dunne to make the relevant phone calls to London, in order to locate her. I'm also expecting a call back from the Commissioner, informing me about how he got on with the F.B.I. and Scotland Yard. I don't believe that our suspects are confined to the family. Donal Hawke must have made enemies all over the world."

"I wonder if someone would come all the way from America to Mayo to murder him," pondered Alexander.

"It would certainly be much easier to get at him at Loughfarraig House, than in one of his properties in America or England or even Dublin," added Muldoon.

"Yes, it was always in the papers, how he loved to come back to his roots in the West of Ireland. It would have been easy enough to find out where he was staying," concluded Alexander.

CHAPTER 15

THE AMERICAN

Back at Loughfarraig House, Alexander and John sat in front of the turf fire, having lunch. They had decided on a delicious fish chowder, with home made brown bread. They were relaxing, sipping their coffee when the receptionist came to their table.

"Inspector Muldoon, there is a phone call for you. You can take it in the office."

John rose from the table and followed the young, red head into the office. Alexander remained seated, watching the turf flames dancing in the hearth. He thought about his family back in Briarstown and, although it had only been a couple of days, he really missed them.

Fifteen minutes later, Muldoon returned to the table.

"That was the Commissioner," he said.

"What news?" asked Alexander.

"Well, he got virtually nowhere with Scotland Yard – not a bit co-operative, it would seem."

"That's no problem really," replied Alexander. "I can use my own contacts from army days to find out all about Donal Hawke's businesses in England. What about the F.B.I.? Any joy there?"

"That's a different story altogether. He was very lucky that he spoke to an extremely helpful young agent, whose own father – also an F.B.I. agent – retired – worked on an investigation into Donal Hawke, going back thirty years. They were never able to prove anything, but his father became very friendly with a man called Bruce Gilbert, whose business was destroyed by Mustelus Developments. The man has spent years trying to prove wrong-doing on the part of Hawke. When Gilbert learned of Hawke's murder, he booked a plane ticket to Ireland.

He is expected to arrive in Shannon tomorrow morning. He is going to rent a car and make his way here. All going well we should expect him at about midday tomorrow."

"That's an extraordinary development," added Alexander.

At 11.45 on the second of January, Bruce Gilbert drove his rental car into the grounds of Loughfarraig House. Alexander and Muldoon were watching out the window of the foyer for his arrival. He was a man in his mid-seventies, slightly balding, looking somewhat dishevelled. His suit was creased and his tie loose. He was carrying a small weekend bag, and a large briefcase which appeared heavy. Alexander and John stood up as he entered the foyer. He made his way to reception.

"I'm Bruce Gilbert. I've booked a room for two nights."

The man had a very evident American accent, so John and Alexander were in no doubt that this indeed was Bruce Gilbert. Inspector Muldoon approached the American and introduced himself.

"Give me fifteen minutes to go to my room and freshen up. I'll meet you here then."

The new arrival grabbed his key and shuffled down the corridor to his room, aided by one of the waiters.

On his return, he was looking a little less frazzled – had changed his clothes into a more casual outfit – jumper and jeans. He was carrying his briefcase which he placed on the floor beside an armchair.

"Let me introduce you to Commandant Alexander de Bruin, who is helping me with this investigation," said Muldoon.

"How do," said Gilbert, shaking Alexander's hand.

"Can we get some coffee here?" asked Gilbert.

"Of course," said Alexander, catching a waiter's eye.

The coffee and scones arrived five minutes later.

"That was a long journey here. It's my first time in Ireland. This is a really beautiful hotel. The driving on the wrong side of the road is a bit much though," continued Gilbert.

The American's thought process seemed to be all over the place. He was exhausted after his long journey from Philadelphia, all the way to the West of Ireland. However, having drunk copious amounts of coffee and eaten three scones, he seemed to be gathering his thoughts together, and started to make sense.

"I hear that rogue, Hawke has been murdered. It's about time someone did him in. I wish that I had had the courage to do it myself years ago."

Alexander made a mental note to check the plane manifest to make sure that Bruce Gilbert arrived in Ireland when he said he did. Otherwise he would make a very viable suspect.

"Can you tell us about your dealings with Donal Hawke?" asked Alexander.

"I can surely," answered Gilbert.

"I wish that I had never laid eyes on the man or his minions. My family had a thriving development company in Philadelphia. It was started by my grandfather. Then my father ran it and finally I took charge. The company was doing very well. The whole community depended on the work. We were expanding – not just building houses, but also hotels. We even renovated the local fire station. Things were surely looking good. Then one morning, this Irishman came into my office. He wanted to buy the company. Of course, I refused. It was a family business and I wanted to hand it down to my own children.

He wouldn't take no for an answer and came back several times. Suddenly, he stopped calling and I was relieved. Then things started to go wrong. It started with small things – like cement put into the plumbing, which caused flooding, electrics blowing for apparently no reason. After a few months it escalated – there were two fires on our sites. Some of our sub-contractors didn't turn up. We couldn't fulfill our contracts. I became very suspicious that we were being sabotaged. Some of my men said that another Irishman was lurking around our sites a lot, a fellow called Smith. Of course I asked the police for help. They weren't able to prove anything. Some of the officers even suggested that I was sloppy. Then, the company itself was investigated for arson. The last straw, I suppose was when two of the men fell from scaffolding. One of the men, James Henry was killed, and the second man John Grimes broke his back, and spent the rest of his life in a wheelchair. He died two years ago. So, I was very near bankruptcy when Hawke came back with another offer. It was a hostile takeover really. I couldn't understand why there weren't other offers but later I deduced that there must have been threats and bribery involved. At the last meeting, all the lawyers were involved. I only got paid a fraction of what the business was worth.

Hawke promised that he would look after the employees. So I signed my company away on that day, knowing full well, in my heart that Hawke had caused our downfall."

"Did he keep his word about looking after the employees?" asked Alexander.

"Of course he didn't. Six months later they were all let go, and he brought in cheap labour – bussed them in and out. Our whole community was badly affected. I was lucky, we had land, so we moved out and started farming. We've been doing that ever since. The kids went to college and have their own lives now."

"So, how did you get involved with that F.B.I. agent?" asked John.

"Well, I kept an eye on Donal Hawke's behaviour. He didn't try the same stunt again in our state, but he moved on and destroyed family companies in other states, and made a fortune in the process. He moved states because of how the law works in America. I contacted the F.B.I. and a young agent was allocated to the case. Apart from that one agent, no one seemed interested. They had bigger fish to fry. Over the years I became very friendly with the agent and we gathered our portfolio of evidence against Mustelus Development. But nothing would stick. Hawke became richer and more powerful. He had lawyers covering his back. The company now has hotels, rental properties and huge developments all over the country.

I'm fairly sure that he has politicians in his pocket. There's a class action suit against the company because of the conditions of his rental properties. Children have become ill. I know that this is still ongoing."

"Why have you brought all this to us?" asked Muldoon. "Do you suspect that someone in America came to Ireland to murder him?"

"I don't give a damn who murdered him – actually I would like to shake his hand. I just want all this to come out. Now, that he's dead and you're doing all this investigating, I had hoped that finally people would be able to get compensation for all the suffering that he has caused. There are families living in penury because of him. I also believe that he behaved in this fashion wherever he went. You'll find that he did the same here in Ireland and in England. I know that as your investigation continues here in Ireland, you are going to uncover fraud, bribery etc. So, I'm handing you my file to make life easier for you and point you in the right direction. He must have used the same methods here. One more thing, I'd really like you to get that Smith fellow – he was his fixer – and a very dangerous man."

Bruce Gilbert handed the briefcase, holding thick wads of information, to John Muldoon, rose from his chair and headed back down the corridor towards his room. His step was more sprightly, as if a great burden had been lifted from his shoulders.

Muldoon opened the briefcase and removed the files. They were divided into six folders – one for each state.

"Let's divide these up – half and half."

Muldoon handed Alexander three of the files.

"We can't study these here under the gaze of anyone who passes through. Better to take them to our rooms and reconvene in two hours," suggested Alexander.

"Good idea," said Muldoon.

CHAPTER 16

THE WILL

The Hawke family assembled in the billiard room of Loughfarraig House, awaiting the arrival of James Byrne, solicitor, and the reading of the will of Donal Hawke.

At exactly 2pm, the door opened.

"Good afternoon, my name is James Byrne. In my possession is the last will and testament of Donal Hawke. This will was made on the 8th December last, in my office in Galway – witnessed by two of my staff. Jack Hawke has been named as executor."

Gerald Moore had arranged the removal of the billiard table earlier that day and in it's stead was a round table to facilitate the family and solicitor.

The family sat quietly around the table as James Byrne began his task.

He explained that there were a number of bequests to valuable staff members of Mustelus Developments – the largest being to Frank Smith. Winnie Hawke seemed to be pleased with her inheritance as was the second Mrs. Hawke – Natalia. It was then explained that Toby would receive a very generous trust fund with the stipulation that it would be managed by his uncle Jack Hawke.

"That's ridiculous!" interjected David Hawke. "We're his parents. I really object to this."

"I'm sorry, Mr. Hawke," replied Byrne, calmly, "but these are your father's wishes."

Both Emily and David glared at the solicitor, and then at Jack who appeared most uncomfortable. Ava placed her hand on Jack's hand and squeezed. Toby looked very confused and his eyes darted from his parents to his uncle and back to his parents again.

David and Emily were becoming more and more agitated. Emily lit a cigarette, inhaled deeply and then blew smoke in Jack's direction. Ava began to cough, then took a sip of water to settle her stomach.

"Get on with it, man, tell us about the business," insisted David.

"According to Donal Hawke's instructions, Jack is to receive 80% of the American business and assets, 40% of the British business and assets and 40% of the Irish business. He has been made President of Mustelus Developments."

"I've always run all the British stuff and Joanne, the Irish stuff," interrupted David. "But I suppose, there's the other 60%, so we'll have the lion's share."

James Byrne took a deep breath before continuing.

"David Hawke is to receive 20% of the British business and assets. Joanne Hawke is to receive 20% of the Irish business and assets."

Both David and Joanne stood up and glared at the "messenger".

"20%," screamed Joanne. "What about the rest of it? Is this some sort of joke?"

Emily stubbed out her cigarette in the Waterford glass ashtray on the table in front of her and immediately lit another. Winnie looked around at her family and a wry smile appeared on her face. David and Joanne were furious while Jack and Ava sat quietly, staring straight ahead.

"May I continue please?"

Joanne and David took their seats again.

"Emma Jones, the youngest child of Donal Hawke is to receive 20% of the American business and assets, 40% of the British business and assets and 40% of the Irish business and assets."

After a moment of shock, pandemonium ensued. Voices were raised in anger and disbelief. David lifted his chair and threw it against the wall. Joanne began to cry. Ava left the room, obviously with morning sickness. The solicitor sat stoically in his chair, looking at the melee – never before had he seen such a reaction to the reading of a will.

Jack then spoke.

"Have you located Emma Jones? Is she aware of this?"

"No, not as yet. I have an address for her in London but I have not been able to contact her," replied Byrne.

"We are going to fight this," shouted David.

"That's your prerogative," answered Byrne.

Alexander and Muldoon had spent nearly two hours studying the files which had been given to them by Bruce Gilbert. They contained a litany of skulduggery, bribes to politicians and police, so called accidents on sites, arson, and dereliction of duty towards tenants. The same modus operandi has been used to take over businesses. Intimidation of anyone who got in the way. And over and over again, there appeared the spectre of Frank Smith the "enforcer". Lawsuits had been taken against Donal Hawke, but many of them had been dropped, for whatever reason. Businesses and families had been destroyed. Still, nothing had ever been proven. Hawke had employed a band of lawyers who would swoop in and sweep everything away, or drown his opponents in paperwork and counter claims. Hawke, Smith and their minions moved from state to state like locusts.

"Well, that was some read," said Alexander.

"What a piece of work," added Muldoon.

The two men were once again seated in their usual spot by the turf fire.

"Donal Hawke had so many enemies. Our suspect pool has just grown exponentially," groaned Muldoon.

"This has opened a real can of worms for us," continued Alexander. "He probably used the same modus operandi in Britain and Ireland. He was like a Mafia Boss. Are we going to uncover a whole web of corruption here in Ireland – politicians, bribery of local council officials? I know he owns some apartments in the city here. There are bound to be disgruntled tenants."

"He had a dodgy reputation always, but I'd have heard through the grapevine if there were guards involved," said Muldoon.

"Let's hope not," added Alexander.

"We're fairly sure that he got his first investment money from the mob in the East End in the forties. He expanded his interests all over Britain, then went into America and only later invested in Ireland. I just hope that there's no paramilitary involvement as well, to add to our difficulties."

"Looks like we are going to stir up a hornet's nest," sighed Muldoon.

"Any idea when the funeral is?"

"Tomorrow morning at 9 o'clock – no Mass – no ceremony at all as per Hawke's wishes – family only. No need for us to attend as we would learn nothing from it. The only people who will attend will be back here after the event."

"I'm going to order some coffee. Would you like some, John?"

"Sure, why not,"

Alexander caught the eye of the young waitress who was passing by. She walked over towards them.

"What can I get you?"

Alexander recognised her as the young girl with whom Monique had been chatting one evening at dinner. He hadn't seen her since. He noticed that her eyes were swollen, as if she had been crying. Her face was as white as a sheet and her hands were shaking as she held her notepad and pen.

"A pot of coffee for two please."

The young woman returned five minutes later with their order and placed it on the table.

"I need to speak to you. I'm in awful trouble. My shift ends in half an hour," she pleaded.

"Of course, no problem at all. We'll meet you in the small sitting room, at the end of the corridor in half an hour," said Alexander reassuringly.

CHAPTER 17

EMMA'S STORY

Alexander and Muldoon sat patiently waiting for the arrival of the young waitress. The door suddenly opened and a very distraught young woman entered the room, tears streaming down her cheeks. She looked at the two men beseechingly. Alexander stood up and led her to a comfortable armchair, facing the couch where Muldoon was seated. He handed her a glass of water. She took it from him gratefully, her hands trembling.

"Please take a moment to compose yourself," said Alexander, wishing with all his heart that Monique was here – she was much better at handling these types of situations.

A few moments passed, and gradually the young woman calmed down a little.

"My name is Emma Jones. I'm Donal Hawke's daughter," she blurted out.

This was not what Alexander and Muldoon had expected. Then Alexander remembered the conversation that Monique had had at dinner with the young waitress with the English accent.

"We are very pleased to make your acquaintance," said Alexander.

"There are a lot of people looking for you," added Muldoon.

"We are very sorry about the loss of your father," continued Alexander.

"I didn't really know what to do. I thought that I was responsible for his death."

Emma began to cry again and started to hyperventilate. Muldoon left the room in search of a brown paper bag, which he found at reception.

On his return, he handed it to Emma, who placed it over her mouth and nose to control her breathing. Alexander told her to take slow, deep breaths. After a few minutes, her breathing returned to normal.

"You see, I have no one here – no one to talk to. He was the only person who knew who I was. The rest of the family aren't aware. He was going to tell them the next day."

"Why do you think that you were responsible for his death?" asked Muldoon.

"Because he fell in the lake."

"Okay, Emma, because this is not making much sense to us, we would like you to start at the very beginning of your story. Slowly tell us how you ended up working here at Loughfarraig House. Perhaps, if you started with how and when you found out that Donal Hawke was your father," said Alexander calmly.

So, Emma began her tale. Both men believed that by allowing someone to tell their story without interruption, unless something had to be clarified, one could build up a whole picture of the person and also what had occurred.

"I never knew who my father was. It didn't matter how many times I asked my mother – she wouldn't tell me. Mum just said that he had left before I was born. We lived in Scotland until I was twelve. She always worked very hard. We always had enough to live on. She was very proud of me as I was very good at school. The teachers always told her that I was "Oxford" material. I think we both believed that I would study at Oxford, so we moved back to London. Mum got a job as a chambermaid at the Regent Palace Hotel. Then a year and a half ago, she got leukemia – poor Mum only lasted six months. She didn't actually tell me who my father was, but she must have known that I would find out when I opened her locked box. The box contained her diary which told the story of how my parents met. His name was there staring at me – Donal Hawke. I also found a gold locket with a photo of my mother and him. I knew who he was. I had seen his photo in the papers. I decided to write to him. I didn't hear back at all, until there was a knock on my door. It was a private detective called Smith. He asked me loads of questions. He took the diary and locket with him to show Mr. Hawke. I didn't hear anything back. I read everything I could about Donal Hawke. I found out about his roots and home in Mayo. So, I applied for a job here and got it. I wanted to be close to where he came from. I had nobody else.

I couldn't believe the coincidence when Mr. Moore told us about the whole Hawke family coming here to Loughfarraig House for Christmas. I made up my mind that I would confront him and tell him who I was. I served them at table a few times. I thought that they were all very rude and arrogant. But, on Christmas Day, I approached him and told him who I was. He wasn't annoyed at all. He looked very closely at me. He told me that I resembled my mother. Then he said that he would meet me down by the lake – down by the jetty, – Christmas night at about ten o'clock."

Alexander and Muldoon looked at each other, both wondering if this young lady was about to confess to murdering her father. Her whole demeanour was now very calm. The more she spoke, the more at ease, she appeared.

"Did you meet him?" asked Muldoon.

"Yes, we met down at the jetty. We had a good chat. He said that he intended getting in touch with me. He didn't want his other children to know that he had accepted that I was his daughter yet. He also said that he had other surprises in store for them."

"Did he say what these surprises might be?" Alexander asked.

"No, he didn't," replied Emma.

"So, what happened next?" Muldoon asked.

"I don't know how it happened, but he slipped on the wooden jetty – it was all slimy – and fell in. Then, the moon went behind a cloud and I couldn't see anything. I heard splashing around. I called out and finally I heard him say, "I'm okay, I'm able to get out.""

"The voice came from over on the right – I thought he had made his way over to the shore."

Then he shouted. "Get back to the hotel, I don't want anyone to see us together yet. I'm fine. I'm going to go in the back door, so no-one sees me in this state."

So, I ran back into the hotel and up to my room thinking that everything was OK. I couldn't believe it when his body was found in the lake the next day. I thought he must have fallen back into the lake again and drowned, that it was my fault for leaving him there. I didn't know what to do, or who to tell. Then I heard that he had been murdered – hit over the head with something. I have been so worried. Everyone is going to think that I murdered him."

"Did you see anyone else around?" Muldoon asked.

"Nobody. I ran in the side door, but I don't think anyone was about. There could have been people down by the sea. That's where some of the staff go out for a smoke. Sure, if someone had seen him in difficulty, they'd have come over to help."

"You'd have thought so," added Alexander.

"I heard the family talking about the funeral tomorrow. I wonder could I go?" Emma asked.

Alexander and Muldoon looked at each other, knowing how troublesome all of this was going to be. The family certainly wouldn't choose to believe Emma's story. They would be delighted if she were proven to be the murderer – she would be out of the will – you can't profit in a will from your misdeeds.

"I suggest that you go back to your room and rest. We will have to inform the family about the recent developments. I also need to inform you that you are a beneficiary of Donal Hawke's will. You have inherited a great amount. Unfortunately that gives you a motive for his murder – that is if you knew about it." concluded Muldoon.

"But I didn't know, this is news to me. I only met him here and we only spoke for a few minutes. I promise you, I knew nothing about this, and I most certainly didn't kill him."

The tears began to well up in her eyes again. She looked beseechingly at Muldoon and Alexander.

"Don't worry, we will get to the truth. We will find the murderer," insisted Alexander.

Somewhat reassured, Emma left the room to return to her quarters.

"What do you think, John?"

"I'm not sure. It sounds like a tall tale. She had a very strong motive – either way. Donal Hawke might have been unpleasant to her. She could easily have whacked him over the head with the oar. She might have killed him to get her inheritance – that is – if she knew about it."

"I'm inclined to believe her – unless she's a great actress," added Alexander.

"If she didn't hit him, as he was trying to get out of the water, then someone was watching, and took advantage of the situation in order to kill him," said Muldoon.

"At least, we now have an approximate time of death. The family seem to have alibis – if you can believe them. I still wouldn't rule them out. Then, if Emma is telling the truth – who was watching?"

"We have to keep an open mind" said John. "From Hawke's history and the people with whom he has done business, it could have been a hit. It was common knowledge that he was going to be in Mayo for Christmas. It wouldn't have taken much sleuthing to fathom that he was in Loughfarraig House."

"There will be a lot of pressure on you to make an arrest, John. It would be very convenient, for all concerned, if Emma were charged and convicted. That would put an end to the investigation into Mustelus Developments – in the three jurisdictions. It would really suit the family and any persons involved in skulduggery."

"There is a very strong case against her. A prosecutor would say that she had means, motive and opportunity – which she had."

"Yes indeed," said Alexander, "but why on earth come forward? There was no suspicion on her. She wasn't seen – or someone would have reported it. You must try to convince the Commissioner that we have grave doubts about her guilt and are more inclined to believe her story."

"I'll make the phone call," said John. "We will also have to inform James Byrne, the solicitor, that Emma has been located."

"That girl is all alone, here." responded Alexander. "The family will not wish to help her. She will need a very good solicitor to represent her, both in sorting out her inheritance, and in defending her against a murder charge, if that transpires. I'm going to ring the Old Rectory. Between the two of them, they should be able to help Emma."

The Brownes, who lived at the Old Rectory knew the law inside out. Lydia was a former District Judge and barrister, Damien a practicing solicitor. The two men left the sitting room to go to their rooms to make the phone calls. The Brownes were very helpful and agreed immediately to represent Emma Jones. Alexander also made a call to Monique to inform her about all the latest developments. She remembered chatting to the young English waitress and offered to help out in any way she could. Monique had great sympathy for Emma Jones, knowing that she could be thrown to the wolves. The Hawkes were a very powerful, wealthy family who would do all they could to destroy the young woman.

It was decided that both Lydia and Monique would make the journey to Loughfarraig House immediately, leaving Damien in Briarstown to hold down the fort and look after all the animals, with the help of the children, who were not due back to boarding school until the 6th January.

Meanwhile, Muldoon had phoned the Garda Commissioner at Garda Headquarters. He imparted all the information to him, – the files from Bruce Gilbert, the shady dealings of the Hawkes' businesses and finally Emma's story. The Commissioner agreed that Emma Jones would not be arrested – that there were many other suspects to be investigated before such a move. He had learned to listen to John Muldoon's opinion since the last case, where a suspect had been arrested prematurely.

Alexander and Muldoon reconvened in the same room. They were both pleased at the outcomes of their phone calls.

"Monique and Lydia are on their way," said Alexander, sounding very relieved. "I have to admit, that I'm not much good at dealing with young women who are distraught. Monique is much better at that sort of thing,"

"Me too," agreed Muldoon. "The phone call to the Commissioner was very positive. He agrees with us, that the investigation into all angles should proceed. Emma Jones is not to be arrested until we have done all our homework."

"That's a relief," said Alexander. "We still have to inform the family about the developments. We will have to tell them about Emma and her encounter with her father down at the lake. We must also point out to them that we believe that there are a large number of other suspects in the frame, and that no one should jump to conclusions."

"I suppose, if Emma wants to go to the funeral tomorrow morning, she could be accompanied by Monique and Lydia," suggested Muldoon.

"The family won't be one bit happy at that," answered Alexander.

"If the girl is innocent, she has every right to be there," responded Muldoon.

"You're correct, John. We will discuss it with Emma and the two ladies when they arrive."

CHAPTER 18

THE BILLIARD ROOM

The Hawke family decided to gather in the billiard room, for afternoon tea. They had a few more arrangements to make for the funeral the next day. Ava was feeling a little better, her morning sickness, not as severe. Winnie was sipping her gin and tonic. Natalia and Francois were sitting in a corner, whispering to each other. Jack was sitting behind his wife. Joanne was twiddling her thumbs, impatiently awaiting the arrival of the eldest son, David and his wife Emily. The door opened. Emily entered the room, followed by her husband, who had a face like thunder.

"You'll never believe who I saw chatting to that Inspector and his side kick," said David. They all looked up at him in anticipation. "Bruce Gilbert – that trouble maker. He must have come all the way from America. He was sitting there, with the other two with folders of information about the businesses in America. He has been a thorn in Dad's side since he took over his company, all those years ago."

"They have no jurisdiction to investigate that, here in Ireland," interjected Emily.

"I know that," continued David, in a malicious tone of voice. "But it could make them suspicious about our company here in Ireland and in Britain. It might open a whole can of worms."

"Is there any chance that we could finish off the preparations for Dad's funeral tomorrow?" Joanne asked impatiently. "It's just going to be ourselves. Does anyone want to say a few words?"

They all looked at each other, nobody volunteering.

"I don't see the point," said Jack. "As you said it's only ourselves – we'll just leave it to the priest. Dad didn't want any fuss anyway."

"We'll get it over and done with – come back here, after the burial," added David.

"When are we going to be able to leave?" Natalia asked, from her seat in the corner. "We can't stay here forever."

She began to weep and Francois put his hand on hers to comfort her.

"Oh for God's sake, stop the playacting, Natalia," snapped Winnie.

Natalia wiped her eyes, sat back in her chair, glaring across at Winnie.

"I'll ask that Inspector after the funeral," said David. "More importantly, we have to plan our next move. We need to contest Dad's will. We can't let that girl take from us what's rightfully ours. We might need to get a whole team of lawyers to fight this – that's what Dad always did. They always overwhelmed the other side."

"She mightn't even be his," suggested Winnie. "You know what some of these girls are like." She took a substantial slug of her drink.

"We should get Frank Smith onto it again," said Emily.

"Frank Smith probably did the investigation to start with," interjected Jack. "He was always Dad's "go-to" man and fixer. I'm sure that Dad was certain that she was his daughter – otherwise he wouldn't make these changes. I think that we would be wasting our time going down that angle. As I said before, I don't think that Dad will have left any loopholes."

"It's alright for you," said Emily. "You've got the Lion's share. You're going to be President of the company. You and that girl will be running things. Imagine it – David only left with 20% of the English business. That's a disgrace, – and you in charge of our son's trust fund. What do you think Joanne? – you are in the same boat as us."

"I agree with David. We are going to fight this."

"What about your father's wishes? Do they not matter?" Ava asked in a quiet tone of voice.

"Poppycock," shouted David, glaring, fearsomely in her direction. "I see that our delicate flower Ava has found her voice."

"Shut up, David," hissed Jack. "You really are a nasty piece of work. Is it any wonder Dad changed his will."

The two men were glaring menacingly at each other, when there was a knock at the door.

"Sorry to disturb," said Alexander, as he and Muldoon entered the billiard room.

The whole family stared at the two men. The atmosphere in the room was tense and awkward.

"What do you want?" David asked with distain in his voice. "I suppose you've come to tell us that you've solved our father's murder?"

"No, Mr. Hawke, unfortunately not," answered Muldoon, "but we have some news to impart."

"Spill it out man," sneered David.

"Your half sister, Emma Jones, has come forward. She is here in the hotel. She is working here as a waitress."

"A waitress? Here?" Emily said. "Was all this planned? It can't be a coincidence."

"Not exactly," interjected Alexander. "Seemingly she had been in contact with David Hawke, her father. He had sent his good friend, Frank Smith, to England to investigate the veracity of her claims. He returned with what Mr. Hawke believed to be proof. Because she had not heard back from your father, she decided to come to Mayo and get a job, somewhere close to where his roots lay. The coincidence, if it is a coincidence, seems to be that he decided to holiday here in Loughfarraig House where she was working. You may not have noticed her, but Emma served you at table, a number of times. She made herself known to her father and they met once for a short conversation on the night of Christmas Day."

Alexander took a breath, looked around his audience and waited for a reaction.

"So, are you saying that she was the last person to see him alive?" David enquired.

"Did she kill him?" Natalia screeched, from her seat in the corner, her eyes wide open, her body trembling.

"She must have murdered him for the inheritance," insisted Emily.

"We don't believe she knew about the inheritance," said Muldoon. "No one seemed to know about it, except Donal Hawke and his solicitors."

Muldoon and Alexander had decided not to tell the family about what had happened at the lake, since they themselves weren't sure of all the circumstances surrounding the events.

"She must be your prime suspect though," said David. "No one else saw him after her."

"Except, the murderer," continued Alexander.

"It has come to our knowledge that Donal Hawke made a great number of enemies in his lifetime. We appear to have a large pool of suspects. Information about his business dealings in America has come into our possession. We intend investigating all aspects of the case, including all those who had a grudge against him and anyone who benefits from his will," concluded Muldoon.

"I suppose you're talking about Bruce Gilbert," interjected David. "I saw you with him. He has been obsessed with revenge against our father, since Dad bought out his business years ago. He has been harassing us for donkey's years. He's nothing but a crackpot. I hope he's on your list of suspects."

"As I said, Mr. Hawke, we will investigate every element of the case. Rest assured, we will leave no stone unturned. We intend to apprehend your father's killer." continued Muldoon.

The members of the Hawke family sat silently for a few moments. Alexander thought that he saw a slight flinch on the face of David Hawke when Muldoon mentioned that he would leave no stone unturned. Alexander was quite sure that the last thing that the Hawkes wanted was for the two men to open up a Pandora's box and all it's dirty secrets.

"One more thing, before we leave you, Emma Jones would like to attend her father's funeral tomorrow," said Muldoon. "She will be accompanied by her legal representative and Mrs. de Bruin."

Muldoon and Alexander did not give the family an opportunity to object. They left the room quickly, leaving the Hawkes slightly numbed from shock.

"How the hell did she organise legal representation so quickly?" David asked, quite bewildered.

Monique and Lydia arrived at Loughfarraig House shortly before 10pm. The two ladies strolled into the reception area with only a weekend case each. Alexander was in the foyer to greet them.

"You got here in one piece," he said. "Lovely to see you both. How was the trip?"

"Exhausting," answered Monique. "It's a very long drive in the dark – although we shared the driving."

"I'll take your bags to the rooms – you can freshen up and I've organised for us to have a late supper in one of the small sitting rooms."

"That's great – I'm starving and I could do with a lovely glass of wine," said Lydia.

"John will be joining us of course."

Lydia's room was just down the corridor from the de Bruins. The ladies unpacked their belongings. Fifteen minutes later they were sitting comfortably in front of a warm turf fire, sipping a Bordeaux.

The waiter arrived with a delicious plate of cold meats and salads, with home made brown bread.

"I've asked Emma Jones to join us later – I told her about 11.15pm. You need to be introduced before the funeral tomorrow morning," said Alexander.

"Thanks for volunteering us for that," smiled Monique.

"Thought you'd be happy," retorted Alexander.

"It's very strange that she ended up working here, where her father and family came on holidays," Lydia added.

John and Alexander gave a very in-depth account of what had transpired since the ladies had returned to Briarstown.

When they recounted Emma's story of Hawke's fall into the lake, Monique and Lydia were a bit sceptical.

"Did you believe her?" Lydia asked.

"Well there was no need for her to come forward. No one had seen the incident – except perhaps, the murderer. I don't think she knew about the will change. She was extremely distressed when she spoke to us. I'm inclined to believe her – it's so farfetched," answered Muldoon.

"The family are going to make her life hell," continued Alexander. "They intend fighting this, tooth and nail. They were very quick to accuse her of murder as well. That's why, we both thought that she was in urgent need of legal help – so here you are Lydia."

"What are the family actually like? I know they came across as arrogant," Monique asked.

"Absolutely dreadful, especially David and his wife Emily. They are leeches of the first order. They are entitled – actually they would run roughshod over anyone. Winnie continues to drink non-stop. Natalie feigns grief but I think she's just waiting around for her inheritance, to take off to warmer climes. Joanne appears apathetic. The French boyfriend, Francois is just a "hanger on". Jack seems to be a little better behaved, but maybe he's just cleverer than his siblings. It's very hard to make Ava out – she's still suffering from morning sickness and says very little. There's one thing on which they are all united and that is getting rid of Emma Jones. They would just be delighted, if she were the murderer," concluded Alexander.

Monique and Lydia found Bruce Gilbert's story very interesting and compelling. They too, realised that if Hawke behaved in such an underhand way in America, he likely did the same in England and Ireland.

"How are you going to find out what went on in England, since Scotland Yard are not being very cooperative?" Lydia asked.

"Don't worry," answered Alexander, "I've made contact with Colonel Johnson – you remember him, Monique – I expect to have all the information we need very soon."

"The Hawkes looked very worried when we mentioned "not leaving any stone unturned". A forensic examination of their business practices is obviously the last thing they want," smiled Muldoon.

"There's probably bribery and corruption involved here in Ireland as well, maybe at a very high level," interjected Lydia. "This could be huge."

"We realise that," sighed Muldoon, "but we have to investigate."

There was a knock on the door at exactly 11.15pm. Emma Jones walked into the cosy room. The two gentlemen stood up and introduced her to Lydia and Monique.

"Please sit down here, beside me," said Monique. "Would you like something to drink?"

"A glass of white wine please," Emma answered.

The company endeavoured to put Emma at her ease. She retold the story of her childhood and finally how she found out who her father was.

Lydia asked her if she was happy to have her as her legal representative. Emma said that she was extremely grateful for all the help she was receiving. Lydia explained to her that she would have to be very strong – that she was firstly a suspect in the murder and secondly that the Hawkes were likely to fight her tooth and nail for her inheritance. She wanted her not to have any discussions with them without her being present. Lydia, Monique and Emma agreed to meet at 8am the following morning to attend Donal Hawke's funeral.

"I'm very tired now," said Emma. "Do you mind if I go to bed?"

"Not at all," Monique answered. "Off you go – you've had a very difficult, stressful time. See you in the morning."

Muldoon and Alexander stood up, as Emma left her seat, made her way to the door and said good night.

"What are your impressions?" Muldoon asked.

"I'm inclined to believe her. I've listened to a lot of liars during my time on the bench and I don't think she's one of them," answered Lydia.

"She's a young girl, all alone in life, who needs our help and protection," added Monique. "If we don't help her, those sharks will eat her up and spit her out."

CHAPTER 19

VICTIMS

At ten o'clock, a fax arrived at Loughfarraig House for Commandant Alexander de Bruin. The receptionist gathered all the sheets of paper together, and went in search of Alexander. He and Muldoon were in the dining room, having breakfast. He received the bundle gratefully. "It's all the information we need, from Colonel Johnson," he said.

"Let's move into our usual office and study it," suggested Muldoon.

The two men took their coffee and headed for the small sitting room, once more. Alexander divided the sheets into sections and the two men studied the information, keenly.

"My goodness," muttered Muldoon. "How on earth did he manage to get away with all this for so many years?"

"Bribery and very good lawyers," sighed Alexander.

The two men spent an hour and a half studying the files. Hawke had destroyed so many lives. He had made thousands of workers redundant. He had built very shoddy flats – more like tenements. People brought law suits against him for accidents and damage to their health. Most of them failed but there were still a few cases pending. One mother of five had died when the balcony of one of the flats collapsed. There was suspicion of intimidation, as well. One other name appeared quite often – Frank Smith.

"He was like a mob boss," explained Muldoon.

"There are so many victims and hence so many suspects," added Alexander.

"What on earth are we going to find here in Ireland? We are in very dangerous waters," concluded Muldoon.

The report on the death of Zoe Bonda, told a tale of bribery, intimidation and corruption. She, her husband Jonas, and five children occupied a flat in an apartment block near Dagenham. The residents had made many complaints to the management over the years. There had been damp and mould throughout the building. The heating rarely worked. Paint kept chipping off the walls. Children were becoming very ill because of the conditions. The block of flats was council owned, built by Mustelus Developments. The laundry was hung out on the balconies to dry. One day, Zoe walked out on to her balcony to bring in the dry clothes, when it collapsed. She fell six stories to her death. Her five children were in the living room, watching television, when they heard the crack and their mother's screams.

Jonas Bonda was doing his shift at the hospital as a cleaner, when the accident happened. Following his wife's death, Jonas tried to sue the development company. A solicitor agreed to take the case "pro bono". An engineer was employed to carry out a survey of the building. His report was staggering – a litany of shoddy work – shortcuts had been taken wherever possible. All aspects of the building lead to safety questions. The materials that had been used were substandard, even for the early sixties. The balconies were deemed unsafe, some of them were disintegrating – it was only a matter of time before a dreadful accident would happen. The report done by the engineer was scathing.

The solicitor believed that he had a very good case – not only for compensation for his client – but also to charge Mustelus Developments with criminal negligence.

Hawke's lawyers produced reports from the time when the block of flats was built – structural engineers – fire engineers – the council. The block passed all elements with flying colours.

Six months into the investigation, the engineer, who had produced the scathing report on behalf of Jonas Bonda's solicitor fell to his death, while out on a cliff walk, near his home.

The police declared it to be a tragic accident. Bonda and his solicitor were very suspicious, but there was nothing they could do. They found it impossible to find another engineer to survey the building on their behalf.

A representative of Donal Hawke – Frank Smith called to Bonda's home and made a once off offer of compensation with the proviso that there would be silence on the matter. Bonda accepted reluctantly – his solicitor knew that it would be dangerous to proceed. So, that was the end of it. There were many more examples of sad cases where Mustelus Developments used the same modus operandi to silence victims. Hawke appeared to have many friends in the criminal fraternity of the East End. There must have been huge pay-outs to people, high up the ladder – in the council, even in the government. But nothing was ever proven. No wonder Scotland Yard was reluctant to help out. All this was evidence of negligence on their part or even corruption amongst the ranks.

There were other reports on building contractors being intimidated and going into liquidation, following accidents on sites and arson – only to be bought out by Hawke.

Donal Hawke made millions and his company grew and grew – leaving many casualties in his wake.

"There seemed to be hundreds of people who were victims of Donal Hawke, who all have a motive to kill him," observed Muldoon.

"I suppose people in Ireland always had an inkling about him. There were a lot of rumours regarding his methods of doing business. However, he created a great many jobs in Ireland. Do you remember, a few years back, there was an article in one of the papers – I think it was "The Morning Times" written by a very good investigative journalist, Joe Winters, casting aspersions on Hawke's character – hinting at corruption. Following the article, Joe Winters was attacked from all sides. He was lambasted by one Government Minister in particular – Jimmy Ward – you know the representative for a north Dublin constituency – he's held that seat for years. The journalist was more or less silenced on the topic of Donal Hawke after that," concluded Alexander.

"It might be a good idea to contact him," suggested Muldoon. "He may have gathered together a whole file on Hawke's businesses in Ireland. I'll phone Sergeant Dunne and put him on the job."

"We really should try to meet with Joe Winters. He may be very keen to help us, now that Donal Hawke has been murdered. I'm sure that the man would love to be vindicated. This would also be a great scoop for him – particularly when he has been silenced on the matter in the past."

Monique, Lydia and Emma arrived back from the funeral just before midday. They all went to their rooms to change their clothes. Muldoon and Alexander met them in the dining room for lunch at 12.30pm.

"Well, how did it go?" Alexander asked the three ladies.

"It was a very strange funeral," said Monique. "A very brief ceremony, devoid of anything really. They just went through the motions. The burial was swift. They never spoke to any of us. David and Emily just glared at Emma throughout. Toby waved across at us, but then his mother whispered something in his ear, so that was the end of that. We left the graveside immediately after the burial and headed straight back here. I presume the Hawkes will arrive any moment now."

"We heard from Colonel Johnson. A fax arrived, shortly after you left. Hawke left a long list of victims in England."

"So, more suspects for you to investigate," muttered Monique.

"We also have to investigate his businesses here in Ireland. I remember an article that I read about Hawke a few years back – not a very flattering one – so John and I have decided to contact the journalist, Joe Winters, who may have gathered some evidence."

"I intend to make an appointment for Emma and I to meet with James Byrne, solicitor, to discuss the will and it's implications," interjected Lydia. "The sooner the better. I will also inform the Hawkes that I am Emma's legal representative and any communication to her should be made through me. I'm not taking any chances with Emma. I suggest that she return to Briarstown with Monique and me. We can't leave her alone here – at the mercy of the Hawkes and their legal team – with your permission of course John. It will give Emma some breathing space – she has a lot to think about – many important decisions to make regarding the company etc."

"Yes, I believe you're right," said Muldoon. "When will you leave?"

"I'll make a phone call straight after lunch to try to see Byrne this afternoon. We can return home with a stop over in Galway for the meeting. I'll speak to the Hawkes as soon as I see them."

Monique was nodding her head as Emma sat in silence, listening intently to the conversation.

"What do you think Emma?" Monique asked.

"I'm fine with whatever you think is best. I'm just so grateful that I'm not alone in all of this."

After lunch, Lydia went in search of the Hawkes. She found them in the billiard room. She imparted her information briskly to them, left the room, walked to the reception to make a phone call to James Byrne, who agreed to see Emma and herself at five o'clock that afternoon in his Galway office.

Monique, Lydia and Emma left Loughfarraig House at a quarter to four, waving goodbye to Muldoon and Alexander, who were standing outside the main door.

"Lydia is a very brilliant, competent woman," said Muldoon.

"She is very impressive," agreed Alexander.

Meanwhile, back in the billiard room, the atmosphere had become very tense, following Lydia's engagement with the family.

"I think we are up against it here," said Jack. "That woman knows what she is doing."

"Stop whining, Jack," hissed David. "Our solicitors will see her off."

"We need to form a plan," interjected Emily.

"This is family business, so there's no need for Natalia or Francois to be here. Please leave the room. You've got your inheritance Natalia," sneered David.

Natalia and Francois stood up and sheepishly left the room.

"I'm going to the bar," said Winnie.

"Of course you are, mother," scoffed David.

The two couples and Joanne sat around a small table, huddled together.

"I have to tell you, that the new solicitor, Byrne, has boxes of Dad's files – one set for me and one for Emma Jones."

"What the hell!" shouted David. "We'll have to stop her getting those – God knows what's in them."

"We can't David, I've rung around a few of our lawyers – they were Dad's property so, his to do with, as he wished."

"Maybe, Jonathan Kelly can help," added Emily.

"I don't believe he can," answered Jack. "None of the businesses were in our names, David. We were just employees. Dad had everything sown up, so that he could do as he wished with them."

"We have two major problems, as I see it," interrupted Ava calmly. "Firstly, Emma Jones will find out everything about the company. We may be able to handle her. We need to get hold of her for a friendly chat. This time, let's all try to be civilised and pleasant to her. That solicitor of hers will have to leave soon – although she told us to communicate with

Emma only through her, we could arrange to bump into her and invite her to join us for a meal – a divide and conquer, I say. Secondly, we are still suspects in this murder. We can never admit to having known about the intended change of will – that would give us all here, a very strong motive – not to mention that Jonathan Kelly would be struck off."

Everyone was very surprised at Ava's intervention – quiet, mousy Ava who hardly ever spoke – certainly rarely voiced a strong opinion on anything.

"Well, well, Ava! There's another side to you that I haven't seen before," said Joanne smirking.

"Shut up! Joanne," said Jack. "Ava is right. I will collect my boxes from Byrne tomorrow, then we'll see what information Emma Jones will receive. As soon as that solicitor leaves, we'll pounce on young Emma and bamboozle her with kindness."

"When are we going to be able to leave here?" Emily asked, lighting a cigarette and inhaling deeply. "Toby will have to go back to school."

"We'll have to play it by ear. One of our drivers can bring him back to school, if necessary," barked David. "I can't believe that Dad has done this to us. He gives you the Lion's share Jack – over 50% of everything. That Emma, cow, gets 33% and Joanne and I are left with only about 7% each. What was he thinking? Then to add insult to injury, you're in charge of our son's trust fund and the execution of his will – bloody hell!" concluded David.

"Let's not fight among ourselves. We have to stick together and resolve this "Emma Jones" problem," said Ava.

"We really have a lot of problems here," added David. "That Inspector and his sidekick are very clever. They are going to investigate the company – looking for potential suspects. We all know that Dad made an awful lot of enemies and that he had extremely dangerous friends. They could easily uncover things that would be detrimental to us all."

"Not to mention, his influential, powerful friends – they must all be hoping that this murder will be solved quickly with none of their dirty linen aired," added Emily.

CHAPTER 20

THE JOURNALIST

"I've managed to contact Joe Winters, the journalist, who did that scathing article on Donal Hawke – well, Sergeant Dunne did, – the man lives in Athlone and is willing to meet us in the Great Southern today at twelve o'clock."

"Great," answered Alexander, tucking into a hearty breakfast. "I rang home early this morning. The three ladies are going to sift through the boxes they got from Byrne, today. They are full of files. Emma is probably going to find it all very overwhelming."

Alexander looked over at the entrance to the dining room to witness the arrival of the Hawkes for breakfast. David and Emily made their way over to where Muldoon and Alexander were seated, while the others took their places at the usual table.

"Good morning gentlemen" greeted Emily smiling. "Have your wife and her friend left?"

"Yes, they went back home yesterday afternoon," answered Alexander.

"That's a pity, I would have liked to have said goodbye," replied Emily, sweetly. "Have either of you seen Emma Jones? We were hoping to invite her for lunch – you know – to get to know her – now that she's part of the family."

"Well that's a pity," replied Alexander. Emma left yesterday afternoon, as well, in the company of my wife and Lydia Browne."

Emily's countenance changed. She was no longer smiling. She looked at her husband.

"I thought she was a suspect in my father's murder – she was the last person to see him alive," blustered David.

"Apart from the murderer, as I said before," replied Muldoon.

"This is all very irregular," added David, storming off and heading to his own table, followed by his wife.

"Lydia and Monique were right. The Hawkes were going to swoop in on that poor girl, as soon as she was left alone," said Alexander.

Muldoon and Alexander finished their breakfast, stood up from the table and made their way towards the exit. They thanked their waiter, Juan, who gave them a broad smile.

"That young fella is looking very pleased with himself," remarked Muldoon.

Two hours later the two men were sitting in the Great Southern Hotel in Galway, waiting for the arrival of Joe Winters. They were sitting in the corner of the foyer, Alexander facing the door. Joe Winters arrived ten minutes late. He was a man in his early fifties – very slim with glasses. He was dressed casually in jeans and a jumper. Winters was carrying a large file, crammed full of sheets of paper.

Alexander stood up, on seeing him, and waved. Winter saw him, walked clumsily towards him, holding on to his large file with difficulty.

"Hello there! I'm Joe Winters," he said.

"Alexander de Bruin, and this is Inspector John Muldoon."

They all sat down, Winters placing his file on the table in front of them.

"Should we have some refreshments first," suggested Alexander.

"That would be great – I'm starving and exhausted. I spent last night and this morning searching out all the information on Donal Hawke and his associates. I didn't get a chance to eat anything."

Muldoon ordered coffee, sandwiches and scones. Having allowed Joe Winters to enjoy his lunch Muldoon said, "As you are aware we are investigating the murder of Donal Hawke. We are aware that you wrote an unflattering article about him and his business dealings, a number of years ago. We are searching out suspects – therefore, if you are aware of any enemies he may have made during these transactions, we would be very grateful for your assistance."

"I have a long complicated tale to tell," said Winters.

"Please proceed, we are in no hurry," added Alexander.

"As you know, I'm an investigative journalist. About ten years ago, a small time builder came to me with a story about corruption in planning in Dublin. I told him that I would look into it but newspaper space was given over mostly to paramilitary activities and disasters, as it still is. I made a few phone calls – I was busy enough doing other projects. A number of people came back to me with the name of a developer who had made millions in England and America and was now operating in Ireland. He was able to buy up land, get planning permission very easily and build substandard buildings. Of course, we are talking of Donal Hawke. He also swooped in to purchase a number of hotels and other properties. There was the suggestion that he used intimidation to put off other potential buyers and investors. The name Frank Smith came up a lot in my investigation. I interviewed a lot of people working for the council. A number of them spoke about bribery, but were too afraid to go on the record. They intimated that the scandal went right up the line. I investigated some of the lifestyles of the people mentioned to me – they seemed to be living far beyond their means.

"Did you report this to the Gardai?" Muldoon asked.

"I had a conversation with an Inspector friend of mine, who told me blatantly that the guards had more to worry about at that time, with all the state security worries. They would not put any sort of manpower into investigating a planning matter, even if there was corruption involved. I suppose, I could have left it there, but I continued to investigate. Bribery and corruption certainly did go up the line – up as far as Jimmy Ward – you know the politician from North Dublin who held his seat for donkey's years. Well, I looked into his lifestyle – he was very wealthy. I doorstepped him, one morning. He was very cagey – he became very angry with me. It was a mystery as to where his wealth came from. He was from a working class area. There was no family wealth. He just had his government salary, but his house, cars and holidays abroad were very suspicious. Of course all these people were very powerful and had friends who could circle the wagons. Then I decided to investigate how Hawke managed to purchase these properties at such reasonable prices. I spoke to one man who had wanted to buy one of the properties but was threatened by Frank Smith. He had told him that he knew where his children went to school, mafia style tactics. Of course, the buyer in question, pulled out of the deal and left the door open for Hawke. I found that the same had happened when it came to buying land that was later zoned for development. To cap it all off, the flats that were built were completely substandard. There were shortcuts taken. The council, of course, did their inspections but not surprisingly – given what we know about bribery – the buildings all passed with flying colours. I actually visited a block of flats built by Mustelus Developments – dreadful conditions – kids getting sick – very, very, shoddy work and of course, the tenants were powerless. They had no means to take on the council or the builder. And so came my article, where I asked all the questions. What a mistake I made! The whole world came down on top of me. Ward went for the jugular. The wagons were circled. The powers that be tried to ruin me. I'm convinced that my phone was tapped. There was a huge amount of pressure put on the editor to fire me. Being the man he was, he refused to do so, but I was removed from investigative journalism into reporting on the arts, where they thought I could do no harm. My career was completely stalled. My family was threatened by Hawke's goons. So we moved out of Dublin to Athlone. You can have all my files. I have another copy of them at home. Now that Hawke is dead, maybe the truth will come out.

"You do know that you've made a suspect of yourself. You certainly had motive to murder Hawke," interjected Alexander.

"I know, but I have an alibi for the time of death. My wife, kids and I spent all of Christmas, from the 24th to the 28th up in Belfast with my wife's family. I never left the property. I have the various names and numbers here for you to check."

Muldoon took the sheet of paper from Winters and placed it in his jacket pocket.

"Thanks for all your help," said Muldoon, "We'll study all the files. We'll contact you if we need any more information."

"There are a lot of names in there, people who would have a motive to kill him – I wouldn't blame them. There are also names of powerful people who were involved with him, who wouldn't want their names made public. Just a warning, mind your backs. I'm sure there are still people who are in Hawke's pocket. It's a very dirty business."

Joe Winters stood up and took his leave. Muldoon and Alexander watched him walk out the door of the hotel.

"I can see a tribunal in the future," whispered Muldoon.

"If it's anything like the last one, the victims will be blamed," said Alexander.

"The suspect pool is getting larger and larger. At least Winters appears to have an alibi. I'll get Sergeant Dunne to check it out."

"We are going to have to sift through his files for potential suspects. Let's get back to Loughfarraig House and start working," said Alexander.

"When this is solved and all the facts are known, this could be a great scoop for Winters – he deserves a break," said Muldoon.

The two men picked up all the files from the table and headed back to Mayo.

Lydia, Monique and Emma began examining the boxes of files pertaining to Mustelus Developments. They began their work at 8am in the large study at The Lodge, in Briarstown. Emma was in much better form – well rested and no longer afraid.

"This is a beautiful, restful place," she had said on first seeing Briarstown. She couldn't believe her luck that she had been taken under the wing of such a clever woman as Lydia Browne. She knew that so many things had to come together for her to be in this much stronger position now – the de Bruins being on holidays at Loughfarraig House – Commandant de Bruin being one of the investigators and Monique being a neighbour of Lydia Browne. Emma had realised that her situation would be so much worse, if she had been left alone to deal with the Hawkes and of course more importantly, in different circumstances, she could have been in jail, charged with the murder of her father Donal Hawke.

Lydia and Monique divided up the files, according to their expertise, as best they could. There was one file which pertained to all the law suits that had been brought against Hawke's company. Most had ended in his favour. It appeared that a number had been settled, out of court. There was a group of lawyers in each country to deal specifically with these law suits – hard nosed – completely ruthless. The ordinary citizen wouldn't have had a chance against them.

Mustelus Developments was extremely prosperous. The property portfolio was worth millions. There was a stockpile of cash in various bank accounts. Monique noticed one particularly dubious looking account which appeared to be a slush fund, out of which came suspicious payments – she guessed that this fund was used to pay his "fixers" – perhaps bribes for government officials, inspectors etc. There were dates of payments and initials with reference to the sites or jobs involved. She knew that it would be very difficult to link these payments to anyone as they were all cash amounts. Emma watched as the two ladies sorted the files into separate piles.

"Can I help?" she asked.

"Of course," answered Monique, picking up a file regarding some of the properties in Ireland, and handing it to Emma.

Monique and Lydia looked at each other convinced that this would be way beyond Emma's comprehension.

They watched as she skimmed through the pages. They wondered how they would be able to avoid embarrassing the young woman – believing that she couldn't possibly have understood what was in front of her.

"If you like, we could just explain everything to you, as we go along," suggested Lydia.

"No need," answered Emma, "I understood all that – quite straight-forward really. If you would like to hand me another one."

"That's quite complicated material," said Monique. "I wouldn't have been able to read it at that speed with any understanding. I don't mean to be insulting but how were you able to do it?"

" I have an eidetic memory. I can also read at speed – scanning real-ly. I remember everything after one reading." Monique and Lydia were quite taken aback by this information.

"Do you retain the information?" Lydia asked, "or is it short term."

"I'm very fortunate, that I can retain it. I suppose you could say that I'm gifted. The teachers were always amazed that I found everything at school so easy. The guidance counsellor insisted on getting me tested when I was fifteen. The educational psychologist did all the tests. She concluded that I had an eidetic memory with a high I.Q. which made studying very easy for me."

"What is your I.Q. score?" Monique asked.

"148," answered Emma.

"So, your in the top 2% of the population."

"I suppose I am. I am a member of MENSA, which again, my guid-ance counsellor insisted on. My mother knew, since I was very small that I was gifted, academically. That's why we moved back to London. I was meant to go to Oxford – studying 4 A levels. I was expected to get A's in them all, but then Mam became ill, so that was the end of that."

"That's quite extraordinary," interjected Lydia. "You'll have no problem scanning these files – this development will certainly make our jobs a lot easier."

"It certainly will," added Monique, handing Emma a number of folders.

Monique and Lydia were quite amazed at Emma's abilities. They watched as this young genius, worked through the files, then explained to them succinctly what was in each. By the day's end, Emma knew everything about Musrelus Developments. She knew everything – she had missed nothing. Monique and Lydia worked extremely hard to try to keep up with her. Emma was a different person when engaged in academic work. She was no longer the shy, uncertain waitress whom they had first encountered at Loughfarraig House.

"You are going to be a very wealthy, powerful young woman," said Monique, as she shut the last folder.

"It will be a very responsible position," added Lydia. "I'd say you will get very little cooperation from the Hawkes. They will undermine you as much as possible. But I must emphasise that Donal Hawke's will is airtight. All their solicitors and lawyers will tell them so."

"There's an awful lot of money there – millions," whispered Emma. "They have done dreadful things to people – ruined their lives and businesses. They are like vultures or sharks."

"That was probably Hawke's plan from the beginning – why else would he have called the company "Mustelus" – the Latin name for the smooth-hound shark," concluded Monique.

The three women put all the files back in their boxes and sat down to supper. They were all very tired after their days work. Emma retired at ten o'clock, leaving Monique and Lydia to have a night cap in the sitting room.

"Well, that was a surprise," said Lydia. "She has quite a brain,"

"Her whole demeanour changed when she started studying the files, – no longer the fragile, scared helpless young girl," added Monique. "I must ring Alexander and inform him about this new development. He is going to be very surprised."

Alexander and Muldoon were sitting in the foyer of Loughfarraig House, sipping a brandy, when the receptionist approached them.

"There's a phone call for you Commandant de Bruin – it's your wife – you can take it in the office – there's no one there at the moment."

Alexander stood up and made his way into the office. He picked up the receiver, listened very carefully to what Monique had to tell him, – then returned to join Muldoon by the fire.

"All okay, I hope?" Muldoon asked.

"All perfectly fine," answered Alexander, staring into the fireplace, where the turf flames were dancing.

"I've had a very interesting conversation with Monique. It transpires that young Emma is quite the genius – an I.Q. of 148 and a member of MENSA. To top it all she has an eidetic memory and can speed read. Between them they were able to get through all the files – Emma has a complete understanding of the workings of Mustelus Developments after just one day. It's quite extraordinary. Lydia, who deals with a lot of clever people in her profession, has never come across the like,"

Alexander and Muldoon sat quietly for a few moments, churning over in their minds, the information that they had just received.

"Was it all an act, then?" wondered Muldoon. "Did she fool us all? Was she really distressed? Did she kill her father?"

"I don't know," sighed Alexander. "She's obviously academically, extremely smart, but that doesn't make her devious or a murderer."

"But, this revelation certainly puts her firmly back on our suspect list," concluded Muldoon.

CHAPTER 20

SCANDAL?

"I've just had a conversation with the Commissioner. I gave him all the information we have. He told me that there was nothing any of us could do here in Ireland about the misdemeanours in either America or Britain. He instructed me to concentrate on Donal Hawke's murder – not on corruption in other jurisdictions. I argued with him that they could easily be linked – if Bruce Gilbert had come all this way from America, to hand his files over to us – then it could be possible that another person, out of revenge, could have done the same. This equally applies to people in Britain whose lives were destroyed by Hawke and his minions. When I told him about Joe Winters, he was even less pleased, but realised that this had to be investigated – at least this alleged corruption was in our own jurisdiction."

Muldoon took his seat opposite Alexander in the dining room, and looked at the breakfast menu.

"Is it possible that someone has gotten to him?" asked Alexander.

"He's probably under pressure. If Winters is right – and I don't believe for a moment that he isn't – well then there are a lot of people who have been bribed by Hawke who could be outed by the end of this."

"Does the Commissioner not think that the information that we have received from America and Britain shows a pattern – a modus operandi that he probably repeated in Ireland as well?"

"Of course he does. But he realised that this could lead to a major political scandal. Most of our manpower is being used to contain the paramilitaries."

"Same in the army," added Alexander.

"Anyway, he finally agreed to give me an extra few men, to do the donkey work. I will use them to check the manifests of the flights from America and Britain, as well as the ferries – see if any suspicious characters arrived in the country shortly before Christmas. It's a long shot anyway. They can compare them with the names of the people mentioned in the files."

"If it's someone from another jurisdiction, I'm afraid that this may never be solved. The number of suspects that we have is astonishing," sighed Alexander.

"The Commissioner also agreed to set up a very small team in Dublin to investigate Winter's allegations. He said that this was going to be done very discreetly. He remembered how Winters was discredited after he wrote the article – the hyenas went after him."

Juan, the waiter from Colombia arrived at their table to take their breakfast order.

"Good morning Juan, how are you today?" Alexander asked.

"Very well thank you Sir," replied Juan with a smile. "Can I take your order, please."

The two men ordered the usual – bacon and eggs, toast and coffee.

Alexander looked out the window and noticed Natalia and Francois, strolling down by the lake.

"I don't think Joanne and Francois' relationship will end in marriage," smiled Muldoon.

"Natalia and himself are being firmly kept out of the loop, I've noticed," added Alexander.

Breakfast arrived and was as delicious as ever. The bacon was crisp, and the eggs were cooked to perfection. The coffee was strong. The scones which followed were scrumptious – dripping with melting butter and strawberry jam.

Natalia and Francois looked very forlorn as they returned to the entrance door.

"There must be a witness who saw Emma with Hawke," stated Muldoon suddenly, staring out the window, where he could just see the little jetty, where Emma claimed her father had accidently fallen in.

"Well, the murderer must have – that is if Emma isn't the culprit. We really need to question everyone again."

"I agree. After the breakfast shift, we can have a chat with the staff again."

"The family will never admit that Jonathan Kelly spilled the beans to his friend David about the impending will change – but we believe that he did – so they all have very strong motives to murder him. I think we can absolutely rule Winnie out – she was too drunk to be able to swing an oar and cosh him over the head."

"Not to mention that they have given each other alibis," concluded Muldoon.

At ten o'clock on the 5th January, a delivery arrived for Jack Hawke at Loughfarraig House, courtesy of James Byrne, solicitor. It was the set of boxes containing the same information as had been handed over previously to Emma Jones and Lydia Browne. The boxes were carried to the billiard room, where the Hawke siblings had gathered with their wives. Francois, Natalia and Winnie were not present. Jack and David opened the boxes and started to sort out the files. They flicked through the pages. David became angrier and angrier. Jack had a look of shock and horror on his face.

"Are you telling me that that bitch has all this information on us – the whole shebang?" David shouted.

"What is it?" asked Emily, puffing on her cigarette.

"Absolutely everything about the business – all the accounts – names of everyone we ever did business with. I can even see the bloody slush fund. It's all there for her to read," concluded David.

"She won't understand a word of it. She's only a waitress," hissed Emily. "The daughter of some sort of an escort."

"Don't be stupid, Emily," barked Frank. "If she doesn't understand it, well, I'm quite sure that her legal representative, Lydia Browne, will."

The Hawke siblings continued to read through the files. Emily and Ava sat quietly by the fireplace, Emily filling the room with her cigarette smoke.

"Will you please stop blowing smoke in my direction – it's making me feel sick," pleaded Ava.

"I'll go outside," snarled Emily, as she hurriedly left the room, banging the door behind her.

"Dad has completely tied us up in knots," said Joanne. "He has given that girl all this power and money. I can't believe that he did this to us.

He didn't even know her. We don't know her. What on earth are we going to do about this?"

"I believe that your Dad has wrapped this all up very neatly. Our hands are tied. Emma Jones has been whisked away so that we can't even get our hands on her, to influence her actions. We can only hope that she was the one who murdered him," interjected Ava.

It was a freezing morning in Briarstown. The children had stabled the ponies the night before to protect them from the elements. Monique awoke early, had a cup of coffee, then called the children who were a little reluctant to get out of bed on the last day of their Christmas holidays. However, they knew that they had their chores to do. Alice, Maeve and Max had a quick snack before donning their wax coats, woolly hats, gloves and wellingtons. Monique decided to allow Emma to sleep in – she was bound to be exhausted after all the work that she had done, the previous day.

Monique, the three children and the two Bernese mountain dogs left the house, went through the courtyard and headed for the stables. The three children ran ahead, followed, excitedly by the dogs. The frost was glistening on the grass. Monique could hear the crunch and crackle underfoot as she watched her breath form a misty cloud. The dogs were chasing each other around the paddock.

The children opened the stable doors. The ponies were delighted to see them. Max, Maeve and Alice removed their lighter stable rugs, replaced them with the heavier, waterproof turnout rugs, fastened the clasps, clipped the lead ropes onto the headcollars and lead them out into the paddock. Once released, the ponies galloped and bucked with delight.

The shovels and wheelbarrows were retrieved from the small barn, so that they could muck out the stables. They shovelled the manure and wet straw into the wheelbarrows and wheeled them out behind the stables to deposit the load onto the manure heap. This would be spread out on the land later on in the year. Even some of Monique's "townie" friends were delighted to use some of it, as compost for their gardens. Max collected a few straw bales from the barn, threw them into the stables, cut the twines with his Swiss army knife – a present from his cousin in Switzerland – and shook out the straw. He used a fork to even it out. He quite enjoyed preparing a comfortable bed for the ponies. The girls distributed the hay into the hay racks. Monique checked that the water coming into the stables was still running. Max ran over to the water trough in the paddock and smashed the top layer of ice with his shovel.

Alice filled the buckets with pony pellets and carried them out to the paddock. The ponies, having galloped around, came towards the buckets, stuck their noses in and ate contentedly. Alice stood beside them, so that they wouldn't steal each other's feed.

Their chores complete, the three children ran around the field with the two dogs. Monique watched, smiling – tomorrow they would be back in boarding school – the 6th of January. She walked back to the house, wondering if Emma was awake.

Emma was in the shower when Monique returned to the house. Monique prepared some scrambled eggs, bacon and toast – she knew that the three children would be starving when they arrived back.

"Good morning, Mrs. de Bruin," greeted Emma as she entered the kitchen.

"Good morning, Emma, I hope you slept well."

"I was out like a light . I must have been exhausted. Yesterday was a long day."

"Take a seat and have some breakfast."

Emma sat down at the kitchen table as Monique placed a welcome plate of eggs and bacon in front of her.

Monique sat down opposite Emma, poured two cups of strong coffee, just as the three children entered the kitchen, chatting and laughing. They had met Emma the day before and greeted her politely.

After breakfast, Max, Alice and Maeve went to their bedrooms to pack their cases for their return to school. They loved their boarding school and friends, so they were looking forward to the "rentree" as their French teacher called it. They had also decided that they would ride out their ponies in the afternoon if the frost had thawed a little.

"We'll go over to the Old Rectory in a while to see Lydia. I'm sure you have some questions for her. You should pick out the files you want to discuss. She has invited us to lunch. She will be on her own as her husband Damien and the kids are visiting a relative."

Emma went into Monique's office to scan through the files. Monique went up to the bedrooms to check on the progress of the preparations being made by the children for their return to school.

Emma and Monique were expected at the Old Rectory at 12.30, so they left The Lodge at 12.20 to make the short walk.

"Wow!" said Emma, as they reached the ornate wrought iron gates – the entrance to the winding avenue, bordered by the majestic oak trees. "This is a beautiful place."

"Yes it is," answered Monique. "The Brownes have lived here for generations."

They walked along the avenue and reached the red bricked, two storey house that dated back to the early 19th century. Emma was in awe as she looked at this house with it's sash windows and shutters, a grass tennis court and small walled garden. Lydia had seen them through the window and was waiting for them at the door.

She greeted them with a broad smile.

"Welcome, welcome, come on in ladies, lunch is served."

"You have a beautiful home, Mrs. Browne," said Emma, as she admired the entrance hall, with it's red flagstones and ornate staircase. She stared at the portraits of the Browne's ancestors, on the walls.

"Thank you, Emma. We are very fortunate. It's been in Damien's family for generations. Come through to the kitchen. I just prepared a light lunch for us – nothing special."

The three ladies ate their selection of cold meats, salads and tasty breads, followed by a delicious apple tart and cream. After lunch they went into the drawing room. Once again Emma was stunned by the beauty of the room, with it's recessed bookcases and log burner under a marble fireplace.

"You're so lucky to live in a place like this, Mrs. Browne. You should see my flat in London – you couldn't swing a cat in it. My mother would be so surprised to see me in a place like this."

"Things are going to change for you Emma," said Monique. "I'm not sure that you realise yet, how much they are going to change. You are now a very wealthy woman with a lot of power. You will have a say in how Mustelus Developments is run from now on."

"Your father Donal Hawke made a decision to leave you all this wealth. We can only guess as to why he gave you a much greater share than Joanne or David. Now it's up to you, to decide, how you are going to use it," said Lydia.

CHAPTER 21

DISAPPEARANCE AND COLLAPSE

Following the breakfast shift, Gerald Moore gathered all his staff, who had been present in the hotel on Christmas night, in the ballroom. Those who were present included, the kitchen staff, waiters, waitresses, bar staff, receptionists and the chambermaids who were in staff quarters on that night. The proprietor, Mr. Moore had informed them that Inspector Muldoon and Commandant de Bruin wished to have a brief word with them.

Alexander and Muldoon had decided that John Muldoon would do all the talking, while Alexander would watch the group, studying their reactions. They were hoping to pick out someone who had information that they had not passed on to the investigators.

"Thank you all for being here," began Muldoon. "I know that each of you has been interviewed individually by one of my officers. I was hoping that in the intervening few days, that one of you may have remembered something from that night. It may be a very small detail that does not appear to be important – something that you saw or heard that seemed slightly strange or out of the ordinary. We would like you all to think again about that night. Were you in your room, looking out the window? Were you smoking nearby and either heard or saw something unusual? Did someone pass you in a corridor, looking distressed or perhaps, out of place? Any little detail at all could be helpful to the investigation. Please give it some serious thought. Come forward, I believe someone knows something."

Alexander was watching the group very intently, looking out for give-away signs. Quite a number of them just looked extremely bored – just waiting to escape. Others listened to John in earnest. There was one young man whose behaviour gave rise to suspicion.

"You may leave now," said John to the gathering.

The employees filed out of the room. The last person to leave shut the door behind them.

"Well, did you notice any reaction?" asked Muldoon.

"Yes indeed I did, Juan the waiter from Colombia looked very agitated. You know the young man who is always smiling and in great humour. Well, he was fidgeting a lot, shuffling his feet from side to side. He avoided eye contact with me completely. He looked extremely worried. It could be nothing, it could be something."

"We'd better have another chat with him. Anything else?" asked Muldoon.

"No, just a lot of eye rolling," smiled Alexander.

Muldoon made his way to the reception, to ask to speak to Juan privately.

"I saw him leave just after the meeting," replied the helpful receptionist.

She then checked the roster which was on the wall beside her.

"He's not due on again until his shift at ten o'clock tonight – he's on the bar for a change."

"Thank you," said Muldoon.

"Do you fancy a walk?" asked Alexander. "I want to clear my head. It's cold outside but not raining."

Ten minutes later the two men, suitably attired in their winter coats and gloves, strolled along the lake shore. The swans and ducks were nowhere to be seen, having taken shelter from the elements. There was very little wind and the lake water was eerily still. They made their way up to the seashore. The tide was coming in. They watched the ebb and flow of the waves, and heard the soft lapping of the water against the rocks. The winter sun was high in the sky – only a few cotton clouds floating above.

"This is such a beautiful, peaceful spot. What a place for a murder!" muttered Muldoon.

The juxtaposition hadn't been lost on either man.

"We'll have a chat with Juan, tonight," suggested Muldoon.

While Alexander and Muldoon were having a light lunch, they were disturbed by a loud commotion in the foyer. They rose from their table and made their way in the direction of the disturbance. Gerald Moore was fussing about, the receptionist was on the phone. Natalia Hawke was being helped onto a couch by two waiters. She was clutching her stomach and screaming. Muldoon walked briskly over to the couch.

"Thank goodness, you're here," said Gerald Moore. "She was ordering a drink at the bar when she screamed, bent over in agony and collapsed. We're calling an ambulance. There's no doctor staying here. I don't know what to do."

Moore looked beseechingly at Muldoon, who moved over to speak to Natalia.

"My stomach and my head, I can't bear it." She screamed again. She was clutching the middle of her stomach, so Muldoon was fairly sure that it wasn't her appendix.

"Did it come on suddenly?" asked Alexander, who had joined the group.

"I felt a bit sick and then I got this awful pain in my stomach, then in my head."

Natalia fainted.

"Oh my God, oh my God, do something," implored Moore.

Muldoon checked her pulse and her breathing. "Her pulse feels normal – her breathing is a bit laboured. How long will the ambulance be?"

"About 45 minutes – it's coming from Castlebar hospital," the receptionist answered.

"I don't think we should move her," added Alexander. "We might do more harm than good. Please, get a blanket to put over her."

One of the waiters ran off in search of a blanket. He returned two minutes later with a woollen throw, which was carefully placed over Natalia. The rest of the Hawke family then made an appearance. They had been in the billiard room when they heard the screams. Francois had been out walking and only became aware of what was happening when he opened the door into the foyer.

"What on earth is wrong with her?" asked Emily, puffing her cigarette.

"She collapsed in pain," answered Gerald Moore.

"Will she be OK?" inquired Joanne.

"An ambulance is on it's way," interjected Muldoon.

"Madam, please take your smoking elsewhere – it can't be helping her," demanded Gerald Moore.

Emily, looking extremely annoyed, moved back towards the billiards room.

Natalia remained unconscious. Muldoon checked her pulse again. Her breathing remained the same.

"Would any of you like to go in the ambulance with her?" asked Alexander, directing his question towards the Hawkes.

There were no takers. They all looked at each other. Francois made his way over towards his partner, Joanne.

"I'm sure she'll be fine," said David. "If you need us we will be in the billiard room." He then led his party down the corridor.

"My goodness! what a crowd!" muttered Gerald Moore.

Forty minutes later, the paramedics arrived into the foyer of Loughfarraig House, checked Natalia's vitals, placed her on a stretcher and carried her to the ambulance. Muldoon gave them his contact details. Alexander and John Muldoon watched the ambulance, sirens blazing, drive down the long winding avenue towards the main road.

"I wonder was she poisoned?" asked Alexander. "Seems too severe a reaction to be just food poisoning."

"Her symptoms are a bit strange," answered Muldoon. "Her pulse rate was fine. There were no chills. She didn't appear to have a high temperature – no redness around the mouth – certainly no foaming at the mouth. When her eyes were open, the pupils were not dilated. She appeared to be in dreadful pain, and being unconscious for so long is obviously very worrying – very confusing. Let's hope there wasn't an attempt on her life, as well."

The two men returned to the foyer. Gerald Moore was still fussing about. There was no sign of any of the Hawkes. The two men sat down by the turf fire.

"These people are callous, they don't care one bit what happened to Natalie. Even Francois, who had been left out on the periphery, along with Natalia recently, showed no sympathy," uttered Alexander.

"I suppose, he knows where his bread is buttered," returned Muldoon. "We don't know what the story is, until we hear something from the hospital. Therefore, we can't investigate anything. I was going to tell the Hawkes that they could leave whenever they wished, but I'd better hold off, in case the news from the hospital points to another crime."

"That de Bruin fellow looked at us with distain, when none of us volunteered to go in the ambulance," said Joanne.

"I had no intention of spending hours at that hospital," hissed Emily. "Life is too short."

"You could hardly expect me to go, in my condition," added Ava cradling her tummy.

"Oh! give it a rest Ava," interrupted Emily. "You'd think you were the only one in the world to ever have a baby."

"Will the two of you shut up bickering," shouted David.

"I'll ring the hospital in a few hours to see how she is," added Joanne.

Francois put his arm around her shoulder to comfort and support her.

"I had hoped that we could leave here today or tomorrow, but I suppose Natalia's little turn will put a halt to that," muttered Emily.

While this conversation was happening, Winnie was sitting by the fire, sipping a gin and tonic. "Hope that Inspector doesn't think that any of us tried to knock off Natalia," she smiled.

"Oh, Mother, don't be absurd," said Joanne. "She just ate something that didn't agree with her."

"Well, she didn't eat anything out of the ordinary – same as the rest of us actually – none of us is doubled up in pain and unconscious to boot," added Winnie.

"Why would any of us want to hurt her?" asked Jack. "She has her inheritance as agreed in the pre-nup. She's out of our lives once all of the legalities are sorted. You're being over melodramatic, Mother."

"Well, we all know that none of us had anything to gain by sending her to the hospital," said David. "This is only a nuisance for us. We have bigger fish to fry. We are going to have to deal with Emma Jones and we don't know what investigations will be initiated by the files that were handed over to the Inspector and his sidekick, together with all the information about our company, available in the boxes that were handed over to our dear half-sister."

Late that afternoon, an unmarked police car arrived at Loughfarraig House. Inspector Muldoon handed over all three files to the young officer – those from Colonel Johnson, regarding the British arm of the Hawkes' company – Bruce Gilbert – the American arm, and Winter's files – into the bribery and corruption in Ireland. Muldoon was relieved to hand this part of the investigation over to the team in Dublin. He wondered to himself whether it would all be a complete waste of time.

"I've just come off the phone to the matron at Castlebar hospital. Natalia is stable. They have done blood tests, x-rays – every test they can think of. They are baffled. She regained consciousness in the ambulance, but continued to fall in and out of consciousness over the last few hours. They are definitely keeping her in overnight to monitor her. I'm to ring after ten o'clock tomorrow morning to check on her situation," said Muldoon, as he and Alexander made their way into the dining room for dinner.

They sat at their usual table and perused the dinner menu. A waiter, who had not served them before, took their order.

"I'm looking forward to having a chat with Juan when he comes on duty," said Alexander. "I'm convinced that he knows something."

"Have you spoken to Monique today? I wonder how she and Lydia are getting on with Emma Jones."

"I intend ringing her tonight, after our chat with Juan."

"I hope something comes up," muttered Muldoon. "Otherwise Emma is going to be in hot water – being the last person that we know of, who saw Donal Hawke alive."

"Clever and all that she is, I find it very hard to think of her as a murderer. The other members of the family had more of a motive – shame about their alibis."

After their dinner Alexander and Muldoon retired to their usual spot in front of the fire, waiting for ten o'clock and the appearance of Juan. Ten o'clock came, but no sign of him. Gerald Moore arrived at the bar at 10.30, in a bit of a tizzy. He was trying to persuade the barman to stay for another few hours. Finally, there appeared to be agreement, although the barman looked far from happy.

"Good evening, gentlemen," said Moore as he approached them, "I hope you enjoyed your meal."

"Excellent as usual," answered Alexander. "We had hoped to have a chat with Juan, when he came on duty tonight," added Muldoon.

"Juan didn't turn up for his shift," said Gerald Moore. "He was due in the bar to relieve Steve at ten o'clock. I have tried his quarters, but there's no sign of him. He has always been very punctual – a very trustworthy young man – always eager to do extra shifts. He has never been late for work before, never mind not turn up at all. I don't know where he could be. There's really nowhere for the staff to go at night. This is very strange altogether,"

"Mr. Moore, telephone call for you," said the receptionist who had walked up behind him.

"Sorry gents, duty calls."

Alexander and Muldoon watched as Gerald Moore hurried into the small office behind the reception to take his phone call.

"This is very suspicious," said Muldoon.

"He certainly looked very worried today when you started asking more questions about that fateful night. He wasn't the same, cheerful, smiling Juan. He was so nervous and fidgety," answered Alexander.

"There's nothing we can do tonight. We certainly can't send out a search party. He may turn up," added Muldoon.

"I think that we can be fairly sure that this isn't a coincidence. He must have witnessed something the night that Donal Hawke was murdered," continued Alexander.

"He could be covering for Emma Jones – they may be friends," sighed Muldoon.

"You're right, John. But where is he now?"

CHAPTER 22

BACK IN BRIARSTOWN

Monique and Emma thanked Lydia for a lovely lunch, and made their way back to The Lodge. Emma was lost in her thoughts as they strolled down the avenue, wrapped up against the cold.

Ten minutes later, they were sitting in the office, where Emma had begun scanning through some files, once more.

"I'll have to let you to it for a while, need to check that the kids are all set for tomorrow."

"That's no problem," answered Emma. "I want to read about some of these cases brought against Mustelus Developments. I've been thinking about what Mrs. Browne said regarding my responsibilities. I have to do the right thing from now on."

"You could make quite a difference to a lot of people," said Monique, as she rose to leave the room.

"We're going to take the ponies out for a ride," said Alice. "The ground is a bit softer now."

"Good idea," responded Monique. "I'll go out with you. The dogs could do with another run around."

Max had very little interest in riding out but gave a hand when required. He was more interested in football. Today, all three children would gallop around the paddock, watched by their mother. Monique was used to Alexander being absent from home for long periods. But, since he retired from the army, they had been apart very little. She watched the children put the ponies through their paces and wished that he was here now, particularly as the three children were going back to boarding school tomorrow. She also hoped that Alexander and

Muldoon would find some evidence to exonerate Emma, as she was growing quite fond of the young woman.

Monique thought about Emma's mother, and the way she worked so hard at menial jobs, to keep them ticking over. She wondered why she had kept the pregnancy a secret from Donal Hawke. Did she not want his influence on Emma's life? Life could have been so much easier for them both, financially, if he had supported them. She realised that no one would ever find out why Katie Jones had kept her secret – she had brought it with her to the grave. She also thought how pitiful and sad it was that Katie had become so ill, just as she realised that Emma would most likely get into Oxford – just as their dreams were going to come true. Some people lead very unhappy lives and then they die.

At eleven thirty that night, the phone rang at The Lodge.

"I'll get it," shouted Max. "It's probably Dad."

It was indeed, Alexander, phoning to chat with the children before their return to school and to bring Monique up to date on all the happenings at Loughfarraig House. When the children had finished talking to their father, Monique took the receiver.

"Well, darling, how are things there?" she asked.

"I must say, today has been very interesting. John had a chat with the Commissioner, who was less than pleased at the prospect of having to investigate bribery and corruption at Government level here in Ireland. However, he agreed to set up a small team in Dublin to look into it and go through all our files. Then the boxes arrived from the solicitors for Jack Hawke – which seemed to cause consternation among their ranks. We also gathered all the staff together to insist that anyone with information come forward. I noticed that Juan, – do you remember him Monique? – the cheerful waiter from Colombia, – was very agitated. So, John and I decided to have another chat with him after dinner tonight – but he was a no show for his shift at the bar. To top it all, Natalia Hawke collapsed in pain. She was taken off to Castlebar hospital by ambulance. John will ring the matron tomorrow morning to check on her."

"You've certainly had a most eventful day," said Monique. "Do you think that Juan saw something, the night of Donal Hawke's murder?"

"It certainly looks that way," answered Alexander. "It would be too much of a coincidence for him to disappear on the night that we want to question him."

"Might he be covering for someone?" ventured Monique.

"I know what you're thinking, Monique. Is he covering for Emma?"

"Well, if he saw him fall into the lake – that it was an accident and Emma's story is true – then why didn't he come forward and support her version of events? Unless he saw her murder him," sighed Monique.

"Yes, that's one scenario, which if true means that you're harbouring a murderer in our own home," muttered Alexander. "Another scenario is that he saw the murderer hit him with the oar as Hawke emerged from the lake, which begs the question – why cover up for that person? There's a simpler explanation of course, which is that he just didn't turn up for his shift and will make an appearance tomorrow. However, Gerald Moore insists that not turning up for work is completely out of character."

"I hope that he's not covering for Emma. She comes across as such a wonderful young woman. She's so bright and clever – really amazing. She spent quite a lot of time today studying the files. She appeared genuinely moved by the predicament of Hawke's victims. She really hopes to be able to make a difference – to change the way the company is run from now on."

"Let's hope she's innocent, Monique. Neither John nor I would relish the prospect of Emma being charged with murder and spending the rest of her life in prison."

"It would really suit the Hawkes, though. They must be terrified of what's going to emerge from the files. Of course, they have no idea about Emma's brilliant mind," continued Monique.

"No, but they certainly know that Lydia is very tuned in. They must be quite worried about what's about to come out. They know that Bruce Gilbert, who has been a thorn in their side for years, handed over files regarding what went on in America. They must realise that this won't all be swept under the carpet again. I'd better let you get to bed. Hope the drop-off to school goes well. I'll give you a buzz tomorrow night."

Monique returned the receiver, stood still for a moment before turning out all the lights and making her way up the stairs to her bedroom. She passed by Emma's room. The light was out – she must be asleep. Doubts began emerging in her head. Is this young woman the kind, empathetic, innocent being that she portrays, or is she a first class actress, with a brilliant mind who is a murderess?

CHAPTER 23

UNANSWERED QUESTIONS

At 8am on the 6th January, John Muldoon went in search of Gerald Moore, to check if Juan had made an appearance.

Moore informed him that there was still no sign of the young Colombian waiter. His room had not been slept in. Muldoon got permission to search Juan's bedroom. At 8.30am Alexander and Muldoon entered the bedroom of the young man. The bed was made, and as Moore had stated – had not been slept in. Alexander opened the wardrobe – all his clothes were still hanging there. His two suitcases were sitting on top of the wardrobe. Muldoon opened the drawers beside the bed – there was a watch, a ring and a few letters in the drawer. Sitting on top of the bedside table was a small lamp and a photo of a young smiling girl of about 18 years of age, with long black hair and big brown eyes.

"This must be the girlfriend that he was always talking about, back in Colombia," said Alexander, as he picked up the framed photo to take a closer look.

"He doesn't seem to have taken any of his clothes, if he has done a runner," added Muldoon.

"I wonder what he saw. Why was he so on edge yesterday when you asked for more information? He can't have left without all his belongings. This is a real conundrum," continued Alexander.

Alexander went over to a small desk by the window.

"There's a writing pad here, with the House's logo on it. There are indentations on the first page here. Other pages have obviously been used and torn out."

"He must send letters back to Colombia to his family and girlfriend. Can't imagine that he would be able to make long distance calls home – anyway, his family may not even have a landline," said Muldoon.

Alexander picked up a pencil that was sitting beside the writing paper and rubbed the tip over the paper to expose the indentations.

"I can't make anything out here – it's not written in English anyway. He must have been writing home."

"We had better leave everything the way we found it," said Muldoon. "There may be a perfectly innocent explanation for all this. If so, we have no business being here at all. He's a young man who may have decided to socialise somewhere and just hasn't returned back here. He's not a missing person as yet."

The two men left the room. Muldoon closed the door behind them. They made their way downstairs and towards the dining room for breakfast.

The Hawke family were seated at their usual spot. David was still sitting at the top of the table. It obviously hadn't dawned on him that he was no longer going to be able to take over his father's position as head of the family and business – Donal Hawke himself had seen to that. Muldoon approached the table to enquire after the health of Natalia Hawke, although he had every intention of checking after 10am himself, with the matron, as planned.

"Last we heard, she was making a good recovery," said Joanne indifferently.

"When can we leave?" interjected Emily.

"I'm not sure, yet," replied Muldoon. "Our investigations here are still not completed. We certainly have to wait until Mrs. Hawke returns from hospital. I will let you know as soon as feasible."

Muldoon made his way back to the table where Alexander was pretending to study the menu whilst keeping a close eye on what was happening at the Hawke table.

"We can't keep them here forever," said Muldoon. "Once Natalia Hawke returns, provided there are no suspicions about her sudden illness, we'll have to let them leave. By the way, I received a fax from head office.

They've checked the manifests from the airlines – they can find no one with any links to Donal Hawke who flew in before his death. Checking the ferries is going to be impossible. They can't get a list of all the passengers – it's also such a busy time of year – just before Christmas. They are doing their best with the ferry lists but I'm not hopeful."

At 10.15am Muldoon rang the hospital to speak to the matron. He was informed that Natalia Hawke appeared to have made a full recovery. Nothing unusual had appeared in any of the tests. The doctors were all confused about her condition. They could find nothing amiss, and did not know why she had been in such pain or what had caused her to collapse. Every test that was available to them had been performed. Her bloods were fine, her x-rays and scans were clear. As far as the health professionals were concerned she was given a clean bill of health. There was the theory that her collapse was stress related. Sometimes when one is under great stress – as in this case – following the murder of her husband – the stress manifests as physical symptoms. The doctors prescribed some anxiety medication. Natalia will be discharged from hospital after 2pm. A taxi has been ordered to return her to Loughfarraig House.

"So, Alexander, Natalia will be back here after three sometime this afternoon. They have a theory about anxiety."

"She didn't come across as particularly distressed following her husband's murder – none of them did. But I suppose, you never can tell," said Alexander.

A phone call was made to Loughfarraig House from Castlebar hospital informing Jack Hawke that Natalia would be returning that afternoon. Jack gathered the family together once again in the billiard room to discuss the situation.

"We might be able to leave here this evening or tomorrow morning at the latest," he said.

"Are we any the wiser as to what happened the silly woman?" asked David. "I'll be very glad when she's out of our lives."

"I wasn't given any information about her condition at all – just that she was being discharged and heading our way," answered Jack.

"What are we going to do about our other problem?" asked Ava.

"I think we should buy Ms. Jones out as soon as possible," interjected David. "She's had nothing all her life – we'll make her an offer she can't refuse. She'll think all her Christmases have come at once."

"You're right of course," said Joanne. "Why would she want to get involved in the business – she wouldn't have a clue about it anyway, much too complicated for her. I also don't believe that Lydia Browne, smart and all as she is, would want to dedicate a whole lot of time to this – I'd say that she would advise her to take the offer."

"I agree," said Jack. "We'll get our solicitors on to it as soon as possible."

"Do you think anything will come of the files that were handed over to Muldoon by our friend Bruce Gilbert – do you think that the company will be investigated?" asked Ava.

"We'll shut that down too. We'll go into court every day if need be. We'll do what Dad always did – every time something is inferred – bring whoever said it to court. We are old hands at this. Dad never lost and neither will we," said David.

"Unless Emma Jones decides that she's going to interfere," added Ava.

"We'll deal with her too," snarled Emily.

"She has the same box of files that we have," said Jack. "Dad made sure of that."

"She'll take the offer, I'm sure," concluded David.

Monique returned to The Lodge at 11.45am, having dropped the three children back to boarding school. Emma had still been asleep in her room when the family had left the house. Monique entered The Lodge and made her way down the corridor towards her office. To her surprise, Emma was sitting at the desk studying some papers.

"Hello Emma, here you are," said Monique, as she entered the room.

"Good morning, Mrs. de Bruin, or is it afternoon," answered Emma.

"It's ten to twelve Emma. Are you long up?"

"I heard you all leaving, got up shortly afterwards. I've been here, studying for a couple of hours."

"I'm going to have some lunch – come and join me in the kitchen," suggested Monique.

The two ladies made their way into the kitchen. Monique prepared a light lunch of cold meats and salad with home made brown bread as Emma laid the table.

"What are you studying?" asked Monique.

"The way Mustelus Developments did business," answered Emma. "They were ruthless. My father and his minions destroyed so many people's lives. His lawyers destroyed anyone who took them on. There was corruption, evidently, as well."

"John Muldoon and Alexander were in possession of files from America, Britain and Ireland that they handed over to Garda Headquarters for investigation," added Monique.

"Do you think anything will come of it?" asked Emma.

"Not so sure," remarked Monique. "There really isn't much they can do about America and Britain – and I'm not certain that anyone here will want to open up a can of worms like this. The journalist Winters was almost destroyed because of his article a few years back and his inference that some "higher ups" were involved here in corruption. Mustelus Developments have very powerful legal teams in each jurisdiction. What really baffles me is, why did your father leave you so much wealth and power, and all the information to cause a great many problems for the company and other members of his family?"

Emma remained silent for a few moments, thinking to herself.

"Maybe he felt some sort of remorse," muttered Emma.

"When Alexander and John spoke to Frank Smith, his fixer and long time friend, he hinted that your mother was the only person who never asked him for anything. There was also mention, I believe from the new solicitor, that he believed that the rest of the family were leeches. Perhaps, your father had an epiphany, realised that he had created a monster and thought perhaps that you might be able to do something about it."

"But, he didn't know me. He wouldn't have known how I would react."

"He knew your mother, Emma. He was probably hoping that you turned out like her and not like him," continued Monique.

"Why didn't he fix it all himself?" asked Emma.

Monique decided that it was probably appropriate for her to inform Emma about her father's state of health before his murder.

"His doctor informed Alexander and John that he had only about six months to live – that was why he had gone to the solicitor to make all the changes to the company and his will. He had intended telling the rest of the family, over the Christmas holidays."

"So, they don't know that he was dying?" whispered Emma.

"No, and they still don't know," replied Monique.

"There was no need to murder him – he would have been dead in six months," muttered Emma.

Monique looked across at the young, innocent looking girl, and wondered if she was talking about herself or someone else. She then began to clear away the dishes and place them in the dishwasher. Emma stood up to help and appeared to be in her own world, miles away from Briarstown.

"I wish I had some time to get to know him," she said suddenly. "Maybe, he regretted some of the things he did in life and we could have worked together."

"That may have been his intention," replied Monique. "He certainly wanted to shake things up in the company. He has left the other children in a much worse position than they would have expected. He didn't appear to like any of them in the end. David has been moved down the pecking order. They certainly came across as a most unpleasant lot, apart from poor Toby. They are going to make things very hard for you, Emma."

"What do you think that they'll do?"

"Well, Lydia believes that their first move will be, to try to buy you out. They will offer you a substantial amount of money, hoping that you will be happy to take it and run. Once rid of you, they will carry on as normal."

"I don't think I want to do that. I could make a big difference. I would like to compensate all those people who have suffered because of my father's actions. I wonder was that what he wanted me to do?"

"I suppose if he just wanted you to be rich, he could have left you a wad of money – instead he bequeathed you a large percentage of each arm of the company and the power that goes with that," concluded Monique.

After the dishes were cleared away, Emma returned back to the office to continue the perusal of the files. Monique went into the back room where the Bernese dogs were sleeping. When they saw her, the two dogs jumped up, wagging their tails. They knew that they were going for a walk. Monique put on her warm winter coat, hat and gloves. She and the two dogs made their way into the paddock. The dogs ran around, chasing each other. Monique walked over to one of the ponies, and rubbed it's nose and mane. The wind was picking up a bit, the hedges rustled. She looked at the bare trees, their branches swaying slightly. The tiny birds were pecking at the bird feeder near the stables.

Monique walked back towards the house. She thought about the murder. She wished that Alexander were home in Briarstown. She also wished that she were positive that Emma wasn't the murderer, and hoped that nothing else dreadful would happen. She thought of Loughfarraig House with all the beauty surrounding it. Suddenly a shiver went down her spine.

At 4.15pm Natalia Hawke arrived back to Loughfarraig House. She was greeted by Gerald Moore in the foyer. Alexander and Muldoon were seated in front of the turf fire, awaiting her arrival.

"She looks extremely well for someone who was at death's door yesterday," said Muldoon.

"She certainly does – she even managed to get her hair done, by the looks of it," replied Alexander.

Natalia's hair and makeup were perfect. She was dressed in a Chanel suit with pink blouse, shoes to match.

"She must have had the clothes etc. delivered to the hospital," suggested Muldoon. "They are different from the ones she was wearing when she collapsed."

"She certainly made a remarkable recovery," added Alexander.

Ava and Emily Hawke appeared from the corridor, followed by Joanne and Francois who were holding hands.

"So glad that you're feeling better," said Emily unconvincingly.

Ava muttered something similar, as Joanne nodded and Francois looked indifferent.

"Come along with us," said Emily. "The others are looking forward to seeing you. They are in the billiard room."

"I was hoping to have a word with her," said Muldoon. "I suppose it will have to wait."

"Are you going to allow the Hawkes to leave, now that Natalia is back, John?"

"I think I'll ask them to stay until tomorrow morning. I really need to have a chat with Natalia. We'll also have to start looking for Juan, if he doesn't make an appearance soon. I'm beginning to think that he must have seen something of significance."

"I also think it's time we told the Hawkes that Donal Hawke had only about six months to live," added Alexander.

"It will certainly be interesting to see their reaction to that piece of news," replied Muldoon.

Fifteen minutes later, Alexander and Muldoon opened the door to the billiard room.

"Sorry to disturb you," said Muldoon. "May we speak to you all? It won't take long."

Winnie was sitting in the corner, gin and tonic in hand. Joanne was sitting on a couch with Francois, while Natalia was seated between Ava and Emily. David and Jack were standing at the fireplace, smoking cigars.

"Can we leave now?" asked Natalia beseechingly.

"I'm afraid that I have to ask you all to stay one more night," answered Muldoon. "I would also like to speak with you about your sudden illness, Mrs. Hawke."

"I'm fine now," she said. "The doctors are convinced that it was stress after the death of my husband."

"Are you making any progress at all with your investigation?" interjected David, blowing cigar smoke in Muldoon's direction.

"There are a number of lines of inquiry," answered Muldoon.

"I'm sure there are," sneered Emily.

"We have another important piece of information to impart to you, regarding your father," added Muldoon. "We have been informed by his doctor that Mr. Hawke was gravely ill, and only had about six months to live. This was borne out by the medical examiner's report."

All the group looked extremely shocked. Natalia began to shake and cry.

"Why didn't he tell us?" shouted David.

"Was it a brain tumour?" asked Emily. "That would explain his will."

"Yes, he mustn't have been in his right mind when he changed his will, we'll be able to challenge it now," hissed Joanne.

"Oh, for God's sake, there was nothing wrong with his brain," said Winnie from her seat in the corner. "Just listen to yourselves."

An awkward silence descended on the company. Natalia was dabbing her eyes with her handkerchief.

"We'll leave it at that for now," said Muldoon, as he and Alexander made their way to the door and made their exit.

Alexander and Muldoon sat down once more in front of the turf fire. Gerald Moore approached them, carrying a tray of coffee and scones.

"Thought you might like some refreshments. There's still no sign of Juan. I'm getting a little worried now. The rest of the staff are beginning to ask where he is. This is so unlike him. He was always doing extra shifts. He was saving up to bring his girlfriend over from Colombia."

Gerald Moore had placed the tray on the table. Alexander and Muldoon were also getting a bit worried.

"Tomorrow morning, if he doesn't appear in the meantime, I will report him as a missing person and begin a search," said Muldoon.

Gerald Moore looked relieved that something was going to happen.

Back in the billiard room, the significance of the information that had been imparted to the family by Inspector Muldoon was beginning to sink in. There was silence, apart from Natalia's whimpering. Francois had his arm around Joanne's shoulder, who was staring into the fireplace. Jack had placed his hand over his wife's and squeezed gently. Winnie was still sitting in the corner, staring, in dismay, over at her children. Emily was chain smoking and David lit another cigar – he was pacing around the room.

"Will you both, please stop smoking," said Ava. "I'm feeling really ill. It's not fair."

"Put out the damn fags," said Winnie. "Why don't you think about others for once."

The group were quite surprised at Winnie's intervention. She usually just sipped her drinks, and said very little.

Emily and David did as they were asked and threw the cigarette and cigar into the fire. Natalia began to shake and weep. The tears streamed down her cheeks.

"Why didn't he tell me that he was sick?" she pleaded. She looked around beseechingly at the others who were quite taken aback by her reaction.

"He didn't tell any of us," replied Ava. "We were all in the dark."

Natalia began to hyperventilate.

"I'll take her outside into the fresh air," offered Francois. "She's very upset."

Natalia got up from the couch unsteadily with Jack's help. Francois took her by the arm, and led her slowly out of the room.

"He's so thoughtful," interjected Joanne. "He's been my rock since Dad died."

Emily flashed a look of suspicion in her direction.

"Glad to hear it," she said.

"I still don't understand why Dad has done all this," said Jack. "He didn't tell us about his imminent death. He made all these changes to the company, together with his new will."

"He found out two things that were earth shattering for him – his incurable illness and his long lost daughter makes an appearance. Maybe the shock affected his thinking," suggested Ava.

"Maybe we could use that argument to fight the will," said Emily enthusiastically.

"I hate to burst your bubble, Emily, but as executor, I made a number of phone calls to our lawyers in America, England and here – unfortunately, as I thought, the will is airtight. We have no comeback at all, as none of the company was legally ours before Dad's death. He could have left it all to the cat – Natalia's pre-nup was safe though. The advice that I've received from all quarters is to "make nice" with our half sister, Miss Emma Jones, and hope that she's greedy and takes our offer," concluded Jack.

"But why on earth did he treat us like this?" said David confusedly.

"I know why he did it," said a voice from the corner. "Take a good look at yourselves. I don't think that any of you really cared that he died. Jack is the best of you – not perfect, but a far sight better than you two." Winnie directed her last observation at David and Joanne.

"Have another drink Mam," sneered David.

"Need I say anymore?" said Winnie.

"I'm sure you're going to anyway," whispered Emily.

"I'll end with this," added Winnie. "Your father, knowing that he was about to meet his maker, may have had some remorse for the way he had conducted himself through the years, he may have wanted to make some reparations to those he had harmed. He knew that there wasn't enough time left, and that things would never change with David in charge. He probably wasn't sure that Jack would be strong enough to stand up to you David, so, perhaps he was hoping that Emma Jones might force a change. We'll now have to wait and see what she'll do."

Nobody had expected this intervention from Winnie. They sat there utterly dumfounded. It had been so easy for people to think of Mrs. Winnie Hawke as the elderly first wife who drank too much and was no longer of any significance – someone who just existed – well past her prime – with nothing to offer. But they had underestimated this woman, who had been married to Donal Hawke for over forty years, who was bright and intelligent and knew exactly what had gone on from the beginning and down through the years. Winnie Hawke was no fool. Disappointment had led her to search out solace in a gin and tonic, but as she had just proven, she was as astute as ever.

Alexander and Muldoon watched as Francois led a very upset, weeping Natalia out into the fresh air. She was wrapped up in a shawl – he had his arm firmly around her shoulder.

"She has reacted very strangely to the news that her husband was terminally ill – she seems much more upset now on hearing that he was dying, than she was when she heard that he had been murdered," said Muldoon.

"It could be the tablets that she was prescribed in the hospital – maybe it's just too much for her. Can't imagine that she's getting much support from the rest of them either," added Alexander.

As the two men sat looking out the window at Francois and Natalia who were strolling towards the lake, a man dressed in hiking gear ran past the window, followed by his collie dog. He opened the door and burst into the foyer. A strong gust of wind followed, causing smoke from the two turf fires to billow out into the foyer. He stood inside the porch for a moment, a look of horror painted on his face, his frightened eyes staring blankly.

Alexander stood up immediately and walked over to the hiker. The man's dog had run in behind him and was now growling.

"What on earth is the matter?" asked Alexander, taking hold of the man's arm.

"There's a body – I found a body – it's awful!"

The man started to shake, the dog continued to growl. Alexander placed the back of his hand in front of the dog's nose, who sniffed it, calmed down and allowed Alexander to pat his head.

"Come and sit down," suggested Alexander, who led the man over towards where Muldoon was sitting.

The man sat on the armchair opposite Muldoon, his dog lay down at his feet.

"This is Inspector Muldoon, what's your name?"

"I'm Joe Quinn. I live in a cottage about three miles from here."

"Would you like a drink to settle your nerves?" asked Muldoon.

"Yes, a whiskey, please," answered Quinn.

Alexander ordered the drink from the waiter who was hovering behind them, wondering what was going on.

The drink was produced very quickly. Joe Quinn drank it in one slug.

"Now tell us what happened," said Muldoon.

"I was walking on the beach with the dog, when he ran over to a big heap of something. He was barking and barking...I went over to see what it was. It was a dead body."

CHAPTER 24

BODY ON THE BEACH

The sun was setting at Loughfarraig House as Muldoon and Alexander followed Joe Quinn and his dog towards the beach. As they looked out to sea, sunbeams streamed through gaps in the fluffy clouds. The rays shone orange and yellow on the horizon, reminiscent of the "Crown of Thorns" on the head of Jesus. The sky above was streaked with stripes of dusky greys and blues. The water was eerily quiet, only gently lapping against the shore. The colours from above were reflected and danced on the surface. To the right, the mountains were dappled with oranges and browns, speckled with greens – some of them in shadow with a quarter still bright from the sun's light. Vermillion on the mountains and death on the beach.

They followed a narrow path on the headland, then carefully descended down to the beach. The pebbles crunched and the seaweed squelched underfoot as they drew nearer to where a crumpled mass lay still. The mass was right on the shoreline, the gentle waves were ebbing and flowing as if carefully checking out what it was, before caressing it, in their embrace.

The dog began to bark as they neared, but couldn't approach the mass, as Joe Quinn had a firm hold of the lead.

"There it is," said Joe, pointing.

"Will you stay here, please. We'll take a look," ordered Muldoon.

Joe Quinn stood still, his dog was straining on the lead as Muldoon and Alexander walked towards the bundle.

They looked down on the sorry sight. It was the body of a young man, who had obviously been dead for hours. He was lying on his back, his face was grey, his eyes half open, fixed and waxy. There was brown sea spaghetti draped over his limbs and torso, like snakes.

"It's Juan," said Alexander sorrowfully.

Muldoon bent down to examine the body more carefully.

"There's a puncture wound in his neck and another one in his chest. There's hardly any sign of blood – it's been washed away," said Muldoon.

He took out a pair of plastic gloves and an evidence bag from the inside pocket of his coat. Although he knew that it was most unlikely that there would be any forensic evidence left on the body, because the seawater would have washed it away, he still had to be careful.

"There's something clutched in his right hand," said Alexander.

Muldoon carefully raised the hand, opened the fingers which released a small wad of paper, and placed it in the evidence bag.

"Looks like a number of fifty pound notes," said Muldoon.

Alexander decided to have a look around. He moved away from the shoreline towards some rocks beneath the headland. He had noticed some fluttering between the rocks.

"John, over here," he shouted suddenly.

Muldoon moved quickly towards him.

"There are a few more £50 notes wedged between the rocks there. The wind must have blown them in this direction," continued Alexander.

Muldoon took out another evidence bag, gently removed the notes and placed them in the bag.

"It's going to be dark soon. We'll have to secure the scene. Will you wait with the body? I'll return to the house to make some phone calls."

Alexander watched as Muldoon, Quinn and the dog headed off in the direction of Loughfarraig House. He was left alone with the body and his thoughts.

He looked down at the lifeless body of the young man – Juan, who had been so full of life, hope and cheer. The young man with the big , brown twinkling eyes and wide grin. He remembered the photograph of the beautiful young girl with the long hair, on his bedside table. Her life would be destroyed too. His family back in Colombia would receive the most harrowing news in the coming days. Alexander stared out to sea, at the beautiful sunset, and then once more at the pathetic sight of a young man whose life has been extinguished by evil. He made another search of the immediate area. He knew that the murder weapon had probably been thrown into the sea. Even if they managed to retrieve it, there would be no forensics found – the sea would have done it's job. Fifteen minutes later Muldoon returned with a sheet of tarpaulin, some tape and posts.

"There's a doctor arriving in half an hour to make a preliminary examination. The medical examiner can't come until tomorrow morning. We'll have to move him after the examination, there's no point in leaving the body here, for the sea to do more damage."

Alexander and Muldoon erected a temporary line of tape, covered the body in the sheet of tarpaulin and waited for the doctor and a group of gardaí from Westport station to arrive, as well as the ambulance from Castlebar hospital. The wind began to pick up slightly as they stood at the seashore.

An hour later, the body of young Juan, the Colombian waiter was on it's way to the morgue in Castlebar hospital. The doctor had proclaimed that he had died from stab wounds to the neck and chest. He couldn't say which stab wound had killed him. There were a few scrapes and scratches on his face and hands, but he couldn't say what had caused them.

Alexander and Muldoon were back in Loughfarraig House. The staff had been quickly gathered together to give statements to the four young gardaí who had arrived from Westport. Muldoon had imparted the bad news to the proprietor, Gerald Moore, and his wife, who were both in shock on hearing of the second murder. The guests were asked to gather in the foyer before dinner. There were only 22 staying, including the Hawkes, Alexander and Muldoon. Fortunately, the same guests had been staying the night before as well – the night that Juan had been murdered.

Gerald Moore offered all the guests an aperatif on their arrival to the foyer. There was a lot of chatter in the room – people did not know what to expect. Everyone was aware that there must be something amiss.

"Ladies and Gentlemen," said Moore in a grave tone of voice. "Unfortunately, there is bad news. The body of one of our staff has been found on the beach. Inspector Muldoon is investigating."

Everyone looked in John Muldoon's direction. He nodded at the congregation.

"It may have been foul play, so there are a number of gardai on the premises who would like to take your details."

"I know some of you may be leaving tomorrow," interrupted Muldoon. "So, if it's more convenient you can be interviewed tonight – if not, tomorrow morning. There is a young officer in the billiard room, so before proceeding to dinner, I would be grateful if you could all give him your details and your preference for an interview time."

The chatter started up again as people began filing down the corridor towards the billiard room.

Alexander and Muldoon were sitting at their usual table in the dining room. Neither of them was very hungry. There was a very subdued atmosphere in the room. All the waiting staff were just going through the motions. The guests were whispering. Even the Hawkes were dining in virtual silence.

"I've sent the young lads home – all the guests have opted to be interviewed tomorrow morning," said Muldoon, as he took a sip of his red wine.

"Are we presuming that the two murders are linked?" asked Alexander.

"It's looking that way," answered Muldoon.

"There was something niggling at me and I've just remembered. Do you recall the day of your arrival, the 28th, having afternoon tea? Well, Juan said something unusual to us – he said that he had some good fortune. He was in flying form, grinning from ear to ear. I told him to use it wisely, to which he answered that maybe his girlfriend would now be able to join him from Colombia. I really think that he must have seen what happened the night of Donal Hawke's murder."

"He was probably blackmailing the murderer," added Muldoon. "Hence the £50 notes in his hand and stuck between the rocks."

"He also looked so anxious and nervous when you spoke to the staff," muttered Alexander.

"This seems to rule out a culprit from outside. Juan must have recognised the person who hit Donal Hawke over the head with an oar."

"We can't rule out someone from his past," interjected Muldoon. "We must keep an open mind. The man had so many enemies. However, the probability now, is that it was someone staying in the hotel or a member of staff."

"If it's the same killer, that rules out Emma Jones and her version of events that night is truthful," continued Alexander.

"We've investigated the other people who were staying here for Christmas – no link has been found between them and the Hawkes," said Muldoon.

"So we'll have to take another close look at the family. I believe that we'll have to ask anyone who was staying in the hotel at the time of both murders to stay put."

"You're right Alexander, I'm sure the Hawkes are going to be delighted!"

"Natalia has an airtight alibi for Juan's murder – being in a hospital bed under observation."

"That poor young lad took on more than he had bargained for. He can't have realised that he was in danger – otherwise he wouldn't have agreed to meet the killer in such a secluded spot," added Muldoon.

"Maybe, the thought of being able to send for his girlfriend blinded him to the dangers," mused Alexander. "Monique is going to be very upset when I tell her the news, tonight."

Monique and Emma Jones were sitting in the lounge watching an old black and white movie when they heard the telephone ring in the office.

"That will be Alexander with all the updates," said Monique cheerfully, as she rose from the couch and quickly made her way into the office.

"Hello there," she said.

"Hello sweetheart," answered Alexander.

"You don't sound very cheerful, darling. What's up?" asked Monique.

"I have some very disturbing news," said Alexander. "Do you remember the young waiter Juan from Colombia? Well, sadly, his body was found, late this afternoon on a secluded part of the beach, on the shoreline. He had been stabbed to death."

"Oh my God," said Monique in shock. "That's dreadful news. He was such a lovely, good humoured young fellow – always smiling. Why would anyone want to kill him?"

"We found a few £50 notes in his clenched fist, a few more caught between rocks. It's looking suspiciously like a blackmail attempt."

"Oh! the poor young fool," sighed Monique.

"Yesterday morning, Muldoon gathered the staff together to ask them to wrack their brains about the night that Donal Hawke was murdered. I noticed that Juan was looking very anxious, so we had decided to have a word with him during his shift at the bar starting at 10pm. He never turned up. He was probably dead at that stage."

"So, I suppose you are working on the theory that Juan saw Donal Hawke's murderer and tried to blackmail them. He was murdered for his trouble."

"That's the most likely scenario, at the moment. Although, we are not ruling out other possibilities."

"Well, Alexander, Emma cannot have murdered Juan. Thank heavens we took her away from there."

After the telephone conversation, Monique made her way back to the lounge where Emma was still watching the film. She became very upset on hearing the news of Juan's murder. She slumped on the couch and began to weep. Emma explained that she had been very fond of Juan. He was a kind hearted young man, who was very conscientious about his work. He was very much in love with his sweetheart in Colombia. His main aim in life was to save up enough money to send for her so that they could get married. Every night after his work, he went to his room to write her a letter. He used to check the post every morning himself, always hoping that a letter would arrive for him. He was so happy and delighted when one did arrive. Juan had told Emma that sometimes it took weeks for the post to arrive from Colombia to Ireland and vice versa.

CHAPTER 25

NOT SO SOLID ALIBIS!

At nine o'clock on the 7th January, the four young guards arrived back to Loughfarraig House to conduct the interviews with the guests who were leaving on that day. There were only twelve guests to be interviewed. They arrived punctually at the preordained time at the billiard room.

The Hawkes and Francois had earlier received the message from Inspector Muldoon that they were required to remain at the house for a further few days in order to help the police with their enquiries.

As predicted, the Hawkes were extremely displeased, and made it known to both Inspector Muldoon and Commandant de Bruin in no uncertain terms. Muldoon made it clear to them that they had little choice in the matter as they were now suspects in two murders – they could either remain and be interviewed in the comfort of Loughfarraig House or be interviewed in a police station. This "Hobson's choice" softened their cough considerably.

The twelve guests had left by noon. After lunch the young guards began to question all members of staff – one by one. Muldoon and Alexander were awaiting the medical examiner's report – although they didn't really believe that they would learn anything new.

A fax arrived for Inspector Muldoon at 3pm. Alexander and he sat down to peruse the report. Time of death was estimated to be between 6pm on the evening of the 6th January and 3am on the 7th January. It was very difficult to pinpoint a time because of the effects of the seawater on the body.

The wounds were inflicted by a small blade – perhaps a Swiss army knife or similar. The medical examiner believed that the fatal wound was the one to the neck. The blood had been washed away by the seawater. The scratches on the hands and feet were most likely caused in the struggle. There was really no forensic evidence because of the effects of the elements on the body. All the finger prints on the notes were smudged – so again no helpful evidence there.

"Nothing to help us at all," muttered John Muldoon. "We knew all this already."

"I believe he died before ten o'clock – otherwise he would have turned up for his shift at the bar," added Alexander.

"So, are we narrowing the time of death down to between 6pm and 10pm?" continued Muldoon.

At four o'clock a young garda arrived with the questionnaires, following their interviews with staff members.

"Any joy?" asked Alexander as he watched Muldoon flick through the papers.

"Yes, here it is. Two of the waiters met Juan in one of the corridors. He told them that he was going for a walk. This was at around 6.15.pm."

"So the poor young lad was probably dead by 7.30 at the latest, if he went straight to the beach to meet his killer," concluded Alexander.

"The Hawkes were all in the dining room before 8 pm as I recall," interjected Muldoon.

"Natalia was in hospital and Emma Jones in Briarstown," added Alexander.

"If someone from his past had murdered Hawke, or if someone had been paid to murder him, there would have been no need for them to hang around this area. Certainly no need to wait around to be blackmailed. Someone coming in from the outside would not have been recognised by Juan. I also find it very difficult to believe that there were two unrelated murders in the space of ten days in a small secluded area like this," continued Muldoon.

"We have to double check that there is absolutely no link between Hawke and the staff members here. If all the staff are cleared – well, that only leaves the family," said Alexander.

At 5.30pm David and Emily Hawke arrived in the sitting room to be interviewed. They had obviously decided that it was in their best interest to cooperate and not irritate the interviewers.

"Can you tell us your movements between 6.15pm and 8pm last evening?" asked Muldoon.

"I was in my room from 6pm," replied Emily." I had a shower and dressed for dinner."

"I went for a walk around the lake for about 45 minutes," answered David. "I left the room at about 6.15 – Emily was in the shower. When I returned it was shortly after 7pm. Emily was putting on her makeup. I jumped in the shower and got dressed. We headed down to dinner at around 7.45pm."

"Did anyone see you on your walk?" asked Muldoon.

"I really don't know," replied David "I didn't notice anyone else. I was having a good think about things."

"Can I ask you again about the night your father died?" said Muldoon.

"Yes," replied David. "After dinner, Natalia went straight to her room, complaining of a headache. The rest of us went into the Long Room for a few drinks. Dad said that he was going out for a breath of fresh air at ten o'clock and never came back. We presumed after a while that he had gone straight to bed after his walk."

"Did anyone leave the Long Room?" interjected Alexander.

"Well, I think that the ladies were in and out to the powder room," answered David.

"But none of us were gone for more than ten or fifteen minutes," interjected Emily.

"I believe Jack and I took turns to go out on the porch to smoke a cigar, as Ava was complaining that the cigar smoke was making her feel sick. I don't remember Francois leaving the room at all, unless he did when I was outside. Joanne would know better. Then we saw mother to her room and we all went our separate ways. Emily and I went to our bedroom and stayed there all night."

"Thank you, that will be all," stated Muldoon.

Emily and David Hawke stood up, and left the room.

"We didn't hear anything about people moving about and going out for smokes the last time we interviewed them," said Muldoon, irritation in his voice.

"We certainly didn't," agreed Alexander.

Jack and Ava Hawke were the next couple to be questioned. They imparted the same story for the night of Hawke's murder. Ava insisted that she was in her room, having a rest before going down to dinner the previous evening. Jack said that he had taken a stroll along the golf course, but also hadn't noticed anyone else.

When it came to Joanne and Francois, Joanne admitted leaving the room to go to the powder room on Christmas night and taking five minutes to take in the air outside. Francois claimed that he had not left the room at all, before he and Joanne went upstairs to their room for the night.

The previous evening, Francois had also taken a walk around the little forest before dressing for dinner and seeing no one. Joanne insisted that she had gone to her room at 5pm the previous evening to read her book and hadn't left until it was time for dinner.

Alexander and Muldoon had decided that it would be a waste of time and energy to question Winnie and Natalia again. All the others agree that Natalia had retired just after dinner on the night of Hawke's murder. The two men also concluded that Winnie could not have murdered either man.

"Well, there we are," sighed Muldoon, "not an alibi in sight."

"Except for one," interjected Alexander. "Everyone agrees that Francois did not leave the Long Room from the time that Hawke left at ten o'clock, to when he and Joanne went upstairs together."

"None of them had a solid alibi for the time that poor Juan was murdered apart for Natalia," added Muldoon.

"So, we are ruling out Winnie and Francois for the murder of Donal Hawke, and Winnie and Natalia for the murder of Juan," concluded Alexander.

"Are we thinking that one of the family members saw the meeting between Donal Hawke and Emma Jones, witnessed Hawke accidentally falling into the lake. Decided to take advantage of the situation to whack him over the head with an oar. Unfortunately, for them, Juan had also seen what had occurred and decided to try blackmail," wondered Muldoon.

"That's a very plausible scenario," concluded Alexander.

"Are we more or less ruling out Emma Jones?" asked Muldoon.

"Well she wasn't being blackmailed by Juan and certainly didn't kill him, so I think we can proceed under that assumption."

The Hawkes had once again gathered together in the billiard room for a conflab, sans Natalia, who was too upset to come down. Francois was present, sitting on the couch with his arm around Joanne's shoulder.

"Well it's obvious that those two believe that whoever killed Dad, also killed that waiter," grunted David.

"And they also think that it was one of us," added Emily with a sneer.

"It appears that Francois is the only one with an alibi, now, for Dad's murder," added Joanne. "The rest of us left the room at some stage or other."

"Are they not looking at Emma Jones anymore?" wondered Ava.

"Not if they believe that the same person committed both murders," said Frank.

"I suppose we had to tell them that we left the room – someone could have seen us," added Joanne.

"Well, I wish someone saw me walking round the lake yesterday when that waiter was being murdered," muttered David.

CHAPTER 26

"TE AMO" AND THE VICISSITUDES OF MAN

By the 9th January, all the checks had been made on the staff of Loughfarraig House. A number of them were from South America and Spain. The others were local young people. The guards found no links at all to the Hawke family.

Unfortunately, no one was able to verify any of the alibis of the Hawkes. There was no witness to the walks taken by the lake, the golf course or the forest. No one could corroborate the ladies account that they were in their rooms on the evening of Juan's murder.

"Of course no one can confirm Emma Jones' version of events on the night that her father was murdered," said Alexander, as he and Muldoon sat reading through all the questionnaires.

"I can't believe that there isn't anyone who can validate any of these stories," added Muldoon.

The young receptionist with the beautiful long red hair made her way over to where the two men were sitting. She was holding a letter in her hand.

"Excuse me, Inspector Muldoon. This letter arrived for Juan, this morning. It's from Colombia. I thought you might like to see it."

Muldoon took hold of the letter and opened it. The letter was written on pink writing paper. It was dated 2nd December, written in Spanish. Neither man spoke Spanish and could only make out parts of it. But at the bottom was written the words "Te Amo, Maria" followed by hearts and x's.

"How very sad," sighed Alexander. "A letter from his sweetheart."

He remembered the photo of the beautiful young girl, with the long black hair and brown eyes that he had seen on Juan's bedside table.

"I wonder does she know yet," said Muldoon, pensively. "Her heart broken, her dreams shattered. I can fax this to Dublin for translation, but I'm sure it's only a love letter."

"Whoever killed that poor young lad, is pure evil," added Alexander.

Once again Alexander thought of the cheerful, young man with the beaming smile. He was so desperate for money so that he could bring his girlfriend to him. He contemplated how unfortunate it was when the innocent get entangled, by chance, in the affairs of the villainous and vicious.

"I don't see how staying here any longer is going to help solve this case," said Muldoon." We have all the statements. We are going to have to allow the Hawkes to leave here, but not the country. We can study all of this just as easily back in Kildare."

"I'm more and more convinced that it was one of the Hawkes in any case," added Alexander. "They were made aware of the impending changes that Donal Hawke was going to make, by David's good friend Jonathan Kelly, and wanted to put a stop to it. The murder itself was opportunistic and whoever did it probably couldn't believe their luck when they saw Donal Hawke fall into the lake. It was very unfortunate for them, that Juan had seen it all."

"Even more unfortunate for poor Juan," added Muldoon.

"And of course, there was no need to murder Donal Hawke at all, seeing as he was terminally ill."

"But, there was," insisted Alexander, "if they wanted him dead before he could change his will. A number of them could be in it together, they all end up loosing a great deal – except for the wives. Winnie's inheritance remained unchanged as did Natalia's pre-nup, and pay-out."

By four o'clock that afternoon, the Hawke party had departed from Loughfarraig House, having left their details, and under orders not to leave the country until further notice. Inspector Muldoon and Alexander thanked Mr. and Mrs. Moore for their hospitality and help, requesting that they be on the lookout for any further information that may come their way. Muldoon gathered all his files together, packed them away into boxes, deposited them in the boot of his car and headed east, back to Kildare.

Alexander took one last walk along the lake shore. He had asked his waiter for some leftover bread so that he could feed the ducks and the swans. When they saw Alexander standing on the jetty, bag of stale bread in hand, the ducks took off from the middle of the lake to fly in his direction. The swans had been sheltering under bushes that acted like a green leafy roof over the corner of the lake. They too glided towards him. He watched as they fought over the pieces of bread. Some of the ducks were so tame and used to this ritual, that they waddled around his feet.

Having fed the ducks and swans, he walked towards the sea, looked out onto the wild Atlantic, the waves crashing on the rocks that jutted out of the water. He listened to the lapping of the waves on shore and the grating of the pebbles as the water retreated back into the sea.

He thought that this was the most beautiful place that he had ever been. This wonderful haven at the edge of a sunset in the west of Ireland, marred now by the vicissitudes of man.

Four hours later, Alexander drove into The Lodge. Monique had been expecting him, saw the car drive in and walked out to greet her husband with a big hug. "So glad you're home, darling," she said enthusiastically, "How was the drive?"

"Not bad at all, very little traffic," answered Alexander. "It's wonderful to see you. Everything OK here?"

The two Bernese mountain dogs had come out with Monique and were jumping up on Alexander, pawing at him for attention, their tails wagging. He patted their heads and spoke soothingly to them. "There, there, good lads."

They made their way into the kitchen where Monique gave the dogs some treats. Finally the Bernese calmed down and settled into their beds.

"Emma has gone to bed. She has been very upset since hearing the news about poor Juan. She is absolutely convinced that it was one of the Hawkes who did this," said Monique, as they both retired to the sitting room.

There was a roaring log fire ablaze in the hearth. The room was cosy. Alexander was very glad to be home. He went over to the drinks cabinet, poured a brandy for himself, and a sherry for his wife. Then they sat down on the couch in front of the fire.

"Emma is probably right," says Alexander. "Looking more and more unlikely that it was someone from outside. It certainly doesn't resemble a planned hit. If we believe Emma's version of events, and both Muldoon and I are leaning that way, it would appear to be opportunistic. John Muldoon has ordered them all to stay in the country."

"Emma has been studying all those files. She has a wonderful mind, Alexander – quite extraordinary. She really took Lydia and I by surprise. Juan's death has made her even more determined to do something about all the people who have been harmed by the Hawkes over the years. She believes that there's real badness in them. We are beginning to understand why her mother wanted nothing to do with them down through the years. Fortunately Emma appears to be their antithesis."

"How is Lydia faring with the legal side of things?" asked Alexander.

"She has decided to co-opt some help. She feels that she needs people more proficient in corporate law. Fortunately there's a firm in Dublin "Hunt and Associates" who deal with this sort of thing – and she knows one of the partners from her university days. Of course they were only delighted to take on a case as big as Mustelus Developments. They are arranging a meeting on 12th January with the other Hawke solicitors to straighten everything out. Seemingly they believe that the will is airtight and that Emma will have her shares and liquid assets very soon indeed. She is going to be an extraordinarily wealthy and powerful young woman."

"I think the Hawkes believe that she is going to be a pushover – seemingly they are in for a bit of a surprise," laughed Alexander.

CHAPTER 27

12TH JANUARY

The offices of "Hunt and Associates" is situated in one of the Victorian red bricked buildings in Rathmines. The large conference room was prepared for a very important meeting. There was a round table in the centre of the room, where the secretary had placed jugs of water, a wonderful Waterford crystal glass for each of the participants and some plates of biscuits.

Everyone arrived on time, at exactly 11am. The three Hawke siblings with their four lawyers filed into the room first to take their seats, followed by two partners from Hunt and Associates, Lydia Browne and Emma Jones.

Introductions made, Jason Hunt opened proceedings by drawing everyone's attention to Donal Hawke's will. Papers had been drawn up for signatures, so that each of Donal Hawke's children would receive their rightful share of the company and liquid assets as per the wishes of the late Donal Hawke.

"My clients wish to buy out Miss Emma Jones," interrupted one of the solicitors. "Jack Hawke, as the executor of the will, has decided to make Miss Jones a very generous offer. We are aware that Miss Jones has no experience in corporate matters, so we believe that it is in the company's best interest, as well of course, in Miss Jones' best interests, to accept the offer."

"We are here today to legally distribute the company shares and assets to the beneficiaries of Donal Hawke's will. That has to be accomplished first and foremost. All documents must be signed. Everything must be lodged in the courts. Once that is complete, Miss Jones can then decide on the next move," interjected Lydia Browne.

The three Hawke siblings moved restlessly in their seats, but said nothing. Their four lawyers sat silently, nodded their heads, then distributed the papers for signature to their clients who reluctantly put their names to the legal documents.

Emma Jones also signed the papers. Lydia sat beside her, very grateful that she had entrusted the proceedings to her good friend Jason Hunt and wondering, as she glanced from David to Jack to Joanne, was she looking across the table at a murderer or murderess. She also realised that this crew would have chewed up poor Emma, despite her intelligence, and spat her out again if she had to deal with them on her own, without the support she had from herself, Monique and Jason Hunt.

The meeting concluded. Everyone walked out of the boardroom – the Hawkes and their lawyers looking somewhat despondent, Emma Jones relieved that, at least, this part of proceedings was over. Lydia and Emma stopped to thank Jason Hunt for his help, then walked out into the fresh air, took a deep breath and headed back to the car. The two women sat into the car, put on their seat belts and stared straight in front of them.

"That went as well as could be expected," said Lydia.

"I have no intention whatsoever of selling to them," added Emma angrily. "They are a shower of gangsters. One of them probably murdered poor Juan. They are just bad, through and through."

"They were certainly trying to pull a fast one there. They thought that we would all be intimidated by their show of strength – four lawyers – each one more slimy and slithery than the next. They must be afraid of what you are going to do with all that information you received about the workings of the company. They would just love you to sell up and disappear out of their lives," continued Lydia.

Lydia put the car in gear, and began the journey back to Briarstown. She wondered how dangerous the Hawkes were, if Emma was in any danger now. She would have to discuss this with Monique and Alexander.

Lydia delivered Emma back to The Lodge. On arrival, Emma retired to her bedroom for a "lie down" as she was complaining of a headache following the stressful meeting in Rathmines. Lydia took advantage of her absence to have a chat with Monique and Alexander.

"Well, how did it go?" asked Monique.

"Legally all went according to plan. One of the Hawke's lawyers made an intervention stating that the three siblings wished to buy Emma out of the company. This was dismissed as irrelevant for that meeting, and all the papers were signed. I've become somewhat worried about Emma's safety, as the Hawkes are suspects in two murders – I was wondering just what are they capable of. Are they dangerous?"

"Their father was certainly a dangerous man," answered Alexander. "He coordinated intimidation, bribery and God knows what else over the years with his "fixer" and long time friend Frank Smith. There was even suspicion about the so called accidental death of an engineer who had written a scathing report about his building practices. I really don't know if any of his children had any hand, act or part in any of this, but as you say, they are suspects in two murders."

"I wouldn't trust them as far as I'd throw them," insisted Lydia." Particularly the eldest son, David – he comes across as a really nasty piece of work."

"So, we are really going to have to look after Emma until all of this has died down," interjected Monique. "Do they know where she is staying?"

"I don't believe so," answered Lydia. "I certainly didn't say anything, but I suppose they have ways and means of finding out."

"I'll have a chat with John Muldoon about it. We'll come up with a plan," concluded Alexander.

The phone rang in Naas Garda Station. The young garda put Alexander straight through to the office of Inspector John Muldoon.

"John Muldoon speaking, how can I help you?"

"Good afternoon John, Alexander here. I need to speak to you about Emma Jones."

Alexander related what had happened in the solicitor's office that morning and Lydia's worries about Emma's safety.

"Lydia took a particular dislike to David Hawke – actually she didn't take to any of them. Have you any thoughts on the matter, John?"

"I can place a squad car at the top of your road. I'll request an armed officer. We're lucky in that there's only one way down to your house. The other end is a cul-de sac. We have all the information on who lives in the area from the last case. Have you any problems allowing Emma stay for a while until this is solved?"

"Not at the moment," replied Alexander. "The children are away at school for the next few weeks, and I can take my own precautions here as well. By the way, is there any news from the Commissioner on whether there is going to be a broader investigation into the company?"

"I'm expecting a phone call in half an hour, to bring me up to speed, from head office. I'm not really very hopeful," concluded Muldoon.

John Muldoon waited patiently for the Commissioner to ring him. The phone rang at 5.30pm. Muldoon picked up the receiver. "Yes Commissioner."

"Just ringing you to give you a briefing on what has been going on here. As you know I organised a small team to sift through all the information. While there's a definite pattern of bribery and corruption in the way Donal Hawke did his business, as I thought, there is nothing at all that we can do about what went on in other jurisdictions. Hawke appears to have had very powerful friends in both America and Britain. When it comes to what went on here – it's all very suspicious, but it could take years. Some of the people mentioned in the journalist Winter's papers, are retired. The politicians have covered their backsides very well. The circling of the wagons has started already. To tell you the truth John, a lot of these fellows are in the same social circle, went to the same private schools, play golf together. We would need a lot of resources to get to the bottom of it all. We don't have enough manpower, nor are we going to get much cooperation. The government wants us concentrating on security – as you know there was another serious incident on the border yesterday. The main instigator of all this bribery and corruption is dead. There is no obvious link to his children. According to our legal advice, the children were only employees of the company, so they had no power. Donal Hawke seems to have kept them out of all the shenanigans. Certainly Frank Smith's name appears a lot, but again, no proof, and he is now an old man. I'll certainly leave the investigation open – maybe in time – if the political atmosphere changes – we might have more luck."

John Muldoon hung up the receiver. He wasn't one bit surprised at what he had just heard. The powers that be did not want this can of worms opened up. The Commissioner's hands were tied. The government had more serious problems to deal with than fraud and corruption in the ranks. They needed to keep the population on side regarding the security of the state. These revelations would have to wait for another day. Alexander was also not surprised when Muldoon recounted to him, his conversation with the Commissioner.

"So, that's that," said Alexander.

"Yes," answered Muldoon. "It's shelved for the time being, well, for the foreseeable future to be honest. All that work that the American did over the years, the work that was done in England and Joe Winter's investigation – all these files will be left in a cupboard to become covered in dust."

"We do have copies," added Alexander. "Emma Jones also has the box of tricks that her father left for her. All may not be completely lost."

"That may be so," stated Muldoon, "but we now need to get back to solving our two murders. The young officers have been all around Loughfarraig House and it's surrounding area, questioning everyone. There doesn't seem to have been any strangers in the vicinity at the times of the murders. All the staff have been checked out – no motives there. All the other guests have been looked into – no motive or connection to the Hawkes – just people on their holidays. So, we are definitely back to the Hawke party."

"None of them has a solid alibi. The men were out walking and no one saw them. No proof that the women were in their rooms at the time of Juan's death. They were all wandering around the place at the time of Donal Hawke's murder, apart from Francois. We have no forensic evidence and no witnesses. We are not going to get them to change their stories. Unless someone comes forward or something else happens we are stymied, but as I always say, murderers tend to make mistakes," concluded Alexander.

Following the conversation with John Muldoon, Alexander made his way into the sitting room where Emma and Monique were chatting.

"As expected, really," stated Alexander. "They are not going to go ahead with the fraud investigation into Mustelus Developments – no interest in rocking the boat, politically – not enough resources with the security situation the way it is. In my opinion they've just circled the wagons. The bribery in local government and further up the ladder may go unpunished – for the moment anyway. John and I are going to concentrate on solving the murders."

"I would be very interested in looking into this," interjected Emma. "Do you think the journalist, Joe Winters would be interested in talking to me?"

"I'm sure he would only be delighted," said Monique. "He got an awful time when his article came out. He was virtually "black balled" for a

time. He's an excellent investigative journalist, but no one would pub-
lish his articles after the politicians etc. went after him. I'm sure he
would love to be vindicated. He was accused of being a liar, of making
up stories. Some of the tabloids went after him as well, delving into his
private life. They were like hyenas picking over a corpse. There was a
concerted effort to destroy his reputation."

"He also believes that his office was bugged," added Alexander.

CHAPTER 28

A BREAK IN THE CASE.

"John Muldoon speaking, how can I help you?" It was unusual to get a phone call to his office at exactly 9am.

"Frank Smith here – we met in Galway – about the death of Donal Hawke."

"Of course I remember you Mr. Smith. What can I do for you?"

"I wasn't completely forthcoming in our last interview. I left out one piece of information. Donal Hawke had asked me last September to watch a member of his family. The information that I've gathered may be relevant to your investigation. I have a file which also contains photographic evidence. Unfortunately, I think I was spotted – getting careless in my old age. I'm not going to give you any further information over the phone. Would you be able to meet me this afternoon or evening at the same place? I can hand it all over then."

"Yes, I certainly can," answered Muldoon. "As you know, it's a long drive. What time will we say?"

"I'll be in the Great Southern at 5pm precisely," replied Frank Smith.

Muldoon replaced the receiver, but almost immediately picked it up again to dial Alexander de Bruin's number.

"Monique de Bruin speaking."

"Good morning Monique, John Muldoon here. I was hoping to speak with Alexander."

"He's out with the dogs at the moment. Can I help you at all?"

Muldoon recounted the conversation that he had just had with Frank Smith. He explained that he wished to ask Alexander to accompany him to Galway. He thought that they may have to stay a few days if the information that Frank Smith had, could lead to a break through in the case.

After the call, Monique put on her wellies and winter coat, and headed out to the fields to give Alexander the news. She walked through the courtyard and out towards the stables. She could see Alexander and the two Bernese in the distance. He caught sight of her and waved.

At three o'clock that afternoon, Muldoon and Alexander checked into The Skeffington Arms Hotel on Eyre Square in Galway, where Muldoon had booked two rooms. This hotel was only a short distance from the Great Southern, where their meeting with Frank Smith would take place.

At 4.50pm the two men walked across the square and up the steps to the grand entrance of the Great Southern. They walked through the foyer and took their seats in the same spot where they had met Smith on the last occasion. The waiters were as attentive as ever. There were only two other couples in the room, who were having afternoon tea.

Alexander noticed the porcelain cake stand, bedecked with an array of tiny crustless sandwiches, and a variety of cakes, scones and colourful buns. The waiter poured the tea with panache mentioning that it was "Darjeeling".

"Who do you think he was watching?" asked Muldoon.

Alexander turned his attention away from the "afternoon tea" ritual.

"I haven't a clue – it could be any of them. It's very strange to have your "fixer" watching a member of your own family. Donal Hawke doesn't seem to have trusted anyone. What a way to live your life!"

"We'll probably be making a visit to one of them following this meeting," stated Muldoon. "They all have their Irish homes within an hours drive of here."

It was now 6pm – Frank Smith was an hour late.

"I'll go to reception and ring his home number. This is strange – didn't seem like the type of man who wasn't punctual. He was waiting for us the last time we met him."

Five minutes later, Muldoon returned, shaking his head, "No answer."

"I presume you have his address John. Perhaps we should call to his house and check."

Smith's home was situated in a quiet leafy cul-de-sac, five minutes drive from U.C.G. The Victorian red brick house was divided into two apartments. Smith occupied the ground floor. Muldoon knocked on the oak door – no answer. He knocked again – still no answer. He noticed a car parked in the driveway.

"I'm going to take a look around the back," said Muldoon.

Both men made their way around the side of the building – no sign of anyone. Alexander peered in one of the sash windows. There were books and papers strewn on the floor, drawers were open and a lamp was on the floor. Then de Bruin saw Frank Smith, lying on his back, behind the couch, blood coming from his mouth and nose, another obvious wound to his chest.

"John, come and take a look at this," ordered Alexander.

Muldoon peered in the window and saw the same sight. He took a deep breath.

"Let's go around the back to see if there's a way in."

All the windows and doors were locked .

"We'll have to make entry," said Muldoon.

He used his elbow to break the glass on the back door, unlocked the door from the inside. He handed Alexander a pair of plastic gloves and shoe covers that he always kept in his jacket pocket. They made their way into the sitting room, and over to Frank Smith.

"He's dead," exclaimed Alexander. "He's been dead for at least a few hours – look at the blush – purple discolouration."

The eyes were half open and waxy. Muldoon located the phone and dialled the garda station. He ordered them to get a forensic team and medical examiner to the crime scene as soon as possible.

"On the surface this looks like a burglary gone wrong. Except there's no sign of a break-in. All the windows and doors were locked."

"A lot of people leave a key under a planter or rock outside the door," suggested Alexander.

"I don't think that Frank Smith was the type of trusting person to leave a spare key for anyone to find," added Muldoon.

"He might have just opened the door to someone who then forced their way in. He was a man in his seventies – no longer physically strong," continued Alexander.

"It's too much of a coincidence that he was about to hand over evidence to us this afternoon," muttered Muldoon. "Let's look for the file and photos without disturbing anything."

The two men made a preliminary search of the apartment.

"It's useless – we can't open up drawers or anything – we'll have to wait until the forensics are finished," groaned Muldoon.

They didn't have long to wait before they could hear the sirens. Two police cars, a forensic van and an ambulance drove into the property. Muldoon and the inspector in charge knew each other – some of his men had been involved in the aftermath of both murders at Loughfarraig House. It was agreed that Muldoon and Alexander would be present as the forensic team did their work.

Two hours later, following a preliminary examination of the body, Frank Smith's remains were transported to the morgue at Galway Regional Hospital and the forensics team had completed their work. No files or photos pertaining to the Hawke family were found.

"A third murder," said Alexander, as he poured coffee into white porcelain cups for Muldoon and himself. They were sitting in a corner of the lounge of The Skeffington Arms Hotel. They were both hungry and exhausted. They tucked into their sandwiches and drank the strong coffee.

"He did say that he thought that he had been spotted," said Muldoon. "If only he had mentioned a name. We are going to have to chase up alibis from the family for this murder now."

"They could have sent someone to do their dirty work, of course," added Alexander.

"I wonder did Frank Smith keep all his files at home. Maybe he kept copies elsewhere."

At eleven o'clock the following morning, a copy of the post mortem and forensics were delivered to the Skeffington Arms Hotel. The teams had agreed to work quickly, as everyone was aware that this was probably the third related murder in a matter of a few weeks. Muldoon had made a call to the Commissioner to appraise him of events. Muldoon was officially put in charge of Frank Smith's murder, with Alexander de Bruin co-opted on to the case as a consultant.

"The only fingerprints found in the apartment were those of Frank Smith. He must never have had any visitors. All the surfaces were spotless. The murderer must have worn gloves. There was a safe in the floor of the bedroom but it only contained his personal papers and twenty thousand pounds in cash. There was absolutely nothing found pertaining to the Hawkes – nothing about them personally or about the business," said Muldoon.

"He probably destroyed anything he had after Donal Hawke's death – apart from the file and photos on whomever he was watching – or maybe he kept them somewhere else," added Alexander.

Muldoon then opened the autopsy file.

"The medical examiner is putting the time of death at between 9am and 3pm. I know he was alive at 9am as I spoke to him. Cause of death is a wound to the heart – a narrow sharp implement was used. There were no defence wounds – he must have been taken by surprise."

"So, our next move is to question the members of the Hawke family. While Frank Smith may have made many enemies down through the years, I think we can safely say that our main suspects are the Hawkes," said Alexander.

"They all live within an hours drive of here," began Muldoon. "They live quite close to each other. Donal Hawke originally bought a rundown manor house, years ago. He renovated it and used it as his Irish home with his wife Winnie. He bought up land close by, and renovated or built new homes for his children. The one he was sharing with Natalia is only a stone's throw from the original one where Winnie Hawke lives. Obviously David and Emily spend a lot of time in England. Jack and Ava reside in the U.S. for much of the year. Joanne is based in Ireland – she also has a house in Dublin and holidays a lot on the continent. As you know, I instructed them not to leave the country, so they are all in their west of Ireland homes presently."

"I presume that we are still of the opinion that Winnie didn't do any of this," said Alexander.

"Yes, I don't think that we'll bother her," replied Muldoon.

Following a phone call to Joanne Hawke's residence, the two men began their 40 minute drive from Galway City to the Mayo Galway border.

"Is Francois here as well?" asked Alexander." No, apparently he had to return to France as a relative is ill," answered Muldoon.

"I thought you told them all to stay put, and not to leave the country."

"Not Francois – he has an alibi for Donal Hawke's murder – remember he didn't leave the Long Room in Loughfarraig House."

"Yes I do remember. He doesn't have an obvious motive, in any case," concluded Alexander.

They arrived at a set of electric gates, pressed the intercom which was answered by a male voice.

"Can I help you?"

"This is Inspector Muldoon and Commandant de Bruin, we have an appointment with Joanne Hawke."

The electric gates slowly opened. Muldoon put the car in gear and travelled along the avenue towards the house. The trees were devoid of leaves, but the lawns were manicured.

A gentleman, who was dressed like a butler of yore opened the door and showed them into a lounge where there was antique furniture, but little warmth. The house did not feel "lived in". Joanne Hawke appeared at the doorway. "What can I do for you gentlemen?" she asked coldly.

"Your father's friend Frank Smith has been murdered. Because of his association with your family, we need to ask you a few questions," said Muldoon.

"The rest of us had very little to do with him, as he was Dad's gopher," she replied.

Muldoon and Alexander were quite taken aback by her reaction to the news. There was no sympathy, no questions as to what happened – complete dismissal – no empathy or care.

"Where were you between 9am yesterday morning and 3pm yesterday afternoon?" asked Muldoon

"I was here until 12 o'clock, then I went for a long drive. I was back at 4.30pm."

"So you don't have an alibi," interjected Alexander.

"Why would I need an alibi, I had nothing to do with the man. Why would I want to kill him?"

Joanne glared intently at Alexander.

"If that's all, Mark will show you out."

"Could you tell us when Francois left for France?" asked Alexander.

"On the 9th. He received a phone call that his aunt was ill. This has obviously nothing to do with him either," she snarled.

"Thank you for your cooperation," stated Muldoon.

Mark, the butler showed them out and closed the door behind them.

Alexander and Muldoon spent the remainder of the day visiting the other Hawke residences and questioning the occupants.

They received a very cool reception from David and Emily who would have preferred to be in England. They too insisted that they had had little communication with Frank Smith, suggesting that he had many enemies. They were each other's alibis.

Jack and Ava were a little more civil, at least offering the men some refreshments. Ava still looked ill and frail. They too had gone for a drive together on the previous afternoon.

Natalia was on her own in the house. She said that she had given the maid and cook the afternoon off on the previous day. She too insisted that she barely knew Frank Smith. She was aware that he was a good friend of her husband's, but that was all. So, she had no alibi at all.

"She's looking much better than she did the last time we saw her," suggested Muldoon, as they drove back towards Galway.

"Yes, she appears to have made an excellent recovery," added Alexander.

Both men were extremely tired after their very trying day. They spent the rest of the journey in silence.

The dinner in The Skeffington Arms was not at all as formal as dinner in Loughfarraig House. The food was very good. The men ordered a red Bordeaux and had a relaxing evening. After their meal, they retired to the Lounge for a night cap.

"Any one of them could have organised someone to do their dirty work," said Muldoon, as he sipped his brandy. "None of them cared one iota about Frank Smith."

"Well, he was watching one of them, whatever they were up to, and he got caught," added Alexander.

"Donal Hawke's murder appeared opportunistic – hit over the head with an oar – a convenient murder weapon. The other two murders were planned. The assailant was carrying a weapon," responded Muldoon. "Both victims were killed in the same way – stabbed to death."

"They probably think that they've covered their tracks now," said Alexander. "Poor Juan killed because he had witnessed the first murder and Frank Smith stabbed to death because he was seen gathering information on one of them."

"So, it seems that Frank Smith was following one of them before they all went to Loughfarraig House, and decided to complete his task after Donal Hawke's murder. I wonder did Frank Smith suspect that whomever he was following, on behalf of Donal Hawke, was also the perpetrator of the first two killings," concluded Alexander.

CHAPTER 29

SOCIOPATHY

In Briarstown, it had started to snow early in the morning. By ten o'clock there was a white blanket covering the fields. Monique had already brought the ponies and horses a bale of hay. They were wearing their winter jackets. The two Bernese mountain dogs frolicked in the fluffy snow. The trees in the copse were devoid of leaves apart from the odd evergreen, their branches skeletal and reaching towards the heavens. The birds happily fed at the two bird tables where Monique had replenished the feeders with seeds and fat balls.

When she returned to The Lodge, Emma was in the kitchen sipping a cup of coffee.

"Good morning Emma," said Monique as she entered the kitchen, then walked towards the kettle and switched it on. "I've just been out in the paddock giving the ponies and horses some hay. There's been quite a fall of snow."

"There certainly has," replied Emma.

"What are your plans today?" asked Monique.

"Still sifting through all the information in the company," retorted Emma. "I was also wondering what is going to happen to Juan's body."

"Mr. Moore has kindly offered to pay for the repatriation of the remains," said Monique, solemnly. "Juan's family have been informed. It must be a dreadful shock for them all."

"I feel so sorry for his girlfriend – they had so many plans. I intend to help them out when everything is settled. I believe that someone in the Hawke family is responsible for all this."

"There's more bad news, Emma," added Monique. "There's been another death – Frank Smith, your father's friend. He was murdered in Galway. He was meant to meet with Alexander and John Muldoon but never turned up. Seemingly, he was watching a member of the family before your father's death. Donal Hawke had reason to suspect something or other. According to Alexander, he thought he had been spotted. So this murder has to be linked to the other two."

"I remember him. He came to my flat in London to investigate my claims. He came across as a very hardy man, but he seemed to have known my mother. I got the impression that he and my father were as thick as thieves."

"Yes, they had known each other since childhood," replied Monique. "Donal Hawke appears to have trusted him implicitly. He was what Alexander called a "fixer" – you've seen it yourself, in the documents – Smith was present whenever Donal Hawke wanted anything resolved to his satisfaction."

"Yes, indeed, he seems to have been involved in a lot of the shady activity that went on over the years – not a very nice man, all told – just like my father," mused Emma.

Monique sat quietly drinking her coffee, pondering all the murders and hoping against hope that Emma wasn't in grave danger. She stared out the window as the snow flakes continued to fall. She thought about the Hawke family – who amongst them was the most likely murderer? She mulled over each character in her head – each more unpleasant than the other. According to Alexander – none of them had a solid alibi for Smith's murder. Monique contemplated the difference between Emma, who appeared to be bright, sensitive and caring – full of empathy for others, and the other Hawke siblings who were selfish, probably dishonest, privileged and entitled. The only conclusion that she could come to, was that Emma was more like her mother.

Monique was jolted out of her reverie by a knock on the front door. Both she and Emma made their way down the hallway and opened the front door.

"Good morning ladies," greeted Lydia Browne cheerfully as she stood at the other side of the threshold, clad in a warm winter coat, hat, gloves and boots.

"Come in out of the snow," laughed Monique.

Lydia removed her boots and outer garments, and followed Monique and Emma into the warm sitting room, where a blazing log fire danced in the hearth.

"What brings you out in this weather?" asked Monique, as the three ladies relaxed in front of the fireplace.

"Just checking up on you both. Damien was a little worried about you – wondering if there was anything that needed doing in Alexander's absence."

"Everything is under control here," replied Monique. "We were just discussing the latest murder. I suppose Alexander has been on to Damien?"

"Yes, he was. He told him all about it. I think he's a little worried about you both being here on your own. Three murders in such a short space of time – and all linked. While he doesn't believe that anyone knows where Emma is, he wants you both to be extremely careful."

"I know, he said the same thing to me last night on the phone," replied Monique. "I'm expecting Robert and Alison to make an appearance at any minute – he has probably been on to them as well. I don't blame him – I think I'd be worried as well if roles were reversed."

"Let's change the subject, Lydia. How are things progressing with Emma's inheritance?"

"So far all is going very smoothly. Donal Hawke had everything wrapped up very nicely indeed – bow and all. No way that the Hawkes can fight it. We've made it very clear that you are not going to sell to them, Emma. Of course they still believe that they will be able to control you – they are going to be in for a big surprise."

"Emma wanted to do something to help Juan's family in Colombia," interjected Monique.

"I see no problem in that at all," replied Lydia. "An interim payment can be made very shortly. That's a very thoughtful, kind thing to do."

"It's the very least that I can do," insisted Emma." His death has been caused by one of my family – I'm sure of it. I wonder if I hadn't contacted Donal Hawke – would Juan be still alive. Did I cause this whole house of cards?"

"You can't think like that Emma," said Monique.

"It probably has got nothing at all to do with you. Remember that Frank Smith was following a member of the family at your father's behest before you ever met him."

Emma began to cry. She placed her head in her hands. Monique sat beside her and put her arm around her shoulder to comfort her.

"Do you mind if I go to my room?" she sobbed.

"Go ahead. You probably need a rest – it's just one shock after another," added Monique.

Emma stood up and quickly headed out of the room. Lydia and Monique heard her footsteps on the stairs as she made her way up to her bedroom.

"She has been so strong for the last while, studying the documents, coming to the realization of what is ahead of her – the amount of wealth and power that she will have," muttered Monique.

"Perhaps, hearing about the latest murder was just too much for her," added Lydia.

"It just became somewhat overwhelming for her, but I'm convinced that she is strong enough to cope. I just hope that we'll find out that all this mayhem has nothing to do with her making contact with Donal Hawke," concluded Monique.

As expected, an army four by four green jeep pulled into the rear entrance to The Lodge that afternoon. Colonel Robert King walked up to the back door, knocked and walked straight in. He placed his great coat and cap on the coat hook in the small hallway.

"Monique," he called "It's only me."

"I'm in the sitting room," Monique replied. "I suppose you are under orders to check up on me," said Monique smiling, as Robert entered the room.

"Are you on your own?"

"My driver is in the car, with Corporal Henry. They will call back for me in two hours. They have an errand to run."

Robert removed his Sam Browne belt and his officer's jacket, placed them on the back of the chair and sat down in an armchair in front of the fire.

"This is a dreadful business," he said. "Three murders, all related, no less."

"Do you really think that Emma is in danger, Robert? I know that Alexander worries because he's so far away from here."

"It depends on the motive for the murders. If the changing of the will is the motive, then she may very well be the next target. If it's something different, then she's probably safe."

"What is your opinion of the murders – from a psychological viewpoint?" asked Monique.

"I believe that one of the original theories – that it was a hit or a disgruntled person from Donal Hawke's past isn't very likely. It really looks to me as if it was a family murder. There was nobody else staying in the hotel with any links to Hawke except his own family and Emma. I believe that someone saw him accidentally fall into the lake, saw Emma run back into the House and took advantage of the situation, picked up the oar, which just happened to be on the shore, and clocked him over the head. Emma would have been the main suspect of course, if there hadn't been two other murders and she did have alibis for both. To me, it looks like someone who knew him very well – we're probably looking at a member of the family."

"There's only one person with a solid alibi for Hawke's murder and that's Francois," interjected Monique, "and anyway I can't imagine what his motive could be."

"The second murder is much more planned and calculated," continued Robert. "Poor Juan, the waiter, obviously witnessed the murder of Donal Hawke and tried to blackmail the culprit. Whoever he was blackmailing brought a blade to the meeting, probably with every intention of killing him. The assailant handed over some cash to put Juan at his ease and then callously stabbed him. From a psychological perspective, they are different types of killings. The first was done without any calculation, like a spur of the moment act, the second is vicious, scheming with design. It's as if there were two different murderers. Then again, once caught in the act, Donal Hawke's killer really had to get rid of the witness. The third murder is very similar to the second – the same method. Frank Smith must have known his killer – there were no defence wounds. Although he was a man in his seventies, I couldn't see someone like him going down without a fight. He must have been taken completely by surprise. According to Alexander, he was following a member of the family from before anyone in the family knew about Emma, which leads me to think that perhaps this has nothing at all to do with her."

"Which one of the family do you think most likely the killer?" asked Monique.

"I wouldn't put it past any of them. They are a very nasty crowd. I don't know who amongst them would actually carry out the act, but I'm in no doubt, that each of them is capable of organising it. But, there was no organisation involved in the first murder. There's a big difference between acting on the spur of the moment and planning a killing – a big difference between reacting to events and being proactive in the taking of a life. If Alexander and Muldoon can find out whom Frank Smith was tailing – then I think they can solve it."

"But Smith was such a loner. Nothing incriminating was found in his home. Perhaps the killer found the evidence and took it away."

"Perhaps – I'm quite sure that the two will get to the bottom of this sooner rather than later," replied Robert, reassuringly. "By the way, how is Emma coping?"

"She is doing extremely well. She's a highly intelligent young woman. She has been sifting through all the documents pertaining to Mustelus Developments. Emma is able to retain all the information. However, she had a kind of collapse today, having heard about the third murder – it was like the straw that broke the camel's back. She is resting at the moment. I'm hopeful that she will recover. Three murders is a lot to take in on top of a huge inheritance coupled with enormous responsibility. She absolutely wants to make amends to as many people as possible who have been so badly affected by the behaviour of Donal Hawke and his minions through the years."

"She's going to get a lot of opposition from the rest of the family," added Robert.

"No doubt," replied Monique, "but Lydia Browne and her associates will be able to guide her through it all. There will be a wall of protection around her. It looks like there will be a few scandals as well – amongst the planners and the politicians. Emma really wants to get to the bottom of all the skulduggery. She also wants to help all the tenants who have been living in squalor. There have been at least two deaths."

"I suppose she can only do her best. I can't really see her being able to get to the whole truth – too many cover-ups – too many powerful, wealthy people involved. She appears to be a very good person."

"I was just thinking about that earlier. She is so different from her half siblings. Their anthesis really. No wonder her mother wanted to steer clear of Donal Hawke and his clan. As if she were afraid that Emma would become infected by them."

"I believe that many of those character traits are inherited. The Hawke children have so many of their father's character flaws – a kind of sociopathy, with little regard for right or wrong, – ignoring the rights and feelings of others. Of course when a sociopath's schemes are frustrated – watch out everyone."

"David Hawke and his wife Emily, I suppose, are the most dislikeable," said Monique.

"Well, they are most obviously callous, but these types are not always the most dangerous. David does not present as the brightest of them. He just tries to run roughshod over everyone. I would be looking more towards the manipulator – but as I said, they all have major sociopathic problems."

Exactly two hours after his arrival, Colonel King's driver returned to collect him. Monique waved him goodbye. She noticed that it had stopped snowing, but it had now begun to freeze. She knew that she would have to give extra feed to the ponies and horses, and was a little regretful that she hadn't taken up Damien Browne's offer to feed the animals.

Monique wrapped up warmly and, accompanied by her two dogs made her way through the snow to the feed-room where there were bins full of nuts and grains. The bins prevented the rats and other vermin from interfering with the animal feed. The ponies and horses had seen her approaching with the buckets and moved in her direction. She gave them their mixture and scattered more hay in the containers. She decided to leave the stable doors open, so that the animals could shelter there if the weather became too inclement for them. Monique knew that they preferred to remain in the paddock. Her job complete, she headed back towards the house. The two Bernese ran ahead of her, hopping like rabbits in the snow. It was getting dark. She knew that tonight the sky would be black, dotted with twinkling stars.

CHAPTER 30

THE KEYRING

Muldoon and Alexander entered the offices of Jonathan Kelly and Son at precisely 10am. Miss Henry was at her desk and rose to show the two gentlemen into the office.

Jonathan Kelly Senior was sitting behind his oak desk as Junior was standing by the window.

"Good morning, gentlemen, please sit down," said Senior, indicating to the two armchairs which had been placed in front of his desk.

Muldoon and Alexander sat down.

"How can we help you?" asked Senior.

"Were you Frank Smith's solicitor?" asked Muldoon.

"Yes, we were," answered Senior, moving slightly in his chair.

"As I'm sure you are aware, Frank Smith has been murdered in his home. We would like you to give us any information you have about him. We found no papers in his home. We don't know if they were kept elsewhere or whether whoever killed him, took them," stated Muldoon.

"We have his will here and the deeds of his residence, but that's it," answered Senior assertively.

"Are either of you aware of any deposit box that he might have, or any other place where he might have kept important documents?" asked Alexander.

The two Kellys glanced at each other. Junior stood absolutely still, pursed his lips and touched his right cheek.

"We are not aware of anything like that," answered Senior, as he stared unblinkingly at Alexander.

"You do know that we will eventually find whatever he has hidden away," added Muldoon." If you impede our investigation, there will be serious consequences for you and your business."

"We have no intention of impeding your investigation. As I have already stated, we only hold his will and his deeds here – nothing else," repeated Senior.

"What about you Jonathan? Have you any idea of where Frank Smith might have kept important documents?" asked Muldoon directing his question at Junior.

"No idea, whatsoever," retorted junior.

"To whom did he leave his estate?" asked Alexander.

"He had distant cousins, living in Bohola – they get everything. His only property is the one he lived in. There's a fair amount of cash. He had no communication with these cousins, so it will be a great surprise for them," concluded Senior.

"Do you know where all his bank accounts are?" asked Muldoon.

"We are aware of the current account and savings account in the Bank of Ireland, here in Galway. We are unaware at the moment of any others, but will have to do our searches for probate," stated Senior.

"Thank you for your assistance," said Muldoon as he rose from his armchair.

Alexander followed suit and both men left the office.

They walked back to the car and sat in.

"Those two are lying through their teeth," muttered Alexander. "They are still trying to protect the Hawkes."

"I know," replied Muldoon. "Young Jonathan had all the giveaway signs – standing absolutely still, pursing his lips, touching his face – trying to look in absolute control, but failing miserably."

"They have placed themselves in a very precarious position. We know that Jonathon Junior tipped off his friend David Hawke about Donal Hawke's intention to change his will. I presume that Jonathon Senior now knows about it – so they have to do the Hawkes' bidding, otherwise they could be struck off if David Hawke spills the beans," interjected Alexander. "They both know fine well that Frank Smith must have kept copies of many of the transactions that he was involved in. I'm presuming that he also kept copies of his evidence on whomsoever he was following on the instructions of Donal Hawke. One doesn't survive so long in this line of work without taking precautions."

"I agree," stated Muldoon. "We'll have to find where he stashed the papers. We need to check the evidence that was taken from his home. There will have to be an account number or keys to a security box, or something that will help us."

"I would say that the killer is in possession of the photos etc. that Smith was going to show us. However, knowing Smith and his ilk, there's another set somewhere," concluded Alexander.

The two men drove to the Garda Station in Galway. They were shown into a room where all the evidence bags collected at Smith's home were being stored. They donned plastic forensic gloves provided, and began to painstakingly sift through all the bags. There were some bank statements from Bank of Ireland – there were two accounts as had been stated by Jonathan Kelly. When they opened the bag containing all the keys that were found, there was one set labelled house, another set labelled car and a lone key on a map of Ireland marble keyring, labelled unknown.

"This looks like a safe deposit key or a locker key," said Muldoon, a slight tone of excitement in his voice.

"So it does," replied Alexander. "Maybe that's the "Holy Grail"."

"We have to keep going through everything with a fine-toothed comb – there must be a hint somewhere. It will be a needle in a haystack if we can't find some sort of clue."

Muldoon and Alexander spent most of the next two hours searching for any indication that might lead them to the illusive documents, but to no avail.

"We need someone who knows about keys to take a look at it," Muldoon said. "There's nothing here. We don't know if it's a key to a box or a locker. A locksmith would probably have a better idea. We don't want to send the men on a wild goose chase, looking through locker rooms all over Galway and Mayo when it might belong to a safety deposit box somewhere in Dublin or even further afield."

"You're right," agreed Alexander.

Muldoon and Alexander made their way to the desk of the officer in charge of the evidence. Muldoon signed out the key, and placed the plastic bag containing the keyring and key into his breast pocket.

An hour later they had located a locksmith, who was highly regarded by the Superintendent in the station, in Salthill.

The locksmith was a very thin man, balding and bespectacled. He took a close look at the key and announced that it was definitely a safe deposit key – like those used in the banks of the bigger towns and cities, such as Galway, Dublin, Limerick and Castlebar. Muldoon and Alexander thanked the man, leaving his shop feeling rather relieved that it wasn't a key to a locker.

The weather had cooled considerably and there was a strong westerly wind coming in from the Atlantic. There weren't many people strolling along the promenade in Salthill. The sky had darkened, the waves were now crashing against the shoreline, throwing foam into the air. Muldoon and Alexander could feel the salty mist from the sea on their faces.

"It's snowing in the east. There was quite a heavy fall yesterday in Briarstown," said Alexander as they struggled somewhat in the wind.

"Those clouds are dark enough for snow," replied Muldoon, turning up the collar of his coat, then placing his hands in his pockets.

"Between the storm when we were in Loughfarraig and the snow now, it's been a bit trying."

"Is Monique able to manage OK in this weather?" asked Muldoon.

"It's no bother to her at all, although I don't like being away when there is a possibility, no matter how unlikely, that Emma may be the next target," muttered Alexander. "The Brownes and Robert King are keeping an eye on them. Monique had an interesting conversation with Robert yesterday afternoon about the possibility of there being two murderers – he was looking at it from a psychological point of view. The first killing being different from the other two. Robert certainly doesn't believe Donal Hawke's killing was a hit."

"But the other two must have stemmed from Donal Hawke's killing," insisted Muldoon.

"Absolutely," agreed Alexander.

When the two men arrived back to The Skeffington Arms Hotel, there were very few people about. They sat in the usual corner and ordered coffee. Muldoon took the plastic evidence bag from his breast pocket and perused again the key hanging from the marble map of Ireland keyring.

"I wonder how hard it will be to find the box," he sighed. "I don't know whether we should delegate this work or are we better off doing it ourselves."

"I don't believe that it is going to be as far away as Dublin or Limerick – more likely Galway or Mayo. I know a manager in Bank of Ireland in Naas – he'll find out where these types of security boxes are kept – that will save us a bit of time – then we'll start at the nearest to us and work outwards," suggested Alexander.

After dinner, Alexander made a phone call to his friend Noel Lacy who was manager of Bank of Ireland Naas, who informed him that not every bank had this facility. There were only nine in total in Ireland. There certainly were two in Galway and one in Castlebar. He also made it quite clear that they would need warrants for them all – under no circumstances would a manager allow anyone access to a safe deposit box without a warrant.

CHAPTER 31

WINNIE POURS TEA

David Hawke had gathered the clan in his country residence. Everyone was present apart from Natalia who was no longer considered a member of the family.

"Well, what's all this about?" asked Winnie, as she sat down in an armchair in front of a very impressive Georgian fireplace.

"I got a phone call from Jonathan Kelly. He and his father have had a visit from Inspector Muldoon and Commandant de Bruin following Frank Smith's murder. They are looking for information on his bank accounts and asking whether they were aware of any safe deposit boxes etc.," answered David. "Jonathan's father is very annoyed at him because he told me about Dad's plans to change his will. However he went along with him."

"Frank Smith knew everything about the business," interjected Jack. "He was involved in every underhanded thing that Dad did."

"None of us can be held responsible for their actions," added Joanne, "All this happened before we became involved, and anyway as we've found out, we were only employees. Frank Smith was the fixer and hard man – he's dead."

"Jonathan got the impression that Muldoon and his sidekick were looking for something specific, something that happened more recently – and that whatever Smith was working on, lead to his murder. Of course the Kellys know where Smith kept all his secrets but didn't tell Muldoon. Jonathon believes that whatever he was working on related to one of us. Jonathon's father is extremely worried that the guards are going to find out that they've kept information about Smith from them."

"None of us has an alibi for Smith's death," added Jack. "And it's quite obvious that the guards believe that the three murders are related, and that we are the prime suspects."

"Whatever Frank Smith was working on must have been at the request of your father," muttered Winnie. "He only worked for him, and Muldoon and de Bruin must believe that he was keeping tabs on one of us, otherwise none of this makes any sense."

The five faces looked, with surprise, across at Winnie, who was sounding completely coherent. They had all noticed a significant change in her since Donal Hawke's death.

"So, does everyone think that he was surveilling one of us? Do the guards believe that whatever he found out was so damning that one of us killed him?" asked Ava in disbelief.

"That seems to be it," snarled Emily, taking a long drag from her cigarette, thus filling the room with smoke.

"I've asked you several times not to smoke in my presence. It makes me feel sick," whispered Ava in a menacing tone.

Emily threw the remainder of the cigarette into the fireplace.

"Well, which one of you has been up to no good?" asked Winnie, staring intently at her three children and two wives.

They all looked at each other aghast.

"Not me," answered Joanne vehemently.

"We all know that Donal didn't like your penchant for younger men," interjected Emily. "By the way where's Francois these days, speaking of younger men?"

"You really are a bitch, Emily – for your information Francois is in France. His aunt is ill. He won't be back for a couple of days. This isn't just a fling either. If I were you, Emily, I'd look closer to home and to your own behaviour and your husband's. Do you really think that Dad approved of either of you – always in debt, spending more money than you ever earned, David's gambling and trips away with his friend Jonathan Kelly and God knows what else. You two are the most likely targets of a surveillance."

"We have no idea either what Jack and Ava are up to in America," said David. "I know it wasn't me, so maybe it was the saintly Ava who is not so gentle and quiet, as we found out recently."

"Will you all stop bickering," shouted Winnie. "Frank Smith was following someone. The guards believe that it was one of the family. For whatever reason, they do not appear to be concentrating on your newly found half sister. They believe that there is information hidden away in some safe or box. When this information comes to light, someone is going to be in very great trouble. The guards are obviously convinced that it is someone in this room. Is there any way, David, that Jonathan Kelly can retrieve this box?"

"No, there isn't, Mother. I've already asked him. He doesn't knows it's exact location. He thinks it's in one of the banks but there's no way for him to get into the bank. He also believes that Muldoon must have the key,"

"None of us did this, Mother," said Jack. "We may have our differences, but on this we agree. Do you really think that any of us could stab someone. The reality is that the same person probably committed all three murders. We are not monsters, Mother."

"I am glad to hear it," said Winnie pensively. "If none of us did this, then who? Someone murdered Donal – left his body in the lake. Then the same person went on to kill the waiter and Frank Smith."

They all sat quietly for a few minutes, then Emily pulled the cord to summon the maid, to ask for some refreshments from the kitchen.

"Agreeing that none of us are murderers here, we must also worry about what else Frank Smith kept in this deposit box of his," interjected Ava. "When all this comes out, the Hawke reputation will be destroyed. Everyone will know how Donal Hawke went about his business. Emma Jones will be in possession of copious amounts of information against us."

"She has no intention of selling her shares to us either. We don't even have any way of contacting her, except through her lawyers. Nobody even knows where she is at the moment," said Jack.

"If I may make a suggestion," said Winnie. "You must all disavow any knowledge of your father's business practices – feign innocence and shock at any revelations that are forthcoming. Sincerely promise that significant changes will be made – agree to cooperate with any investigation that may be instigated. Bring Miss Emma Jones into the fold. She may be easily manipulated – she may not. From now on, you'd better all stick together, stop all the squabbling amongst yourselves. Your whole futures are at stake. Remember that this whole sorry affair may be flavour of the month in the media when it all comes out, but we all know that if we all sit tight, make the right noises, everyone will get fed up with it and something more interesting, more scandalous will come along. Just play the game. Get a good P.R. person on the job – seemingly that's all the rage in America. They can spin everything round and round until everyone is dizzy,"

The maid entered the room with a tray of sandwiches, cakes, tea and coffee.

"Shall I be mother?" said Winnie, as she poured the tea into the china cups.

Meanwhile in Briarstown, Emma Jones had regained her composure, having rested for some time. She resumed her study of all the documents. After a few hours she came across the article that Joe Winters had written on Mustelus, following which she examined the aftermath – the circling of the wagons, the character assassination, the virtual destruction of a very good investigative journalist's career. She now had all the proof that was required to vindicate Winters.

According to Monique, those at Garda Headquarters were loath to open up an investigation, probably pressured by those in high places. She was determined to rectify the situation. She would hand over names, dates, planning irregularities, payouts. There would certainly be a shake up in Government and councils.

"Glad to see you are feeling better," said Monique as she entered the office, "I think you were doing too much. Such a lot has happened to you in the last few months. You hadn't even recovered from your mother's death when Donal Hawke was murdered."

"You're right Monique, I'm not superwoman. By the way, I've just read the article that Joe Winters wrote about "Mustelus", and what happened to him afterwards."

"That was dreadful, his reputation was called into question. Alexander was always convinced that they tapped his phone."

"Who are they?"

"Probably that politician Jimmy Ward whom Winters mentioned by his initials. Everyone knew who he was talking about – he's been in the Dail for donkey's years – a right slithery character."

"I can see several payments to him, in the files that Donal Hawke left me. There's a slush fund that seems to have been managed by the late Frank Smith. He organised all the hush payments, the bribery payments. There are even hints that he used scare tactics to silence people who stood up to Donal Hawke. The information that I have would corroborate almost everything that he accused my father of in his article. Winters could be vindicated."

"You would need to contact him to see if he wants to get involved in all this again. Perhaps he would like some revenge for the way he was treated by quite a number of people in high places," continued Monique. "I also don't believe that cooperating with him would put you in any more danger – once it's out there in the ether – the people accused of wrong doing, including professional misconduct, will be helpless. They won't be able to insinuate that Winters is a liar anymore, because it will be backed up by your proof. He wouldn't be shut down again. Alex has his contact details. I'll get them for you and you can give him a ring. If he says no, well you'll have done your best. There is a large group of other victims that you can help."

CHAPTER 32

MIGUEL

Juan's father Miguel flew into Shannon airport to collect his son's body. Gerald Moore had paid for his ticket from Colombia. He had also organised for the repatriation of the body. Muldoon and Alexander were standing on the tarmac, together with Gerald Moore and a Spanish speaking waiter from Loughfarraig House. The steps were placed at the exit door of the plane. The passengers began to alight. Muldoon was present as an official representative, but also wanted to talk to Miguel – to find out if he had any information which might throw some light on Juan's murder.

The passengers filed down the steps. Finally a small, thin, dark haired man appeared at the door, carrying a small, tattered looking case. He was wearing a suit and tie, but obviously wasn't used to wearing formal clothing. He looked shattered and exhausted. His face was wrinkled and gaunt. His eyes were sunken in their sockets, the skin beneath was swollen and red. They were looking at a broken man, who was wracked with grief.

As Miguel stepped onto the ground, Muldoon approached him. The Spanish speaking waiter was at his side. Miguel stood for a moment, his gaze darting all around – like a deer in the headlights.

The Spanish speaking waiter translated what Muldoon said.

"I'm Inspector Muldoon, I wish to offer my sincere condolences and that of the Irish Government. I am the officer in charge of your son's case."

Alexander and Gerald Moore were introduced to the stricken man. It was explained to him that they were going to travel to Loughfarraig

House where he would spend two days before returning to Colombia with his son's body. Miguel thanked everybody profusely for their help. He said that he wanted to see the place where his son lived and died. He was keen to speak to Juan's friends. Miguel wanted to know everything about his son's life in the West of Ireland, before his untimely death.

Gerald Moore, Miguel and the young waiter travelled to Loughfarraig in Moore's car, and Alexander and Muldoon in another vehicle. The journey lasted nearly three long hours. They eventually took the turn into the long avenue which normally produced feelings of great joy. But today, everything looked forlorn. The naked branches reached up beseechingly to the heavens. The birds weren't singing. As they reached the lake, the water was moving and shimmering, but there was no sign of the ducks and swans, as if they were in mourning and hiding away from the gaze of the world. It was drizzling, the clouds were dark and the wind was howling sorrowfully.

Mrs. Moore was standing at the door to greet them. She shook Miguel's hand, but then gave him a hug before leading him into the warmth of the Long Room. He sat down in front of the turf fire as directed.

Miguel now looked amazed at the beauty of Loughfarraig House. He gratefully drank the coffee and ate the array of sandwiches and scones that were placed in front of him. The young Spanish speaking waiter was beginning to look exhausted, so Gerald Moore dismissed him, not before thanking him for his efforts and asking him to locate someone else who spoke Spanish.

Mrs. Moore showed Miguel to his guest room. Once more he was stunned at the opulence of it all. She arranged to show him Juan's quarters after he had taken a rest. He had been travelling for hours, as there was no direct flight from Colombia to Ireland, and needed some sleep.

Alexander and Muldoon sat in the foyer in their usual chairs beside the warm turf fire. Muldoon had decided that they should both spend two days with Miguel and then escort him back to Shannon, onto the plane for his sad journey back to Colombia with his son's body. It had taken quite a lot of organising to repatriate the body. A number of favours were called in. Gerald Moore had been very generous. Juan came from a very poor family, who lived in a small village, so it was known that they would never have been able to afford a return flight to Ireland for Miguel and the expense of bringing Juan's body home. Juan's family were practicing Catholics so it was very important for them to be able to perform the funeral rites.

Later that afternoon, Miguel informed Muldoon that he and Juan's mother had received a letter from Juan once a month. He wrote to his girlfriend, Maria, quite often. Sometimes she would receive several letters together because of the way the post was delivered in Colombia. The last letter that the parents had received was dated the 10th November. Maria's last letter was dated the 12th December – the Christmas cards had been posted in November, so that they would arrive in time. Miguel informed Muldoon and Alexander that Juan sounded very happy and was saving like mad so that Maria could join him in Ireland.

The two men soon realised that Miguel was of no help to them at all in solving the murders. None of them had received a letter from Juan since Donal Hawke's death. He never telephoned them as it was much too expensive to make such a long distance phone call.

Miguel became very emotional when he visited Juan's bedroom. All his belongings had been carefully placed in a cardboard box, including the photo of Maria that he kept on his bedside table, and other photos of his parents and siblings. He had very few possessions – just his work uniforms and other clothing. Maria's letters were in a large envelope. Miguel didn't know whether to keep them or burn them. He would later decide to return them to Maria, who could make the decision, after all they were private correspondence between the two young sweethearts.

Miguel spent time chatting with Juan's work colleagues. He wanted to know everything that the young man had done since beginning his work in Loughfarraig. He appeared to get some solace from listening to the young people relating stories about his son. By evening time Miguel looked less agitated. He was content that Juan had been happy in the West of Ireland, had some good friends and a kind, thoughtful employer. He chose to have dinner in the staff quarters saying that he would feel a little awkward having dinner with Muldoon and Alexander, who couldn't speak his language. It was fairly obvious that the poor man had never dined in a place like Loughfarraig House before, and would be completely out of his depth. He looked much more at ease in the company of Juan's friends.

Gerald Moore had organised a small prayer service in Juan's memory the following morning at eleven o'clock. The parish priest had been invited to lead the ceremony in the billiard room where a photo of Juan, smiling as he always did, sat on a linen bedecked table, with candles flickering and two beautiful arrangements of flowers. The young priest was very kind to Miguel. He said some of the prayers in Latin. Gerald Moore read a poem . Finally, there were hymns led by Mrs. Moore, who had a beautiful singing voice. A very emotional Miguel, thanked everyone, tears running down his cheeks. Mrs. Moore put her arm around his shoulders, once more, to comfort him.

After some refreshments the group donned their coats, gloves and hats and made their way to the beach. The wind was howling. There was drizzle as they made their way to the back of the house and towards the sandy seashore. The tide was ebbing and flowing. Seagulls were screeching in the distance. Just as they reached the spot where Juan's body had lain, the drizzle stopped, the clouds parted and the sun peeped through. Alexander watched Miguel's reaction as he looked down at the sand, then took in the awesome wonder of the place. He knew what he was thinking – how could such a dreadful thing have befallen his wonderful young son in a landscape so breathtakingly beautiful. Mrs. Moore handed each person present a red rose. In turn they threw them into the sea, and watched them bobbing on the water, the waves taking them in and out at first and then the tide took them towards the open expanse of the sea. One large wave appeared and crashed on the delicate petals as the sun went in behind the clouds once more.

The young priest said a decade of the rosary – one of the sorrowful mysteries. Miguel had taken a rosary beads out of his pocket, kissed the cross and ran the beads through his fingers as the priest went through the ritual – "Our Father... Ten Hail Marys and the Glory Be To The Father," – everyone joined in – some in English, some in Spanish. The company then walked slowly back to the hotel, where the chef had prepared a fish chowder with home made brown bread, followed by apple tart and cream.

Later that afternoon, Miguel could be seen down at the seashore, staring out at the expanse of the wild Atlantic, lost in his thoughts.

While John Muldoon was making last minute arrangements for the transportation of Juan's remains to Shannon Airport the following morning, Alexander decided to take a walk over to the lake. He went down to the small jetty, where Emma Jones had met her father Donal Hawke – where he had slipped on the greasy wood and fallen into the lake. He looked out at the water now which was moving and shimmering. The ducks and swans were swimming in his direction, hoping that he had some stale bread with which to feed them. He opened the bag filled with leftovers from lunch, threw the pieces of bread and scones into the lake. The ducks quacked and squabbled. When the bag was empty, he made his way along the edge of the lake to where Donal Hawke had emerged after his mishap, only to be clocked over the head with an oar. He turned and looked back at the old house and up towards the window of Juan's bedroom, from where there was a perfect view of the jetty and the side of the lake where Donal Hawke was murdered. If the moon had made an appearance – which it must have – Juan could have seen everything. "What bad luck," thought Alexander, "to have been standing at your window at that precise moment."

There was also a very clear view of the lake from the patio area where the staff smoked during their breaks. Juan could have seen the accident and the murder from either vantage point. The poor fellow thought that it was his lucky night, that he had found a way of paying for his sweetheart Maria to join him. Alexander then strolled to the back of the house towards the beach, climbed down over the stones and onto the sand. He looked out onto the wild Atlantic, the waves crashing against the rocks jutting up out of the water. As he neared where Juan's body was found, he saw Miguel, again, standing very still, staring out to sea – a sad forlorn figure. It began to drizzle, then to rain heavily. Miguel still stood there, not moving a muscle. His hair became drenched, the water dribbled down his face. Alexander had his umbrella to protect him against the elements. He walked over towards the solitary figure. He placed the umbrella over their heads. Both men stood staring out to sea.

That was one of the most difficult trips I've ever had to make," said Muldoon as he and Alexander arrived back to the Skeffington Arms Hotel.

They were both exhausted. They had driven Miguel to Shannon airport. Juan's coffin was loaded onto the plane. Before the coffin was placed in the cargo hold, a priest said a few prayers and blessed it with Holy Water. Muldoon and Alexander stood solemnly beside Miguel. The tears welled up in his eyes, but he tried to compose himself. Finally the two men watched as Juan's father climbed up the steps to the door of the plane, where he was greeted by an airhostess. He turned briefly and waved goodbye to the two men standing on the tarmac, who, he hoped, would solve his son's murder.

Alexander and John Muldoon sat in the lounge and ordered two brandies. They were both silent for a few minutes, needing a bit of rest after their trying day.

"That poor man has a long trip home. Then he has to face his wife and children," said Muldoon.

"Don't forget poor Maria – her hopes and dreams shattered," added Alexander.

"They must lead such a different life to us, in their little village. I really admire Miguel – he's so stoic and brave. To have made this journey was so courageous. I'm sure that he has never been out of Colombia."

"You're right," said Alexander, "The consul had to arrange an emergency passport and visa for him."

"Gerald Moore is also to be admired. He went to great expense and lengths to arrange the return flights and the repatriation of the remains. Not everyone would have been so generous," continued Muldoon.

The two men became silent again, lost in their thoughts – both feeling great sorrow for Miguel who was now flying across the Atlantic, his beloved son in the cargo hold.

CHAPTER 33

SUSTENANCE

When Alexander awoke the following morning, he felt great anger towards whoever had murdered Juan, and caused such grief to his family and sweetheart. He was an innocent who had become embroiled in a very dirty business by sheer accident.

Talk about being in the wrong place at the wrong time. Despite the fact that Juan became involved in blackmail, both he and Muldoon felt great sympathy for him. It was much more difficult to experience compassion for someone like Donal Hawke, who himself had caused such hardship to others, or Frank Smith, who, like Hawke had little empathy for people – both men implicated in suspicious deaths, use of violent tactics to get what they wanted, intimidation of people in less advantageous positions than themselves – no, it was virtually impossible to feel sorrow for what had befallen them. He shook himself out of his sullen humour and decided to ring Monique – he wanted to expunge such dark thoughts from his head. He dialled the number of The Lodge. After five rings, the receiver was picked up.

"Hello, Monique de Bruin speaking."

"Hello darling, it's me."

"Alexander, how wonderful to hear your voice, you didn't ring last night."

"I'm sorry my love. John and I were absolutely exhausted. I actually fell asleep on the bed. When I woke up it was too late to ring you."

"It's OK – don't worry about it. How did it go with Juan's father and the trip back to Shannon Airport?"

"It was quite dreadful really. The whole experience of seeing the coffin being loaded onto the plane was reminiscent of that dreadful tragedy when I was overseas."

"I thought it might be awful for you Alex."

"Not as awful as for poor Miguel – what a dreadful cross to bear. Anyway, Monique, it's done. John and I must get on with solving this case. We must try to locate Frank Smith's box of tricks. Enough about that. How is everything at home?"

"Snow is still on the ground, but we are managing. All the animals are fine. The dogs absolutely love being out in the snow. Emma is back to herself after her wobble – I think it was just exhaustion and the realisation of what is ahead of her. She read the article that Joe Winters wrote a few years back and seems to be keen enough to contact him with all the proof that she has."

"If he writes another article, it will certainly put the cat among the pigeons. Those planners and politicians will finally get their comeuppance, and rightly so," said Alexander cheerfully.

"Have you any idea of when you'll be home Alex? We are perfectly fine here, but I just miss you."

"I miss you very much too. Perhaps in a day or two – depending on how we get on locating this mystery deposit box."

Following his conversation with Monique, Alexander was in much better humour. He was now ready to face the day. Muldoon and he met in the dining room for breakfast at ten o'clock.

"How did you sleep?" asked Alexander as they perused the breakfast menu.

"I was out like a light," answered Muldoon.

"I don't want to go through a day like that again. It's really emotionally draining – much worse than being physically tired."

A young dark haired waitress, who didn't look much older than fifteen arrived with a pot of coffee, brown bread and toast. Alexander poured the strong coffee for both of them.

"Well, what's the plan for today?" he asked.

"Need to put those warrants for the banks in motion," replied Muldoon, as he buttered his toast. "That could take a few days, depending on the judge."

They were both very hungry that morning, and so ordered a full Irish breakfast which they normally didn't eat. But, for some reason, that they didn't quite understand, it all tasted delicious.

Having completed the paperwork for the warrants, Muldoon suggested that they both return to Kildare for a few days. There didn't seem to be anything else for them to do in Galway until they received permission to search the bank vaults. They packed their bags, paid their bill at reception and gladly headed east.

Three and a half hours later, Alexander walked in the back door of The Lodge, to Monique's delight. They hugged each other and made their way into the office to where Emma was seated at a desk.

"Welcome back, Commandant de Bruin," said Emma, with a smile on her face, "You must be glad to be home."

"I certainly am," replied Alexander. "I hear that you've been very busy."

"That's for sure," retorted Emma. "I don't know what I'd have done without you all. I can't believe my good fortune. Any luck with solving the murders?"

"We are making some progress," said Alexander. "Inspector Muldoon and I are sure that they are all linked, so when we solve one, we'll have solved them all," he concluded.

"I'm sorry that I didn't meet Juan's father," added Emma.

"It wasn't really feasible to bring you all the way back to Loughfarraig. He met Juan's other friends. We had a little ceremony down by the beach. He's a lovely man, but obviously grief stricken. We all did what we could to make it as easy as possible for him."

"I think I'll just walk the land, if you two ladies will excuse me. I'll take the dogs with me."

He needed to clear his head. He pulled on his wellingtons, donned his waxed jacket, grabbed the dogs' leads and stepped out into the courtyard. The two dogs were very happy to see their master. They jumped all over him as he petted their long fluffy ears. The Bernese mountain dogs barked excitedly. The snow crunched underfoot. Alexander's warm breath turned to fog as he strode towards the paddock. The three ponies trotted over towards him. He rubbed their manes and noses. He checked that there was hay in the container. Alexander inspected the fencing. Icicles had formed between the slats like tiny stalactites. All the fields were covered in a blanket of white snow. He walked around the boundary, every so often ice cracked underfoot where there had been a puddle of water that had turned to ice. The bird feeders in the copse were half full. Tiny finches and a robin were eating the fatballs. A red fox scurried across one of the paddocks in search of food. He contemplated how hard this type of weather was on wildlife. Then his mind wandered again, and he thought about Juan's coffin being loaded onto the plane and what it reminded him of – the dreadful tragedy that had occurred while serving abroad on a mission in the Lebanon – the shot that rang out in the guard room – the dreadful accident – the efforts to save his friend – the realisation that no more could be done. The group of officers and men had stood around in disbelief. The body was covered in a blanket, but still blood seeped through. The medic and Chaplain were called. Their dear friend was pronounced dead, but they all knew that already. Alexander was the officer picked to accompany the coffin home, draped in the tricolour.

Once more there was a crackle underfoot which snapped him out of his reverie. He looked across the field and saw Damien Browne waving at him. He strode in his direction to greet him.

"I see you're back, Alexander. It's great to see you. I'm sure Monique is delighted that you're back home. Any news of the case?"

"Not much more really," replied Alexander, as he walked beside his friend. They made their way towards The Old Rectory. They climbed up the stone steps, through the old oak door, and into the hallway. They both removed their coats and gloves. They left the two dogs at the front of the house to play in the snow.

"We've more or less come to the conclusion that it must be one of the family, particularly after the death of Frank Smith. He was meant to meet with John Muldoon and myself at the Great Southern, but never showed. He said that he had information on someone whom he had been following on the instructions of Donal Hawke."

"It really must be one of the family so," concluded Damien.

"I hear that Lydia has been working hard on Emma Jones' behalf. Monique said that she and her colleagues have everything more or less tied up."

"It sure looks that way," retorted Damien. "She is very impressed by the young woman, bright as a button, it seems. Have you ruled her out completely?"

"Unless she has been working in cahoots with another party," responded Alexander. "She was in Briarstown during the second and third murders. Muldoon and I will have to think carefully about the possibility of two murderers. According to Robert King the psychology of the killings is different."

An hour later, Alexander was strolling across the snow, his feet sinking into the small drifts. He looked back and waved at his friend, and reflected on friendship – what it meant to him. Aristotle believed that friendship was "The art of holding up a mirror to each other's souls." Alexander believed that it was solidarity and sustenance. He then visualised the rows of men in army uniform shoulder to shoulder, surrounding the widow and children around the graveside like a comfort blanket, as the coffin was lowered into the dark earth as the last post was played. "Anyone without an Anam Cara is like a body without a head."

Monique was waiting for her husband to return. She knew what was going through his mind. She knew what memories would have been evoked by the repatriation of Juan's body to Colombia. It had all happened a long time ago now, but none of them had ever forgotten the sorrow. His wife would have known that something dreadful had happened when she opened the door to an Officer and Chaplain in full uniform. There would have been no hope.

Monique heard the back door opening. She heard Alexander's footsteps in the hall. She opened the door and they hugged for a long while, each knowing what the other was thinking – no need to say anything.

"I have no duty to be anyone's Friend and no man in the world has a duty to be mine. No claims, no shadow of necessity. Friendship is unnecessary, like philosophy, like art, like the universe itself...it has no survival value; rather it is one of those things which give value to survival." C.S. Lewis.

CHAPTER 34

WHERE CAN IT BE?

Alexander bounded up the stairs to Inspector Muldoon's office in Naas Garda Station. They were meeting to discuss the suspects in the murders. He knocked on the office door.

"Come in," said Muldoon.

Alexander opened the door and entered the room. There was John Muldoon, sitting at his desk. Behind him was his chalkboard, where he had written all the names of the suspects in different colours. In one column, in white chalk were the individual names of all the suspects – in another column, the couples who could be in cahoots. There were arrows leading from one to the other in different colours which at this stage only made sense to Muldoon himself.

"Good morning, John," said Alexander. "I see you've been hard at work, not sure about the coloured arrows."

"It will all become clear," laughed Muldoon, "when we've discussed them all."

Alexander sat in a chair at the side of the table. Both men faced the chalkboard.

"As you can see, in the first column is a list of suspects for the Donal Hawke murder – David, Emily, Jack, Ava, Joanne, Natalia Hawke and Emma Jones. Just below them I have placed Winnie Hawke and Francois Dupont. Winnie is highly unlikely and Francois was the only person who couldn't have killed him, as he never left the Long Room in Loughfarraig. As you see, we are only going to deal with those who are family members or in the company of a family member, at the moment. In the second column there is the list of people who were present at the time of Juan's murder. I have again placed Winnie below as she is highly unlikely to have stabbed him, together with Natalia, who was in hospital at the time.

In the third column we have a list of possibilities for Frank Smith's murder. Once again you can see that I have, more or less, ruled Winnie herself out. No one else has a solid alibi, except perhaps Francois, who was supposedly in France. The arrows show people who could have been working together – so it's like a spider's web."

"So, let's talk motive for the first murder. Emma Jones, who may have just wanted revenge. Perhaps their meeting at the lake didn't go as well as planned. Yet, he had changed his will in her favour, and was pleased that she had come forward," said Alexander.

"The other siblings and their wives had a very strong motive for killing Donal Hawke. He was going to change his will. We are fairly certain that Jonathan Kelly told his good friend David Hawke about the impending changes, who in turn probably informed everyone else. The two wives, Winnie and Natalia didn't seem to have a motive as their portion of their inheritance wasn't going to change – unless they have a different motive – perhaps a wish that he would just be gone out of their lives. The only person with an outright alibi is Francois, who never left the room. The means – the oar – was just a weapon that was available. They all had opportunity, except Francois, as each one of them left the Long Room at some stage that night. Even Natalia had opportunity – she could have left her bedroom," stated Muldoon.

"The motive for Juan's murder is obvious. He saw Donal Hawke's killer and attempted to blackmail them. The means was the knife which was brought to the scene – so premeditated probably. Everyone had opportunity except for Natalia who was in hospital, and Emma who was in Briarstown. The motive for Frank Smith's murder was to silence him. He had been seen surveilling someone whom Donal Hawke suspected of something. The method again was the knife – definitely premeditated. Everyone of them, apart from Emma and Francois had opportunity. If the same person committed all three murders, we are left with David, Emily, Jack, Ava and Joanne – their motive is clear. However if there are two killers, it makes life a lot more complicated," concluded Alexander.

"I can't see how Emma could have an accomplice, nor do I think that Winnie killed her ex-husband. According to you, she was drunk most of the time at Loughfarraig. I believe that the other two killings stemmed from the first."

"Let's hope we find the box that the key from Smith's home opens, and that there's evidence there about whom he was following. Otherwise I fear that we may be a bit stumped. We have too many suspects and our only witness is dead."

"Do we think that Emma is in any danger?" asked Muldoon.

"If one of the Hawkes killed their father to stop any changes to the will – well it's too late now. Lydia Browne has organised for Emma to make her own will, so that bumping her off won't make any difference to the Hawkes. The Hawkes will have to be notified, otherwise they would still have a motive – it's a protection mechanism. Once that is in place, she's probably safe. Of course, if she killed him herself, she's perfectly safe," concluded Alexander.

The two men turned to the blackboard and studied intently the columns of names and arrows leading in all directions, linking together different people. "Oh what a web, we weave…"

The following afternoon, Muldoon received a phone call from the Superintendent at Galway Garda Station. They had obtained the search warrants for the deposit boxes in the banks. Officers had been deployed from early morning to visit each of the buildings, Smith's key in hand. Unfortunately the key did not fit any of the deposit boxes in the banks. Needless to say Inspector Muldoon was very disappointed at this news as they seemed to be now back at square one. This had been their great hope of solving the murders quickly. Before hanging up the receiver, the Superintendent had one piece of interesting news for Inspector Muldoon – one of the bank managers had imparted a suggestion on seeing the key. He had spent time working in America and had come across some private safes, the keys to which resembled the one on the marble map of Ireland keyring. So, he suggested that what they were looking for may not be in a bank depository, but rather in a private safe in someone's home. This titbit gave Muldoon pause for thought. There was no sign of a safe anywhere in Frank Smith's home, so he must have entrusted the safe to someone else. But who? He didn't appear to have any close friends apart from Donal Hawke. He didn't have any other properties in Ireland. The safe must be close enough to his home, so that he could have access fairly quickly to it. He must have copies of whatever information he has gathered together with the photos. Muldoon was now hoping against hope that he really had kept copies and that his killer didn't take the only evidence available. Muldoon was wracking his brain – where on earth could the safe be? Who on earth was keeping it for Frank Smith?

Alexander wasn't best pleased when Muldoon rang him with the news.

"Where on earth could it be?" he wondered.

"I suppose it could be in a friend's house, but what friend?" replied Muldoon. "Is it something that you could leave in a solicitor's office?– maybe the Kelly's. I wouldn't put it past Jonathan Junior to be in possession of it, I really thought that they were lying to us the last time that we were questioning them."

"Would you be able to get a warrant to search their offices?" asked Alexander.

"I don't really know. Our suspicions are very tenuous. What can we say? That we believe that they are dishonest – that young Jonathan breached client confidentiality by passing on information to David Hawke – we have no proof and hell will freeze over before either of them will admit it. I'll put out some feelers, but I wouldn't hold my breath."

"This is a real setback," sighed Alexander. "We could get the young guards to hand out questionnaires to each house, asking if anyone had information on the movements of Frank Kelly in the weeks leading up to his murder – just as part of the inquiry. He might have been seen entering some premises or other."

"Good idea," retorted Alexander. "Maybe some appeal on the News on T.V. and radio, and in the papers – cover all angles."

"Will do," responded Muldoon.

"Nil desperandum," added Alexander. "Something will come up – it usually does."

"Forever the optimist," laughed Muldoon, "but fortunately you have been proven right in the past."

The following evening, after The News on RTE at 6pm, Inspector Muldoon asked the public for their help. He sounded very efficient and came across very well. A photo of Frank Smith was shown to the nation. Muldoon stated that the Gardai wished to trace the movements of the murdered man during the weeks prior to his death. There were various telephone numbers shown on screen. This appeal was repeated after the late news as well.

Muldoon was quite pleased with how it had gone. There were ten guards manning the phones. Following the broadcast, hundreds of sightings were reported – unfortunately Smith had been seen in Belfast, Cork, Wexford, on trains, planes and ferries – sometimes at the same time. It would take quite some time to decipher what was relevant from what were crank calls. However, the guards were used to this. It happened every time there was an appeal of this sort. Nevertheless, some gem of information was usually found. It might take some time and some tedious work but finally, there would be a tiny morsel glistening like a diamond.

CHAPTER 35

NEW BEGINNINGS

Emma Jones was very well prepared for the meeting with the Hawke siblings and their lawyers. Lydia Browne had informed her that everything was in order. The Hawkes had decided against contesting the will. They had accepted that Donal Hawke had made sure that everything would move ahead as he had planned. This meeting was to determine how they would all work together.

Following pleasantries, everyone sat around the oval shaped table in the boardroom. Winnie Hawke was also present, although she did not hold any shares in the company. Emma had been asked if she objected to her presence. Her reply was in the negative. Lydia had suggested that she may be there to try to keep some control over the children.

Jack, as chairman opened the meeting by welcoming Emma to the company and family. He apologised for any perceived negativity towards her in the past, explaining that all these changes put in motion by his father's death had come as a great shock to them all. Emma accepted this with magnanimity. It was suggested that Emma should acquire a personal assistant, a secretary and other staff members that may be of help to her in her new position. Emma thanked Jack for his kind words, said that she would organise her own staff – (the last thing she wanted was to have a spy for the Hawkes working in close proximity to her).

David and Emily did not look at all happy but held their council for the first hour of the meeting. Joanne sat quietly as did Ava. Winnie added some words of welcome. There was no intervention by the lawyers on either side.

Jack ended his speech by asking Emma if she had any questions or requests.

Emma opened her briefcase which held the notes that she had prepared.

"I have quite a number of changes that I would like to make. As you know I received the same box of documents that you all did from our father's solicitor. There are a large number of people and businesses which have been harmed by Mustelus. I would like to try to rectify the situation as far as possible. I think we should start by improving the living conditions of our tenants. Before we even do that, I would hope that we could settle any outstanding cases against the company and compensate these people. We need to wipe the slate clean. We must become an ethical company."

"That's ridiculous!" interjected David in an agitated tone of voice. "It will cost the company a fortune."

"There are millions in the bank," retorted Emma, "I have all the figures here. We can easily afford to do this work. The company is still making millions in profit each year. We can set aside a percentage of the profits as a compensation fund."

"What on earth do you know about running a business?" asked Emily.

"I know what's right and what's wrong," answered Emma. "I can read reports and bank statements. I understand profit and loss. Whether you like it or not, I'm going to insist that Mustelus will be run ethically from now on. It's a highly profitable company. We don't need to cut corners. We don't need to silence our detractors. There will be no more need for "fixers" or bribery. We need to keep the properties in good order. I don't want any more avoidable accidents, or children becoming ill because of damp or mould."

"If I may make an observation," interjected Lydia.

"Go ahead," said Jack.

"My associates and I have trawled through all the documents. Because you were employees of the company and not share holders – because your father kept you all far away from his misdemeanours and malpractices – none of you can be held responsible for what happened in the past. Whether you were aware of it or not is not obvious, and a question for yourselves and your consciences. So, here you have the opportunity to start anew – a clean slate. There may be findings against the company in the near future. No doubt some of the bribery scandals will come to the fore. There will probably be very bad press for a time. But when the air clears, the company will be under new management. You all have the opportunity to right the wrongs and be seen to do so. As you have all probably noticed, Emma Jones is a very clever, capable young woman who could be a great asset to the company. If you all work together, you could all do great things. There are a lot of people depending on you all. The company can be extremely profitable without making enemies."

The gathering sat quietly for a few minutes. Winnie was the first to speak.

"I think that it all makes perfect sense," she said. "Your father must have had an epiphany. He was terminally ill. A daughter whom he had never met or even knew of, came into his life. He must have felt some guilt about his misconduct down through the years. He must have looked at all your behaviours, your entitlement, your overindulgence, gambling and wondered what to do about it. Well, he made these changes. These are his wishes and I think we should try doing things differently, treating people with more respect. We really don't have a choice if we want the company to succeed."

"Okay, Mother," agreed Jack." We'll settle the outstanding cases, and begin improving the living conditions of our tenants."

Joanne agreed and David nodded reluctantly.

"What happens when the press comes after us?" muttered David.

"We'll explain that there will be major changes, that compensation will be paid. As Mrs. Browne has suggested, we will tell the world that the company is under new management," concluded Winnie.

"Perhaps we should change the name. "Mustelus" is dreadful," said Emma. "We are no longer going to be sharks."

"We'll give it some thought," said Ava, speaking for the first time.

"There's a question of where I'm going to live. There are a number of properties available, belonging to the company. Can you suggest which one would suit me?" asked Emma.

"There's a beautiful Georgian House in Bray which is vacant, that would suit very well. You'll need staff of course, a car and a driver," answered Winnie.

"I'll organise all that," added Jack.

"If you don't mind, I'll employ my own staff," said Emma.

"As you wish," replied Jack.

A week later, Emma Jones had moved into her new home in Bray. The house is quite beautiful, bright and spacious. It's an end of terrace Victorian property which was built in around 1880. She adored the ceiling roses and cornices, the marble fireplaces and window shutters. Walking along the Victorian promenade and plaza along the sea front brought her great joy and solace. She still found it hard to believe that her life had changed so much.

The de Bruins, Brownes, Kings, Muldoon and Emma Jones herself were not fooled by the sudden transformation of the Hawke family from being what they always were – selfish, dishonest, entitled, a downright nasty crowd to being altruistic, empathetic and reformed. They were still murder suspects, and would love to have never met Emma Jones. They had been backed into a corner, so had to agree to amend their ways. Time would tell how they would react to their new situation. Rats and corners and leopards and spots come to mind.

Corporal Tim Mc Grath knocked on the door of "Ventum Maris" the new home of Emma Jones in Bray. When Emma had first seen the name engraved in the stone wall of the old house, she had asked Monique what it meant. "Seabreeze" was the answer. She thought that it was a fitting name for a beautiful old house near the sea.

Corporal McGrath was a tall young man in his early twenties, with blond cropped hair, blue eyes and a cheeky grin. He had only just returned from a six month deployment abroad and was on leave. Alexander had thought of him immediately when the question of some sort of protection for Emma emerged together with her need for a driver. This young man could fill both roles for a few weeks at least, or until the murder was solved.

Tim McGrath was the son of Sergeant Major John McGrath, who was well known to Alexander de Bruin. As a newly commissioned Second Lieutenant, McGrath was Alexander's first Platoon Sergeant, in the 3rd Infantry Battalion in Connolly Barracks in the Curragh Camp. His son Tim was as fine a man as his father, who Alexander insisted was the best sergeant that he had ever known.

The door was opened by the newly appointed housekeeper. She showed McGrath into the parlour and asked him to wait. Five minutes later Emma entered the room. Tim rose from his chair, and greeted her cheerfully.

"I'm Tim McGrath. I'm under strict orders to look after you for a few weeks," he smiled.

Emma blushed and replied "I'm Emma Jones," as she moved towards him, her hand outstretched.

They shook hands, after which followed an awkward silence.

"I believe I'm to stay here in the house," Tim finally said.

"Yes, I'll show you to your room. Mary has prepared it. I hope you'll be comfortable."

"Don't worry, I'm sure it will be like the Ritz, compared to army accommodation abroad," he laughed.

Emma led the way upstairs to a very large bedroom on the first floor. There was a dressing room and bathroom adjacent to it.

"This will do me very nicely," he grinned. "I just have a case in the car – by the way, that's a beautiful vehicle that I'll be driving you around in."

"It certainly is," replied Emma. "I'm not used to this at all, you know. It's all new to me."

"I know. Commandant de Bruin explained everything to me. I'm sure you'll work it all out. I'll help any way I can. I have six weeks leave after my tour of duty. Did you want me to drive you anywhere today?"

"I'll think about it. Just get unpacked and I'll get Mary to prepare us something to eat. See you downstairs in half an hour."

"Yes Maam," said Tim McGrath with a broad grin.

Half an hour later, the two young people were sitting at a coffee table in the parlour, eating sandwiches and cake, and drinking freshly brewed coffee. Emma related her life story to the young corporal. He regaled her with stories from his army life – some serious – some funny. Before they realised the time, they had spent two hours chatting and laughing. Emma was very happy to spend time in the company of someone closer to her own age. She was delighted to be able to relax a bit, not to think about all the work ahead of her, all the responsibilities she now had. She was looking forward to being driven around by this very handsome, very charming, very kind young man.

CHAPTER 36

THE SECOND ARTICLE

J oe Winters arrived at precisely 10am as arranged, to meet with
Emma Jones in her home in Bray. He had brought with him his array of documents pertaining to Mustelus and Donal Hawke's dealings
with planners and politicians in Ireland. He was greeted warmly by the
young woman. Emma had thought a great deal about Joe Winters and
how his whole career had been all but destroyed by her father. She had
wanted to make amends and was delighted that he had taken her up
on her invitation. She had offered him some refreshments but he had
refused – obviously very keen to get down to work.

"I read your article," said Emma. "You really hit the nail on the head."

"That article nearly destroyed me. They all came after me – called me
a liar. That politician Ward was particularly vicious and of course Donal
Hawke was so powerful and wealthy, with friends in high places. I suppose the country wasn't ready for that kind of scandal, either. I knew
what I wrote was true, but I suppose I needed more corroboration."

"Well I have it all here. My father left me a box full of evidence. I have
payments, dates – it's absolutely obvious who these people are. You'll be
able to write the article again – this time with all the proof that anyone
will ever need. You'll be vindicated."

"What do the rest of your family think of this?" asked Winters. "I don't
think that they are going to be too pleased."

"There's nothing that they can do about it. They know that it will probably happen. They were handed the same information that I was. I intend to make sure that there are changes in the company. There will be
reparations to those who have suffered."

Joe Winters spent several hours perusing all the details in Emma's files. He was able to link up the payments made to people, to the allegations that he had made all those years ago. He breathed a sigh of relief. Finally, all those gangsters who had become rich through the receipt of bribes, all those who had tried to destroy his life, would finally get their comeuppance – their fair and deserved punishment for their corruption down through the years. The editors and programme makers who had wanted very little to do with him over the last number of years, would now be tripping over each other to get hold of his story. He was particularly looking forward to seeing Ward's smug smile being wiped from his face.

"Et puis La vengeance se mange tres-bien froide, comme on dit vulgairement."

Three days later Joe Winter's article appeared in the "Morning News." It caused quite a stir. There were questions in the Dail. Ward went into hiding. Journalists were camped outside his home in North Dublin. The Garda Commissioner sent for Muldoon, who arrived at his office, knowing that he was in for an earful.

"I gave you strict instructions that this was to be put to bed. I told you in no uncertain terms that we would not be investigating this matter," he shouted.

"I did not investigate it," insisted Muldoon.

"How did the press get hold of all this information?"

"I did not give this information to any journalist, nor did Commandant de Bruin," stated Muldoon.

"I have been getting phone calls all morning from all quarters," continued the Commissioner. "This is Joe Winters again."

"To be fair, Commissioner, it was Joe Winters who handed us information on this planning scandal which we handed on to you."

"Where did he get all this corroborating evidence?" asked the Commissioner.

"From Donal Hawke himself. Hawke left it all to be handed over to his daughter Emma Jones, who is quoted in the article. She is a woman with a conscience. The Gardai had every opportunity to investigate this and chose not to. Now it has come back to bite us. It's out in the public arena now, so it will have to be investigated thoroughly."

"Bloody hell, Muldoon – this is a fine mess."

"I agree, Sir, but perhaps it's fine time that the mess was cleaned up. We have all the names and dates."

"I know, Inspector, but I'm going to have to divert my scarce resources to deal with this. It's the timing. In my opinion the security of the state trumps fraud any day. The journalists and media in general are going to be like hyenas around this story. I suppose the sooner files are sent to the D.P.P. and arrests are made the better."

Muldoon was relieved to see the Commissioner calm down a little. He knew the amount of pressure he was under. The Commissioner realised that he had made a mistake by wishing this particular problem away – now it would have to be solved.

Over the next few days, there was a raft of resignations in various planning offices throughout Ireland. A few politicians also resigned their seats "for family reasons". There was a feeding frenzy in the media. Muldoon and Alexander knew that this would last until the next bomb went off, and innocent civilians were killed or maimed.

CHAPTER 37

AN UNFORESEEN DEVELOPMENT

The weather had improved. The snow was no longer on the ground. The temperature was a few degrees warmer. Alexander, Monique and the two Bernese mountain dogs strolled from the house to the paddock. The ponies and horses were grazing. There really wasn't enough grass to nourish them, so Alexander carried a bale of hay over to the feeder. Monique dispensed nuts and grain into their individual buckets – she was always amazed the way they chose their own buckets – rarely would you see two of them heading for the same feed bucket. The job complete, they then located the wheelbarrows and shovels to clean out the stables. They replaced the dirty bedding with clean straw and deposited the muck onto the compost heap. They decided to check the riding gear in the tack room. The children normally took care of their own saddles and bridles, but it was a long school term, and the leather needed polishing and buffing. Monique and Alexander sat on the benches and applied saddle soap. Monique found this whole ritual quite soothing.

"Did Muldoon get into much bother with the Commissioner over Winter's article?" she asked.

"The Commissioner had to vent his frustration on someone – he was really annoyed that he had to invest scarce resources on fraud instead of national security. He was very annoyed when Muldoon went into his office, but calmed down after a while – he knew fine well that we didn't give Winters any information – he had most of it already – it just had to be confirmed by someone, and it was quite obvious that all the evidence was handed over by Emma Jones."

"It was an excellent article. No one could now be under any illusion about the existence of skullduggery in the planning departments. I'm very glad that they are all caught now. It's an awful business when we can't trust our politicians and planners," said Monique.

"The Dail can certainly do without the likes of Ward in it's midst. The guards won't have that much work to do anyway. Donal Hawke left all the relevant information behind him. I hope that this will be a lesson to anyone thinking of getting involved in bribery," added Alexander.

"I don't know," sighed Monique. "I think that there will always be dishonest people around, willing to do quite a lot for money. The powers that be will just have to make it harder for them."

"Emma seems to be delighted with young Tim McGrath. That was a good idea of yours."

"Well as you know, Muldoon and I aren't sure whether Emma is in any danger or not. It doesn't make sense really that she is, now that she made her own will. The Hawkes have been made aware of it, so they would have nothing to gain by bumping her off. They have more to gain by cooperating with her. But, we didn't want to take any chances. She needed a driver to get her to meetings etc. The poor girl never had the opportunity to learn how to drive, so she hasn't a licence."

"Tim McGrath was a very good choice, lucky that he was available," interjected Monique.

"Yes, it certainly was," replied Alexander. "He was just back from his tour of duty in the Middle East. Seemingly he's a chip off the old block. His father Sergeant Major McGrath is a very fine man and a wonderful soldier. Tim has six weeks leave, so being a single young man, he was only delighted to oblige us. We decided that it would be a good idea for him to stay in the house with Emma – just in case. He's a very capable young man and by all reports an accomplished soldier. It is expected that he will be recommended for the Potential Officer's course next year, according to Robert King."

"That's wonderful news for him. I'm sure that he will take great care of Emma. She will feel more relaxed and confident with someone she can trust in the house with her. She will certainly feel safer. Emma is a wonderful young woman, and so determined. She is going to do her best to make things right for as many people as possible."

"The information she handed over to Winters was invaluable to the article. It was interesting to see how no blame can be attributed to the

Hawke children. Donal Hawke made sure of that. He kept them out of his shenanigans. Winters even made sure that it was obvious that from now on, things would be different in Mustelus, with Emma Jones' influence. I suppose it was only fair to give her the opportunity to rectify things. No one wins if everything implodes. Better to give her the time to bring the company around. Anyway, Winter's reputation which was virtually destroyed by Ward and his minions, has now been restored."

"Do you believe that the Hawke children knew nothing about all the bribery and corruption?" asked Monique.

"Of course not. I'm quite sure that they were well aware of most of it, particularly when they were older. They certainly turned a blind eye. I'm certain that they were in the know when it came to their father's "fixer" Frank Smith. It just suited them all to stay schtum and reap the many rewards. Winnie was married to the man for forty years – she's not a stupid woman. She may have turned to alcohol for solace in latter years, but you can't live with someone for that length of time without really getting to know his character."

"Emma is going to have to be very careful when dealing with them," interjected Monique. "They are not trustworthy. They would knife her in the back if they got the chance. Lydia said that she and her colleagues have them nicely tied up, but that she wouldn't put anything past them. She only hopes that putting in the safeguards of Emma making her will and informing the Hawkes about it will constrain them in what they might do to harm her."

"I hope that when you said "knife her in the back," you meant it figuratively," muttered Alexander.

"So do I" said Monique, with a sigh.

Alexander and Monique wiped away the excess soap from the saddles and bridles, and polished the leather with a soft cloth. They replaced the saddles onto their tack stand, and bridles onto their hooks, all ready for when the children came home from school the following weekend. Alexander closed the tack room door behind him. Monique linked Alexander's arm and the couple walked through the field together towards the house, while the dogs chased each other ahead of them.

Later that evening, the phone rang in The Lodge.

"Monique de Bruin speaking."

"It's Emma, Mrs. de Bruin, just rang to give you an update on everything."

"How lovely to hear from you, Emma. How are you coping with everything?"

"So far, so good," replied Emma. "My plans are beginning to fall into place. As you know I've already met up with Joe Winters. I think his career will take off again after this scoop. I thought his article was excellent. No one can doubt all he is claiming now. I've given him the proof, as promised."

"You're right. The article was excellent. A lot of corrupt people will be caught in the net. It might give others pause for thought before taking bribes from developers again. There should be a level playing field, where honest people can do well. How are you getting along with the Hawkes? Are you making any progress with them?"

"I may be," answered Emma. "At least they've made promises. Jack Hawke is flying out tonight to America. He is going to meet with Bruce Gilbert – you remember the American who flew into Shannon after my father's death, and gave files of documents to Commandant de Bruin and Inspector Muldoon. Jack had promised to arrange to make amends in America and to begin whatever renovations were needed to improve the living conditions in Mustelus properties."

"I thought that the Hawkes weren't allowed to leave the country?" asked Monique.

"Oh! both Jack and David can leave if it's for business. Inspector Muldoon cleared it."

"I see," replied Monique. "Is David heading to England then?"

"Next week. He is much more reluctant to honour the promises that were made at the board meeting. But, I suppose he's outvoted now. His wife, Emily is very negative about my plans. She wants the company to keep every penny it has. However, I think that Jack and Joanne have come to terms with the facts, and will reluctantly cooperate. Winnie Hawke seems to be having an influence on matters as well. She has become involved again since my father's death."

"How about Joanne and the Irish end of things?"

"I'm going to Mayo tomorrow. She has invited me to her country home for a few days, where we can discuss our plans for the Irish arm of the company. I want to get started on helping our tenants here."

Monique took a deep intake of breath. She became anxious at the thought of Emma being at the mercy of any of the Hawkes.

"If I may give my opinion, Emma – I'm not at all sure that you should stay with Joanne."

"Don't worry, Monique," laughed Emma. "I declined her offer to stay at her home. I've booked three nights at Loughfarraig House. I will go to Joanne's house for a number of meetings, but I certainly don't trust any of them enough to stay under their roof. I want to pay my respects to Mr. Moore and his wife. I also want to visit the place where Juan died. I know that the Moores have been very generous towards Juan's family. He is in contact with them, so I may ask for his input into how I may best help them."

"You're right – the Moores have definitely stepped up to the plate. I'm sure, also, that they'll be delighted to see you again and you will get re-acquainted with your friends still working at the hotel. I presume Tim will drive you?"

"Oh! of course. I've booked two rooms for us."

"How are you two getting along?" asked Monique.

"He's wonderful! – he really is. I feel so safe here now. He's also great company and so interesting. He told me all about his family and his army life. I never realised how fascinating army life was. He knows so much about the world. I'd be lost without him." Emma took a breath and added, "of course Mary is a great housekeeper and Joan is a very efficient P.A.. Thanks to you and Commandant de Bruin and Lydia Browne, I'm surrounded by great people."

"I'm very glad that everything is working out for you, Emma. Let me know how your trip to the west of Ireland goes. Be wary of Joanne Hawke. Keep your wits about you," advised Monique.

"I certainly will, Mrs. de Bruin, and thanks again for everything. I'll ring you when I get back to Bray."

Monique replaced the receiver, stood quietly for a moment, looking out the window.

"I wonder what Alexander is going to think about this unforeseen development," she thought to herself.

Monique strolled into the office where her husband was working on a ledger. When she entered the room, he raised his head and smiled.

"Who was that on the phone?" he asked.

"Emma with an update on everything," she replied.

"I hope young Tim McGrath is looking after her well," said Alexander.

"It would appear that he's doing a superb job," replied Monique with a smile.

"What are you smirking about?" asked Alexander with a confused tone.

"I believe that Emma is smitten by our young Corporal. When I asked her about him, she was effervescent with enthusiasm. She actually said that she'd be lost without him."

"Do you think that anything inappropriate has happened between them?" asked Alexander, anxiety in his voice.

"I don't think so, but I'm not sure. She informed me that they were both travelling to Loughfarraig tomorrow for a few days. She said that she had booked two rooms. Do you know if Tim has a girlfriend? I don't want Emma to get hurt."

"No, he's definitely not involved with anyone, that's why he was available for this job while on leave," retorted Alexander. "He's a decent young chap like the rest of his family. He knows how vulnerable and on her own Emma is. I really don't believe that he would take advantage of the situation. Why is she travelling west in any case?"

Monique explained to Alexander all about the progress of Emma's plans – about Jack heading to America that evening – David reluctantly travelling to England next week – Joanne seemingly agreeing to make improvements to their tenants living conditions here in Ireland. She also reassured him that Emma was not naive in her endeavours – she was well aware that the Hawkes were anything but trustworthy – Emma intended to tread carefully.

"I never thought about romantic entanglements when Robert and I arranged for Tim McGrath to take on this job of driver and protector," said Alexander. "We were just thinking about getting a very suitable candidate for the job," Alexander mused.

"Of course you didn't darling," responded Monique. "I'm sure they'll both be fine."

CHAPTER 38

A CLOSE CALL

At 2.30pm the following day, the telephone rang at The Lodge. Monique and Alexander were in the kitchen having a cup of coffee.

"I'll get it," said Alexander, as he rose from his chair and headed towards the office. He was gone for fifteen minutes. Finally he re-entered the kitchen. Monique could see that he was very pale, as if he had had some sort of shock.

"What's wrong darling, you look as if you've seen a ghost? Who was that on the phone?" asked Monique, anxiously.

"That was John Muldoon. There's been an accident – well, not an accident – an attempted murder," answered Alexander. "In Mayo, on the road to Loughfarraig. Tim and Emma. They're alive. Both are in Castlebar hospital. It happened this morning at 11.45am. John got a telephone call half an hour ago from the guards in Castlebar."

"What happened?" asked Monique. "Emma told me yesterday that she and Tim were going to travel west today."

"Tim was able to give a full statement to the guards. He's not badly hurt. Emma has a head injury," continued Alexander. "Seemingly, they left Bray at 7.30am this morning, so that they could arrive early. Emma had a meeting planned with Joanne Hawke at her country residence this afternoon. According to him, they were travelling on that very boggy road from Westport to Loughfarraig when a jeep sped up behind them, clipped the right rear side of the car and shunted them off the road and into the bog. There was nothing that Tim could do. The car went out of control and rolled over. His left shoulder was dislocated. He knew the pain, his shoulder had been dislocated before when playing rugby. The car landed on it's roof. He looked across at Emma who was not conscious – a dribble of blood was coming from her ear. To top it all he could smell petrol, so he had to act fast. He managed to get out of the car. He had to pop his shoulder blade back into it's socket. He then took Emma from the car, still unconscious. Tim was fairly sure that she didn't have any spinal injuries, but he didn't have any choice in any case as he was afraid that the car would catch fire. He carried her away from the car and onto the road. The car did catch fire.

Unfortunately they were on the road for nearly twenty minutes before a farmer arrived on a tractor. The farmer lived nearby, so called an ambulance. The ambulance and gardai arrived 45 minutes later, and they were both transported to Castlebar hospital. The medics were amazed that Tim was able to pop his shoulder blade back into place – the pain must have been horrendous and then to be able to remove Emma from the car and carry her to safety. When John Muldoon got the phone call, Emma had not yet regained consciousness. The doctors think that they may have to relieve pressure from the brain if the swelling increases – they are monitoring her very carefully."

"That's dreadful news," said Monique in shock. "We'll have to drive there a.s.a.p.. Emma has no one else."

"I agree, and I'm responsible for organising Tim to be her driver. I must ring his father Sergeant Major McGrath immediately and let him know what's happened. At least the young lad has only minor injuries. I really didn't think that this would happen, after all the precautions that were put in place. It has to be one of the Hawkes who tried to kill her. Emma doesn't have any other enemies."

"You go ahead and ring Tim's father. I'll run over to the Brownes with the dogs and ask them to look after the animals for a few days. Lydia will be very upset as well. She is very fond of Emma."

An hour later, Alexander and Monique were travelling west. All the arrangements were made with the Brownes. They had travelled via Newbridge to pick up some clothes from Sergeant Major McGrath for his son. Monique had packed everything that Emma might need, as the suitcases had gone up in flames in the car. Muldoon and Sergeant Dunne were travelling separately to Castlebar.

It was 7.30pm when the de Bruins arrived at Catlebar hospital. They went up to the receptionist, explained who they were and why they were there at 7.30 in the evening. She informed them that Inspector Muldoon was already there and had left instructions that they be allowed into the ward as soon as they arrived. The young receptionist picked up the phone to ring the ward. A few minutes later John Muldoon made an appearance in the hall. Alexander and Monique approached him immediately.

"Well, what's the news?" asked Alexander.

"Emma has not regained consciousness yet, but they have done a scan and the swelling isn't getting any worse. They hope that she will recover without an operation."

"That's good news," interjected Monique. "Can we see her?"

"Yes, she's in intensive care. Young Tim hasn't left her bedside. He's a wonderful young man. He saved her life, with his quick thinking."

Alexander and Monique followed Muldoon down the corridor, which was painted white and smelled of disinfectant – the usual hospital smell that made Monique feel queasy. The corridor was eerily quiet until they approached the intensive care where there were machines beeping and nurses checking patient's drips. In a corner, they could see Emma, a drip attached to one arm. Tim McGrath was sitting in a chair beside her bed, one arm in a sling, the other resting on the bed, while he held Emma's hand and looked at her intently. Her breathing was shallow and her eyes shut.

When Corporal McGrath saw the three approaching, he released Emma's hand and stood up.

"Please sit down Tim," said Alexander, kindly. "Just came back to check on you both."

"You three go and get a cup of coffee. I'll sit with Emma for a while. You look as if you could do with a break and something to eat Tim," said Monique.

"Thank you Mrs. de Bruin," said Tim gratefully.

The three men made their way to the canteen. There were sandwiches, tea and coffee available.

"Wouldn't bother with the coffee, it's dreadful," said Muldoon.

They bought three teas and sandwiches, then sat at a table in the corner. There were only a few more people there – obviously nursing staff on a break.

"There was nothing I could do, Commandant de Bruin. The jeep just appeared behind us. I thought he wanted to overtake us, so I pulled over as far as I could. Then he hit us and the car went off the road and flipped over. Emma could have been killed."

"You both could have been killed. Because of your quick thinking, Emma is alive Tim. You could have done no more. As far as we are all concerned, you did a wonderful job."

"Are you absolutely sure that this was done on purpose?" asked Muldoon. "Is there any chance at all that it was an accident?"

"None at all," replied Tim Mc Grath. "Whoever was driving that jeep tried to kill us."

"I'm going to put an officer on the ward. They might try again," stated Muldoon. He stood up and headed towards reception to make a phone call to the Garda Station.

"I'm very sorry that this has happened to you Tim. I really didn't think that you would be in this sort of danger." said Alexander.

"I'm not sorry Sir, I am very glad that I was there for Emma. She is a remarkable person. It appears that the west of Ireland is more dangerous for me than the Middle East," he grinned.

Alexander was happy that young Tim hadn't lost his sense of humour.

"I'd like to get back to Emma now, Sir," insisted Tim.

"Absolutely," retorted Alexander, as both men stood up, left the canteen and walked down the white corridor towards the ward. They met Muldoon en route.

"The officer will be here to guard the ward in ten minutes," he said.

Monique was still sitting by Emma's bed. She was holding her hand and speaking gently to her. As yet, there was no response. She stood up as the others approached. Tim sat down in her place and took hold of Emma's hand.

An hour later Muldoon, Alexander and Monique were sitting in front of a blazing turf fire in Loughfarraig House. They had been greeted warmly by Mr. and Mrs. Moore and provided with a late supper of sandwiches, cake and tea. Tim McGrath had decided to wait beside Emma's bed for another while, hoping to see some improvement. Muldoon had organised a car for him for when he felt ready to leave the hospital.

After supper Alexander ordered two brandies and a sherry. They had much to discuss.

"Was there any evidence at the crash site?" asked Alexander.

"Just skid marks on the road. Emma's car was destroyed by the fire and all evidence with it. Tim can only say that it was a dark coloured jeep – probably dark grey or black. Everything happened so quickly," answered Muldoon. "The jeep itself must be damaged by the impact, but we have to find it. There was no one else on the road it seems, at the time. They were lucky that the farmer came along when he did – otherwise they could have been on the side of the road for hours."

"We now believe that it must be one of the family, or someone close to them, I presume," said Alexander.

"But they can gain nothing by this – getting rid of Emma would not improve their circumstances in any way. They were told that she had made a will – to protect her," interjected Monique, confusion in her voice.

"This is all extremely strange," continued Muldoon.

"Who would have a motive to kill all four people? We can certainly rule out anyone from Donal Hawke's past at this stage."

"According to Emma, Jack Hawke is in America"

"Is this true, John?" asked Monique.

"I gave them all permission to leave the country for business. I'll check his flight," retorted Muldoon.

"Let's recap," said Alexander. "Donal Hawke was murdered most likely by a member of his family. The only one in the group with a solid alibi is Francois Dupont, Joanne Hawke's boyfriend. Donal Hawke had changed his will, but his family believed that he was going to change his will after the Christmas holidays thanks to David Hawke's long time friend and solicitor Jonathan Kelly. No one seemed to know that Donal Hawke had only six months to live.

Juan was murdered, we are nearly 100% sure because he had witnessed the murder, and was blackmailing the killer. The only people with a solid alibi for this killing are Natalia, who was in hospital and Emma who was in Briarstown.

Next, Frank Smith, who was about to impart some information to us regarding surveillance he had undertaken for Donal Hawke on someone or other in his family. He told us that he thought that he had been seen. Smith was murdered with the same, or similar, weapon as Juan. Finally, Emma was run off the road and nearly killed by a jeep on her way to Loughfarraig and later to meet Joanne Hawke."

"We have to find out who knew that Emma would be on the road. They must have been lying in wait. They just couldn't have happened upon her," interjected Muldoon.

"It could have only been one of the family," insisted Monique. "We knew that she was travelling to Mayo, Tim McGrath could have mentioned it to someone, I suppose. Her housekeeper and P.A. probably knew, but none of these people have any motive to harm her. Joanne Hawke knew, because they had meetings planned. She probably told her own family, her boyfriend Francois and maybe some friends. Nothing makes any sense except that one of the Hawkes did it or organised it."

As they sat sipping their drinks and pondering the facts of the case, Gerald Moore approached Alexander.

"Commandant de Bruin, there's a telephone call for you. You can take it in my office," he said.

Alexander rose from his armchair and followed Moore into the small office behind reception. He sat down at the small desk, and picked up the receiver.

"Alexander de Bruin speaking," he said, waiting in anticipation for an answer, being fairly certain that it was someone calling from Castlebar hospital about Emma's condition.

"Sir, it's me, Corporal McGrath," came the voice from the other end of the line.

"Tim, what's the news?"

"It's good news, Sir. Emma regained consciousness about twenty minutes ago. The doctor has seen her and believes that she will make a full recovery. She is sitting up in the bed at the moment, and has asked for a cup of tea. I can't believe that she is going to be fine. I'm so relieved."

"That's wonderful news, Tim. I'll tell the others. Monique will be so happy. Are you coming back to the hotel?"

"I'll wait with her another while, Sir, until she wants to get some sleep. Then the driver will take me to Loughfarraig House. It will be very late when I get there, so I probably won't see you until tomorrow morning."

"Thanks for letting me know, Tim. Give our regards to Emma. Tell her we will see her sometime tomorrow. Goodnight."

"Goodbye, Sir,"

Alexander left the office and returned to where Monique and Muldoon were sitting, anxiously awaiting his return. They were delighted to hear the excellent news of Emma's recovery.

Muldoon retired to his room shortly after the phone call. Alexander and Monique decided to take a stroll along the seashore before going to bed. The sky was pitch black. The stars twinkled brightly and there was a full moon. It was a calm night, the breeze only whispered and the lapping of the waves was a gentle gurgling. They linked arms as they slowly walked on the pebbles which crunched beneath their feet, and looked out onto the expanse of the dark Atlantic ocean.

They both thought about Tim and Emma, and wondered if there was a love story to follow.

CHAPTER 39

THE DOCTOR AND THE MYSTERY

When Alexander and Monique arrived down for breakfast the following morning, an excited, grinning Tim McGrath was waiting for them in the lobby.

"Morning Sir, Morning Ma'am," he greeted them.

"Good morning Tim," said Monique, "What time did you get back last night?"

"It was nearly one thirty," replied Tim. "The driver was very good to wait around for me so long in the hospital."

"How is your shoulder?" asked Alexander.

"Not too bad, Sir. I got loads of painkillers. I was wondering what time you were going in to the hospital?" asked Tim impatiently.

"We'll go in after breakfast Tim. Come and join us," said Monique. "We'll just wait for Inspector Muldoon to arrive."

As they sat eating a scrumptious breakfast, Tim recounted how Emma's eyelids began to move, her breathing seemed to change and she suddenly opened her eyes and looked over at him. She asked him what had happened. She couldn't remember anything about the accident. She complained about a headache, but that was all. The doctors and nurses arrived. They gave her some painkillers. The doctor examined her, and was very happy with her condition.

"Has anything else occurred to you, Tim, about the accident?" asked Muldoon.

"Not a thing, Inspector," replied Tim. "Just as I said, the jeep just appeared out of the blue and shunted us off the road. I couldn't see the driver. I don't even know if it was a man or a woman. It just all happened so quickly."

"Here's the plan, Tim," interjected Monique. "I'll drive you to the hospital while the two men here proceed with their investigation. I'll see you in the foyer in fifteen minutes. I'm sure that Emma will be delighted to have some visitors."

An hour later Monique parked the car near the entrance to the hospital. She and Tim walked quickly up the steps that led to the automatic doors which opened as they approached. They proceeded down the white corridor until they reached the Intensive Care Ward. A nurse intercepted them just as they were about to enter the ward.

"Are you here to visit Ms. Jones?" she asked, having recognised Tim from the day before.

"She has been moved to a private room down the corridor, there on the left – number 5."

"Thank you so much," returned Monique. "How is she doing, I'm a friend, Mrs. de Bruin."

"She had a very good night. The doctor is doing his rounds and will see her soon. You can have a chat with him then."

Tim knocked at the door of Room 5.

"Come in," said a voice from inside.

As they entered the room they were delighted to see Emma, sitting upright in the bed, a smile on her face. Tim went over to her, took her hand and kissed it. She beamed at him.

"Mrs. de Bruin, how lovely to see you."

"You too Emma. We are all so happy that you are okay. You gave us all a dreadful fright."

Monique sat down on a chair beside the bed. She noticed an enormous bouquet of flowers sitting on a small table by the window.

"Where did the flowers come from?" she asked.

"Oh! from the Hawkes," replied Emma.

"How did they know that you were here?" asked Monique with a tone of suspicion.

"I asked one of the nurses to ring Joanne to explain my absence, first thing this morning. The flowers arrived a few hours later."

Monique rose from her chair and went over to inspect the flowers and the note which read "Get well soon, Emma. Best wishes from the Hawke family."

Monique wondered how sincere was the sentiment expressed in the note. Suddenly the door opened and a distinguished looking man in his early fifties entered the room wearing a white coat and stethoscope around his neck. There were two nurses with him – one very young and cheerful looking, with a pretty smile and blond hair tied back in a bun underneath her nurse's cap. The second nurse was more serious looking, with a lot more experience under her belt.

"Good morning Ms. Jones," said the doctor. "You are looking well rested."

He looked at her chart, then approached the patient to shine a light into her eyes.

"How is your shoulder, young man?" he said to Tim.

"Not bad at all, doctor," replied Tim.

"This is my good friend Mrs. de Bruin," said Emma. "She has taken care of me since my father's death."

"I wonder could I have a word with you in my office," said the doctor.

"Of course," said Monique, as she followed the entourage out of the room, down the corridor towards the doctor's office. The two nurses continued with their rounds as Monique was shown to a seat in front of the doctor's desk, which was cluttered with files and other paperwork.

"I just wanted to let you know about Emma's state of health. She's an extremely lucky young woman to have recovered so quickly from the head injury – it could have been so much worse. We were afraid at first that there might have been a major bleed. Luckily we didn't have to operate. Tim, her companion, informed me that it was deliberate. Emma told me that she has no family, and that you have taken her under your wing. While she is making a good recovery, she will need some check ups in the next few weeks. Are you the right person to talk to on this matter? I would like to be able to contact you regarding her treatment. She has consented to this."

"That's no problem. We will make sure that she attends her follow up appointments. Thank you so much for everything that you've done for her."

"This is a very strange coincidence you know. I was the doctor on duty when Natalia Hawke was admitted. We couldn't find a thing wrong with her. She seemed completely healthy – heartbeat, pulse, X-rays, scans – we did the whole gambit of tests – not a thing amiss. It's very strange indeed," he muttered.

"There has been a lot of strangeness around the Hawke family of late – three murders and an attempted murder," added Monique.

"Yes absolutely – but we couldn't find a single thing wrong with her," he muttered under his breath.

"This doctor certainly didn't like mysteries," thought Monique to herself.

CHAPTER 40

LIAISONS

As Alexander and Muldoon came to a halt in front of Joanne Hawke's country residence, they noticed that there were cars parked at the side of the house, but no sign of a dark coloured jeep with damage.

"It wouldn't be parked for all to see," said Alexander with a wry smile.

The two men climbed the six steps to the front door and knocked.

The butler opened the door and showed them into the parlour where Joanne and Francois were standing at the window.

"Please take a seat gentlemen," said Joanne, indicating two armchairs on either side of the beautiful fireplace. She and Francois sat on the couch facing the two visitors.

"How can we help you?" asked Joanne.

"As you already know, there was an attempt on Emma Jones' life on Tuesday morning on the road to Loughfarraig House. A jeep ran them off the road. We are endeavouring to locate the jeep. Do you own such a vehicle?" asked Muldoon.

"I own a jeep," answered Joanne. "It's parked in the garage behind the house. I would say nearly every landowner has a jeep around here."

"What colour is it?" asked Alexander.

"It's green. You're welcome to examine it."

"We'll do that on our way out," said Muldoon.

"Who else knew that Emma Jones was on her way to Loughfarraig?" asked Alexander.

"We all did," answered Joanne. "I hope you don't think that one of us is responsible? We have all come to terms with her existence. We don't have a choice. None of us would have anything to gain by her death – the opposite in fact. We are tied to her now, for better or worse. Jack is in America doing her bidding. She and I were due to have a meeting about changes in the company here in Ireland on Tuesday afternoon."

"Can you tell me where you were on Tuesday morning?" asked Muldoon.

"I was here on the estate. I was riding out on the far end where the stables are."

"Can anyone vouch for you?"

"No, I was on my own for several hours."

"What about you Monsieur Dupont? Where were you on the morning of the incident?" continued Muldoon.

"I was travelling back from Limerick where I had business with a friend," answered Francois.

"Francois has nothing to do with any of this," insisted Joanne. "He has nothing to do with Emma Jones. Why would he run her off the road? Are you sure it wasn't just an accident?"

"We are quite sure it wasn't an accident. Her driver remembers the whole incident and is extremely reliable," retorted Alexander.

Alexander and Muldoon sat into the car, having checked the jeep in the garage, and set off down the avenue.

"Did you notice that neither of them even asked how Emma was?" said Alexander.

"Yes, and no alibi once again. Just because that jeep isn't the one involved in the accident, doesn't mean that there isn't another one on the estate somewhere. Joanne could have easily run them off the road, while she was supposedly out riding on her own."

"We really haven't checked out Francois Dupont. I found him a bit shifty today," added Alexander. "Well, we know that he has an alibi for Donal Hawke's murder – in fact he's the only person who couldn't have murdered him. And he was in France when Frank Smith was murdered," said Muldoon.

"I've a feeling that he is hiding something. I think that he knows something. If it's OK with you I'm going to contact my friend in the

Gendarmerie and ask him to check him out. Just to put my mind at ease," concluded Alexander.

"Go ahead – we have nothing to lose. Is that one of the men you worked with in France on the French Colonel's murder?"

"Yes, we've kept in touch. He will be happy to help us out – it will be easier and quicker than you going through official channels. There might be nothing to it. Dupont may well be above board, and not involved at all."

Ava Hawke was the only member of the family with an alibi, as she was indisposed at her home. There was a nurse in attendance. David and Emily Hawke alibied each other as there were no members of staff in the house at the time. It was difficult to take them at their word. However, they all insisted, like Joanne, that they had accepted the new situation with Emma Jones and had no reason to harm her.

When Alexander and Muldoon arrived back at Loughfarraig House, Monique was waiting for them.

"Well, any joy?" she asked as the two men joined her in the Long Room.

"Not really," answered Alexander. "No worthwhile alibis again, except for Ava Hawke, who is in the clear. How did you get on at the hospital? How is Emma?"

"In very good form, considering everything that she has been through. She will need some follow up treatment according to the doctor. He was a bit of a strange fellow – I'd say one of these geniuses who is excellent at his job, but with very few social skills. He even seemed a bit obsessed with not being able to find something wrong with Natalia Hawke the day she was taken ill here. Anyway, I promised him that we would make sure that Emma attended her follow up appointments. He was insistent."

"Did Tim come back with you?" asked Alexander.

"No, he wanted to stay on. One of the guards will drive him back later on this evening. Emma isn't the only one who is smitten. Tim obviously has very strong feelings for her. There is definitely a romance blossoming there."

"Should we be worried?" asked Alexander.

"I don't believe so," replied Monique. "Tim is a wonderful young man – completely trustworthy. It would have been very difficult for Emma to meet someone in the future, who would love her for herself, and not for her new found fortune. How could she ever be sure? This is different. These two young people were thrown together by circumstances. There was no design here. Tim was doing you a favour. Poor Emma has endured a very tough few years. She has no one in the world. She deserves some happiness. She certainly can't trust the Hawkes and will always have to stay one step ahead of them. Perhaps she has found love and someone she can trust implicitly. I, for one would be very pleased if it worked out for them."

"Well, you certainly have given this some thought," said Alexander, with a smile. "Have you a wedding venue in mind."

"Very funny," retorted Monique.

Tim McGrath returned to Loughfarraig House at eight o'clock, just in time to join Muldoon and the de Bruins for dinner.

The food was delicious and everyone enjoyed a few glasses of Bordeaux. Gerald Moore was as attentive as usual and asked sincerely after Emma.

"They are hoping to discharge her tomorrow. She was hoping to stay here for a few days – will that be possible?" asked Tim. "She wants to do what she had planned."

"We'll have to think about that, Tim," replied Muldoon. "There may be another attempt on her life. Let's sleep on it. She's safe in the hospital with the guard at the door, keeping watch. There would be more opportunity here for the assailant to make a move."

"I don't understand why anyone would want to harm Emma. She's such a good person, who just wants to improve the lives of other people," whispered Tim.

"Nor do we," agreed Monique. "We thought that we had protected her."

It was decided that Emma would not stay at Loughfarraig House for safety reasons. Sergeant Dunne drove Tim and Emma to a hotel just outside Ennis, where they checked in under a false name. They were to stay there until instructed otherwise by Inspector Muldoon. Monique headed back to Briarstown to take care of the house and animals. Alexander and Muldoon stayed on at Loughfarraig, hoping that something would break in the case.

There had been a great response to the appeals. The gardai sifted through the phone calls. The owner of a hotel in Limerick recognised

Frank Smith from the photo which had been shown on the news. Alexander and Muldoon decided to pay him a visit. It took a good three hours to get there. The hotel itself was very secluded. There was a long avenue to the front of the building. The facade was draped in ivy. To the side was a beautiful U-plan conservatory with a curving cast-iron roof and ornate cresting and finial. The moulded cornice and arcaded glazing made it one of the most appealing conservatories that Alexander had ever seen.

"A lovely secluded place to hide away," said Alexander as they entered the building.

The bar area was mostly made up of snugs, where couples could have privacy. They made themselves known to the receptionist, who located the proprietor, James Irwin, a very handsome man in his mid forties, dressed in a made to measure suit.

"How do you do gentlemen, I'm James Irwin. Let's take a seat."

The two men followed him to one of the snugs.

"I'm Inspector Muldoon. This is my associate Commandant de Bruin. I've been informed that you may have some information for us concerning Frank Smith, who was murdered."

"Yes, I recognised his photo on the news. He was here a number of times. He was always on his own. The first time that I saw him was last July or August. Most of our guests stay with us. Some of the locals come in for a meal, but I know them all. He just came in, ordered a drink and sat in one of the snugs – usually the one right in the corner. He never stayed or even dined with us. He always seemed to be on the lookout for someone or other."

"When was the last time you saw him?" asked Alexander.

"It was four days before his death. Same ritual as ever. He arrived – looked around furtively, took his seat in the snug, ordered a drink and watched everyone carefully."

"Do you have any idea whom he might have been following?" asked Muldoon.

"There was one particular couple who stayed here each time that Smith made an appearance, and he was definitely spotted by the lady on the last occasion. I was greeting the couple at reception, which has a view of the bar. Smith stuck his head out of the snug. She became very agitated when she saw him and ran down the corridor. Smith knew that he had been seen and hid behind the panel. The young man was somewhat perturbed and confused and went in search of his companion. At that stage, Smith quickly got up and left the premises."

"Do you know the name of the couple," asked Alexander.

"Well, they always checked in as Mr. and Mrs. Johnson. They just gave their address as Galway City."

"Could you describe them," asked Muldoon.

"The man was in his late twenties, dark hair, quite tall and slim. It was difficult to see the woman. She looked somewhat older, but always wore a scarf, so couldn't see her hair, and dark glasses. She was of medium height, about five five and slim. She always wore a tweed coat. One more thing – the man spoke with an accent – French, I think."

"Thank you so much for your cooperation, Mr. Irwin. This has been very helpful," said Muldoon as he stood up, extending his hand. James Irwin shook his hand followed by Alexander's. They said goodbye and made their way back to the car.

"Who do you know, involved in the case, with a French accent," muttered Muldoon.

"Francois Dupont. His description also fits perfectly. But who was the woman?"

"It's such a vague description. She obviously didn't want to be recognised – the scarf, the dark glasses and the tweed coat, – 5ft.5 – slim build. All the women involved could fit that description except Winnie Hawke. It could also be some other woman who was having an affair with Francois – not involved in the case."

"But," interjected Alexander, "Irvin said that she was upset when she spotted Smith in the bar. She must have recognised him and knew that they were being followed. It must be one of the Hawke women – whoever she was, she recognised Frank Smith."

"We can't be sure that that's the sequence of events – perhaps Francois recognised him, and warned her to move away. Witness statements aren't always completely reliable."

"If this was Francois Dupont, it's highly unlikely that the woman was Joanne Hawke. Why would she have to hide away in a hotel with her lover? Her father and the rest of the family knew all about Francois. Why would Frank Smith have been asked by Donal Hawke to follow his daughter and her lover in any case?"

"We will have to get a photo of Francois, and show it to James Irwin. If he recognises him, at least we'll have one half of the puzzle," concluded Muldoon.

"I'm not sure that Donal Hawke would have been bothered to have Francois followed to prove he is having an affair with someone else. Joanne has a reputation for having younger lovers, and replacing them quite often. It probably was the woman that was being followed," said Alexander.

"So, was it Emily, Ava or Natalia? I suppose he would have cared if Emily or Ava were cheating on one of his sons."

"We have forgotten a very important fact here – Francois did not murder Donal Hawke. The rest of the Hawke family will attest to that. He was also, supposedly visiting a sick aunt in France when Frank Smith was murdered," continued Alexander.

The two men made the long journey back to Loughfarraig House. It was getting dark as they drove along the avenue. The lake was still, the sun was setting on the horizon, a halo of yellow and pink touched the heavens.

CHAPTER 41

REVELATIONS

Inspector John Muldoon was first down to breakfast at Loughfarraig House. As he took his seat in the dining room, Gerald Moore approached him with a large brown envelope.

"This fax arrived this morning for your attention, or that of Commandant de Bruin."

"Thank you, Mr. Moore," said Muldoon, taking hold of the envelope and opening it to reveal a number of pages of print, all written in French. Inspector Muldoon's school French was not really up to the task. He could make out sentences, here and there, and could guess at others. He waited patiently for Alexander to arrive down for breakfast. The fax was a "Rapport de Police" sent by Alexander's friend in the Gendarmerie in Paris. It was a lengthy document, which must contain the life story of Francois Dupont.

"Good morning John," greeted Alexander, as he took his place at the breakfast table, took the linen napkin and placed it on his lap. "What have you got there?"

"It's the report on Francois Dupont from your friend in the Gendarmerie. Unfortunately I can only understand some of it," answered Muldoon. "What is escroc?"

"A scoundrel," answered Alexander

"I can see "imposteur" but what is a "menteur?"

"A liar – sounds very promising," laughed Alexander.

"He seems to have had a problem with authority in his youth," said Muldoon pointing to the sentence "d'avoir des antecedents de probleme avec l'autorite quand il etait jeune,"

"There's also mention of a criminal record," added Alexander – "that's a "casier judiciaire."

"He spent time in prison when he was 18 – look "passe six mois en prison guard il avait 18 ans pour vol avec effraction".

"What's vol avec effraction?"

"Burglary," replied Alexander. "I think it might be better if I read through it all, and translated it for you."

"One more thing," said Muldoon, "What does "Les femmes ont ete trompees par lui" mean?"

"Women were duped by him," answered Alexander.

They decided to put the pages away and enjoy breakfast. Then Alexander would study the document and relate the contents to Muldoon.

They reconvened in the small sitting room at 11.am. Alexander sat down beside Muldoon with a handwritten translation of the fax in his hand.

He began to read. "Francois Dupont was born into quite a wealthy family in Nantes. He was sent to the best schools and was a very clever boy. However, he had problems with authority and was expelled from two schools. Despite not having done a lot of study, he managed to get a place in the Sorbonne, but that didn't last. He was caught cheating in an exam, and was sent down, as they say. He got in with a bad crowd when he was eighteen – he was caught burglarising the home of wealthy friends of his parents. He was imprisoned for six months. At this stage, his family gave up on him, so cut him off.

Francois is a very good looking, well educated charming young man, so he put these charms to work – usually on older wealthy women, from whom he received cash and gifts, They were duped by him. Some made investments in fictitious businesses and art work, which one of his friends painted, "in the style of" some of the masters. The police were made aware of what he was up to by one woman who reported him. The other women were too ashamed to come forward, and some seemed to be genuinely in love with him. He is a very clever "escroc", "imposteur" and "menteur". He was also known by two other names, Francois Henri and Francois Moreau. He does not have a sick aunt. All his family are well and haven't seen him in years. He did not travel to France in the last four months unless he came by ferry and his passport wasn't checked which happens sometimes. He wasn't on any manifest. He hasn't been in any trouble for two years, or at least he hasn't come to the attention of the police in France."

Alexander stopped reading from his translation and looked at Muldoon.

"Well, that's it – he's a right piece of work. Of course his relationship with Joanne started about a year and a half ago – he must have thought that he landed on his feet."

"I wonder where he went when he told her that he was in France, or away on business?"

"It would appear that he was meeting his lover, at least on some of these occasions," replied Alexander. "However, there is no sign at all of any violence towards anyone on his record. He used his charm and good looks to lure women into his web. Even the burglary was a burglary – no violence or intimidation. He knew that his parents' wealthy friends were away on holidays and robbed their houses. He wasn't a very good burglar at that – he left his fingerprints behind. And as we keep saying, he could not have killed Donal Hawke."

"But it is unlikely that he was in France, as Joanne Hawke said, when Frank Smith was murdered, especially as he doesn't have a sick aunt," added Muldoon.

"This is all very confusing. Francois appears to have found his meal ticket with Joanne Hawke. They gave the impression of being very close. He was very attentive to her at Loughfarraig. Why on earth would he jeopardise his future in the Hawke family with all their millions to see another woman. Why would he need a second mark?" wondered Alexander.

"Joanne has a reputation of having relationships with younger men but then moving on when she got bored. Perhaps he sensed this and had found another woman to dupe," continued Muldoon.

"I really got the impression that she had fallen for him," said Alexander. "So did Monique – and she's very good at spotting these sort of things."

"We'll have to question him again," stated Muldoon. "Joanne Hawke isn't going to be best pleased when she finds out about him."

"Perhaps she already knows and has fallen for him, warts and all, despite his past," suggested Alexander.

"But, she seems to believe that he was in France taking care of a sick aunt, and also that he has business interests, in parts of Ireland. This next interview is going to be very interesting indeed."

Before Muldoon and Alexander got the opportunity to arrange another interview with Francois Dupont, one more snippet of information came to light which might help to move the case along. The parish priest, who knew both Frank Smith and Donal Hawke rang the helpline stating that he had information about Frank Smith that might be helpful. He stated that he had seen Smith two days before his death. Father John Kenny had been curate and parish priest in the community where both Smith and Hawke had spent their childhood, for over sixty years. He was originally from Doneraile in County Cork, but loved his small Mayo parish, where everyone knew everyone else. The two boys were about ten when Fr. Kenny arrived in the parish as a young priest.

Alexander and Muldoon arrived at the presbytery at the preordained time. It was a beautiful old house, clad in ivy and red brick. There was a short avenue leading up to the front door. The front garden was very well maintained. A white wrought iron table and chairs stood near the small conservatory on the lawn. There were two trellises, which were adorned with roses in summer time.

The door was opened by a small, plump woman in her sixties. She had silver hair, tied back in a bun, wore a tweed skirt with an apron, and a navy jumper with a lace collar.

"Good morning gentlemen, the Father is expecting you – he's in the parlour by the fire. I'm Gladys Aherne, the housekeeper."

Gladys led the two men into a cosy parlour with a blazing fire. The couches were adorned with cushions whose covers had been embroidered by hand. There was a screen in front of the fire, also embroidered with the design of a horse.

In front of the fire, sat a very old man, probably in his late eighties with white hair, wearing spectacles. He had obviously been writing some sort of sermon as there was a notebook and pen alongside a Bible, on the side table beside the armchair.

"The two gentlemen have arrived Father," said Gladys, as Alexander and Muldoon took a few steps into the parlour.

"Thank you, Gladys," said the Father. "Please take a seat." He indicated to the couch opposite his armchair.

"I'll make some tea," said Gladys, as she left the room.

"Gladys takes such good care of me," added Father Kenny. "She's been with me for over forty years. Her aunt was my housekeeper before her. She never married, but dedicated her whole life to the parish. She looks after all my paper work as well."

Alexander and Muldoon looked at this very frail man, whose life had been spent in the service of God and his flock. Although physically weak, his mind was still razor sharp.

"I'm Inspector Muldoon and this is my colleague Commandant de Bruin."

"So, an army man," interjected the Father.

"Retired, Father," answered Alexander. "Just helping out with this case."

"A very good friend of mine was Chaplain in the Curragh Camp, but way before your time. Were you stationed in the Curragh?"

"For most of my time," answered Alexander, "apart from my trips abroad and different secondments."

"Are you close to solving these murders?" enquired Fr. Kenny.

"Not there yet," answered Muldoon. "We need the public's help. People like yourself, who may have invaluable information. You rang the garda helpline, stating that you had seen Frank Smith, shortly before his death."

Before the priest could reply, the door opened and Gladys pushed a dumbwaiter into the room.

"Tea is served," she said with a smile.

There was an aroma of freshly baked bread. Two plates of goodies sat on the top shelf of the dumbwaiter – warm white soda bread, buttered and covered with homemade raspberry jam on one, slices of rhubarb tart and cream on the other plate. The best china was on the bottom shelf with a "Queen Anne" pattern, a sugar bowl with a silver tongs, a very pretty milk jug and china teapot. Gladys had used loose leaf-tea and there was a silver tea strainer and holder beside the teapot. The tea was poured and the three men enjoyed the delicious home made bread and tart.

"I've known both Donal Hawke and Frank Smith since they were boys. They were about ten when I arrived as a curate to the parish. I was only twenty five myself. I was very involved with the school, so I knew all the children well. The two boys were always together. Donal was the really clever one, but there was also something not quite right about him. He didn't seem to care very much about others. Frank followed him around like a puppy – always doing his bidding. Frank's mother was a very religious woman – the church was very important to her. Neither family had much money. As you know Donal Hawke left first and went off to England. Frank followed a few years later. Frank came back quite often. He adored his mother. He always sent her money. He even offered to buy her a new house, but she was happy in her old home. Once Frank started making money – whatever way it was made, his mother was never short of money again. I don't believe that Frank was religious, but he used to help out the church here a lot – I believe because it was so important to his mother. She's buried here in the graveyard. He placed a fine looking marble tombstone on her grave."

"Did he visit here a lot since her death?" asked Muldoon.

"Yes, he used to spend time in the church, on his own. I presume he was praying – although I never thought that he was a great believer. He'd call in to see me as well, and we'd have a cuppa and chat. Actually about twenty years ago, the church roof was in disrepair. There was a storm one night, and the sacristy was completely flooded. Frank offered to foot the bill for the repairs. He organised the men to more or less rebuild the sacristy and fix the roof – he supervised the whole thing himself. They did a great job. The roof has weathered many a storm since. He also funded some repairs to the presbytery. Frank has been a very good friend to this parish. He was here two days before his death. He visited me here – we had a chat about Donal Hawke. He said that he was definitely retiring after he had finished one job that Donal had asked him to do. He said that he had no intention of working for the Hawke children. He also told me about Donal Hawke's daughter – said that he was pleased that she had come forward – she was different from the other children – more like her mother whom Frank had also known. Then he told me that he wanted some quiet time, alone, in the church, as he always did, and that was the last I saw of him. Next thing, I heard that he was murdered. I suppose I've always known that the two of them might come to a sticky end. However, I'll be forever grateful to Frank for his help with the church, especially the rebuilding of the sacristy. Funny thing though – when the sacristy was finished it seemed smaller."

Alexander and Muldoon looked at each other. A light bulb had gone off in their heads. They were both thinking the same thing.

"Could we visit the church on our way out, Father?" asked Muldoon.

"Of course. It's always open," replied Father Kenny. "We have no need to lock it around these parts."

Alexander and Muldoon stood up, thanked the elderly priest for his hospitality and assistance and took their leave, saying goodbye to Gladys Aherne, who closed the door behind them.

They walked the short distance from the presbytery to the Church. It was a beautiful little church with stained glass windows. The old oak doors opened into a small hallway with flyers of all sorts pinned to a notice board. There was a holy water font made of marble just inside the door. Both men dipped their fingers into the font, and then made the sign of the cross – force of habit. All the wood was shining – the church was immaculately clean. The hymn books were stacked at the end of each pew. There were beautiful flowers on the altar. They made their way to the altar, genuflected, then noticed the door which led to the sacristy.

Inside the sacristy, the priest's vestments were hanging in an open wardrobe. They noticed a cupboard with a glass door, which contained the wine for the consecration. There were bibles and hymn books stacked on a small corner table. They admired the shining wood panelling on two of the walls. There was a sacred heart painting with a lighted candle beneath. The eyes of the painting seemed to follow you wherever you moved. Every house in Ireland used to have one of these pictures looking down at the family – sometimes used by the parents to scare the children to behave, as God was watching them.

"The room certainly does look narrower than it should," stated Muldoon.

"This inside wall seems to be jutting in."

He tapped the timber, but nothing seemed amiss.

"I think there could be a hidden space behind the timber," interjected Alexander, as he began to check for a hidden panel or some means of opening up a little door. He painstakingly moved his hands along the wood. In one corner, he felt a small lever, which he moved upwards. It made a clicking sound and one panel moved slightly.

"I think we've found it," exclaimed Alexander, clicking it shut again. "But I don't think that we should open it without Father Kenny's permission."

"You're right. It would be a huge invasion into his personal space. This is a sacred place to him, after all. We need to tread carefully," agreed Muldoon.

"Have you the key with you, John?"

"Yes, it's in my breast pocket," answered Muldoon, tapping his jacket.

"Poor Father Kenny is going to get an awful shock if Frank Smith has been using this sacristy as a hiding place for all sorts," added Alexander. The two men decided to return to the presbytery to inform Father Kenny of their find.

"Back again, so soon," said Gladys, as she opened the front door. "Come on through. Father is still in the parlour, working on his sermon."

Father Kenny looked up from his notes as Alexander and Muldoon entered the room.

"Is there something wrong?" he asked.

"I think we may have found a hidden space in the sacristy, Father. We located a lever, but didn't want to open it and look inside without your permission," stated Alexander.

"I thought you might have been looking for something when you asked to visit the church," sighed the old man.

"We are very sorry about this intrusion, Father," said Muldoon.

"I'll come with you," said Father Kenny, as he pushed himself up from the armchair, with some difficulty. He took hold of the walking stick which was leaning against the fireplace. Gladys had collected his coat from the stand in the hallway, and helped the frail old man to put it on. He looked dejected as he led the way back to the church. As they passed the graveyard, he pointed to an ornate marble headstone.

"That's where Frank Smith's mother is buried."

It was indeed a beautiful rich green marble headstone with gold lettering. There were pebbles on the grave and shrubs and planters atop.

"He took very good care of it," said Father Kenny.

The priest shuffled up the aisle of his little church, followed by Muldoon and Alexander. The walking stick made an eerie clack, clack on the wooden floor, which echoed throughout the church – a sound of sadness and disappointment. The Father entered the sacristy first and stared disbelievingly at the wooden panels. Muldoon and Alexander stood behind him.

"Where is this lever?" he asked.

Alexander pointed to the corner where he had found it. "It was very hard to find," he said.

"Open it up," instructed Father Kenny, stoically, staring at the wall.

Alexander lifted the tiny lever which clicked. He then moved the panels which showed a door, which resembled a safe. Muldoon removed the key from his breast pocket, inserted it into the keyhole which released a mechanism. He pulled open the safe door which revealed a treasure trove. The secret space ran the length of the wall. There were shelves containing video tapes, ledgers, files, camera equipment and in one corner there were wads of money – Irish money, English money, francs and dollars. There were thousands of pounds worth of cash. In another corner there were ten gold bars. The three men stood staring at the contents in astonishment. Father Kenny had a look of disdain and horror on his face.

"Frank Smith used this place of God, this sanctuary, as a hiding place for his ill gotten gains, and whatever else he had stored here," exclaimed Father Kenny, teetering a little, having to steady himself with his walking stick. Tears welled up in his eyes.

"I'm so sorry, Father. This has been an awful shock for you," said Muldoon. "Would you like to sit down?"

"Yes, I'll go out in front of the altar and pray," returned the priest.

Alexander helped him from the sacristy, until they reached the first pew in front of the altar. He left him sitting there, lost in his thoughts and prayers.

"What should we do now?" asked Alexander as he returned to join Muldoon, who handed him a pair of plastic gloves.

"Lets hope he kept a copy of the file and photos of whoever he was following," answered Muldoon. "And that his murderer didn't take the only copy from Frank Smith's home, the day he killed him."

The two men carefully checked each file. There were video tapes dating from ten years before – Lord only knows what was on them. There were ledgers with financial transactions from the USA and Britain – pay offs – probably going back years. In one box they located a revolver with ammunition. This was the life story of a gangster. Finally, Alexander picked up a file containing dates, times,descriptions of rendez-vous and of course, the photos which gave the game away.

CHAPTER 42

NEWS FROM BOGOTA

"Commissioner, Sir, there's a phone call for you from Colombia. It's the Police Chief. He said that he has information about a murder here in Ireland," said Garda John Willis excitedly, as he entered the office of the Commissioner.

"I presume he speaks English, put him through John."

After two rings, the Commissioner picked up the receiver and introduced himself.

"This is Carlos Gonzalez speaking, I am Chief of Police in Bogota, Colombia."

"What can I do to help you?"

"It's what I can do to help you and the police in Ireland," replied Gonzalez. "I have come into possession of a letter sent from Ireland describing the murder of a man called Donal Hawke."

"How did that come about?" asked the Commissioner.

"The girlfriend of another victim in your country received a letter a few days ago. Her boyfriend Juan, was also stabbed to death in your country. You seem to have a lot of murders over there," laughed the Police Chief.

"Not usually," answered the Commissioner.

"But, you have bombs and shootings, it's always on the news," interjected Gonzalez indignantly.

"That's a different story – that's our terrorist problem, there are very few other murders."

The Commissioner knew that it was going to be virtually impossible to explain to this man, at the other end of the world, the policing complications in Ireland.

"Whatever you say," said Gonzalez. "This letter that has come into my possession is very interesting. It was posted from Ireland on the 29th December, but only arrived in Colombia less than a week ago. It must have been lost. Maria, the young woman travelled to Bogota to give it to me – she said that she wanted to make sure that it would not be lost again. She said that her boyfriend Juan wrote to her nearly every day. He was working in a beautiful hotel in the west of Ireland. He was murdered on a beach there. It was clear from the letter that he saw who killed the very rich business man. He was going to blackmail the murderer, and with the money, he was going to send for his girlfriend."

"Can you fax the letter to me?" asked the Commissioner.

"It is being translated into English, as we speak. As soon as I am happy that it is a true translation, it will be faxed to you immediately. I will also fax the original letter as well. I need the fax number where it is to be sent to."

"It would be best to send it to the officer in charge of the case, Inspector Muldoon. He is staying in the west of Ireland, in the same premises where poor Juan was murdered, and also Donal Hawke. I will fax all the details to your office."

"Certainly," said Gonzalez. "Has he nearly solved the case?"

While the Commissioner did not want to share much information with an officer from another jurisdiction, he thought he could give him a few details as he was being so helpful, and in any case, much of it was already in the papers.

"There has been a third murder, linked to the first two – a man who was an employee and a close associate of Donal Hawke. He seems to have been stabbed, also, because he came into some damning information. To top it all, there was an attempt on the life of a young woman also linked to the other murders. So, to put it mildly, Inspector Muldoon has his hands full at the moment."

"Does he think that there is only one killer or might there be more?" asked the Chief of Police.

"He is not sure, as yet. The murders of young Juan and the associate of Donal Hawke, Frank Smith are very similar – both stabbed – probably by someone that they both knew. The murder of Donal Hawke, the wealthy business man does not appear to have been well planned – more opportunistic really – hit over the head with an oar and was pushed or fell into the lake. Inspector Muldoon and his colleagues are checking alibis and keeping an open mind."

"So, that is what Juan witnessed – the murder of a businessman with an oar. When you read what he has written, I am sure that it will help your Inspector to solve all the crimes."

"I hope you are right Chief Gonzalez. You have been very helpful and very thorough. I will let you know what happens if you like."

"Oh yes, I would be very interested in the solving of this case, especially as one of the victims is Colombian," concluded Gonzalez.

The Commissioner replaced the receiver, searched for a phone number in the index cards, picked up the receiver again and dialled a Mayo number.

"Loughfarraig House Hotel, Laura speaking, how can I help you?" came the cheerful voice on the other end of the line.

"May I speak to Inspector Muldoon or Commandant de Bruin please?"

"I'm sorry Sir, but I saw them leaving the house about an hour ago. May I take a message for them?"

"Yes. A very important fax will arrive for Inspector Muldoon in a few hours. Please deliver it to them as soon as they return to the hotel. It is vital they read it as soon as possible."

"Yes, I will indeed, Sir," replied Laura, just as cheerfully.

Gerald Moore approached the reception, having heard part of the conversation.

"Who was that on the phone Laura?" asked Moore.

"He didn't actually give his name, Mr. Moore, but he sounded very serious and important,"

"What did he say?" asked Moore, slightly impatiently.

"He wanted to speak to the Inspector or the Commandant to tell them that a very important fax was going to arrive here for them. We have to tell them the minute we see them."

Gerald Moore was hoping that there was going to be a break in the case. He just wanted the whole dreadful saga to be over. Two murders at his beloved Loughfarraig House. Who would have thought such a thing. All his guests who visit here, come for the peace and tranquillity – not to be part of some horror show. He knew that the whole business was affecting his wife very badly. She was especially upset about the death of poor Juan. Mrs. Moore always looked after the staff so well. She treated them like members of the family. She had been so moved by the sadness and stoicism of Juan's father Miguel. He thought about the little prayer service that they had had at the spot on the beach where Juan's body had been found – all his wife's idea. She always knew how to behave and what to say. Suddenly he heard the beeping of the fax machine.

CHAPTER 43

AN ENGAGEMENT

"How is your shoulder this morning, Tim?" asked Emma as she kissed him on the cheek.

"It feels a lot better, thanks," replied Tim. "I may be able to remove the sling tomorrow."

She linked his other arm and cuddled into him.

"I'm so glad that we met – so very glad that Commandant de Bruin picked you as my protector," whispered Emma.

"So am I, my love," returned Tim, kissing Emma fondly on the forehead. "It seems to have been fate."

"I wish all this awfulness was over," said Emma. "Just hope no one else gets hurt."

"I know that Commandant de Bruin will get to the bottom of all this – he always does," replied Tim reassuringly.

"That was more fate or good luck – the de Bruins being on holiday where you were working when Donal Hawke was murdered."

"Yes, I'm sure that I would have been in right trouble without them. I'm not sure that someone else would have believed my story about my father falling in the lake. And if Mrs. de Bruin hadn't taken me away to her home in Briarstown, I would have been a prime suspect in Juan's murder."

"I wonder who he could have seen hitting your father over the head?" asked Tim.

"I wish he hadn't seen anything. He'd be still alive now. Sometimes I wish that I had never contacted my father. I can't help thinking that it all goes back to that."

"And maybe, it has nothing at all to do with you – anyway you're not responsible for the actions of others," stated Tim.

"If it's nothing to do with me, why did someone try to run us off the road?" whispered Emma.

"I see what you mean," agreed Tim.

The couple went downstairs to the dining room to have breakfast. All the staff believed that they were a married couple. Muldoon thought that it would be a better cover story. Nobody knew where they were, apart from Muldoon, the de Bruins and Sergeant Michael Dunne who drove them there.

"It doesn't seem to make any sense for one of the Hawkes to want to kill you," said Tim, buttering his warm toast. "Mrs. Lydia Browne made sure that they knew that they would be worse off if something happened to you. Yet, who else do you even know here in Ireland?"

"You're right, Tim. It would have been a different kettle of fish if I had died before I made my will," whispered Emma, as one of the waiters came within earshot.

"Can I get you anything else?" asked the waiter.

"No thank you. Breakfast was delicious," answered Emma.

Tim nodded his head in concurrence. The waiter cleared the plates and used cutlery from the table. The couple sat sipping their coffee for a few minutes, then left the table to return to their room.

"I really need to talk to you, Emma," said Tim in a very serious tone of voice.

"What is it?" asked Emma.

"You know that this isn't just a fling for me. I think that I fell in love with you the moment I saw you in Bray. I was hoping that you felt the same way."

Emma walked over to Tim, put her arms around his neck and kissed him gently.

"Of course I feel the same, Tim. You're the most wonderful thing that's ever happened to me. I couldn't believe it when I saw you. I've never met anyone like you."

The couple embraced tightly They held each other for a long while, Emma's head resting on his chest.

"I never want to let you go," he whispered.

That afternoon, Tim and Emma took a stroll in the grounds of their hotel. They held hands as they walked among the trees and shrubs. It was still very cold, so they wrapped up tightly in winter garb.

"We must make plans for when things get back to normal," stated Tim.

"Of course," answered Emma, "Would you like to help me to run my part of the company? I'm going to have to keep the Hawkes in check. I could do with your support."

"Of course I'll support you in any way I can, but I really want to continue my career in the army. Colonel King is putting me forward for the potential officer's course. I've always wanted to become an officer. We are an army family – it's in our blood."

"That's fantastic news, Tim. Of course you must do as you wish. You'd make a wonderful officer."

"There will be trips abroad and duties on the border. That's what being an army wife is all about."

"Is that some sort of a proposal?" laughed Emma.

Tim blushed, as the last sentence had just slipped out. This was not the way he had planned to propose.

"If you'll have me," said Tim, getting down on one knee and taking Emma's hand in his.

"Of course, I'll marry you, my love," answered Emma, tears welling up in her eyes. "I've never been so happy."

The phone rang at the Lodge in Briarstown.

"Monique de Bruin speaking."

"Mrs. de Bruin, it's Emma."

"How lovely to hear from you. I hope everything is okay. With a bit of luck, Alexander and John will solve the murders soon, and you'll be able to go home. How is Tim?"

"We are both great," answered Emma. "I have some wonderful news to tell you."

"Well, enlighten me," said Monique.

"You won't believe what's happened. Tim and I are engaged to be married. I know that you'll probably say that it's all happened too quickly – that we only know each other for a short while – that we were thrown together in very strange circumstances – that he saved my life and I might feel in his debt – that maybe my emotions are all mixed up – but none of this matters. He feels the same about me. He loves me," said Emma excitedly, without pausing for breath.

"Calm yourself, Emma, I'm not going to say any of those things. Of course, you're both in love – I saw it with my own eyes when you were in hospital. You're both very lucky to have found each other – a love like that doesn't come around very often. When it does, grab it with all your might and never let go."

"So, you don't think that we're mad. Tim was afraid that you and Commandant de Bruin mightn't approve."

"Of course, we approve. You are two wonderful young people who deserve happiness. You were meant for each other. I couldn't be more pleased for you both. I'm certain that Alexander will feel the same way when he hears the news."

"Tim is going to stay in the army. I suggested that he come to work with me, but he loves his army life, so it looks like I'll be an army wife."

"You'll love it. It's like one big supportive family. Even after retirement you feel part of it. Pass on our congratulations to Tim, and I wish you Emma, every happiness in the world."

At the hotel in Ennis, Emma replaced the receiver, took a deep breath, and waited for Tim to return to the room. He had gone for a short walk to give her some privacy to make the phone call.

Five minutes later she heard the key in the door and Tim entered the room, a look of apprehension on his face.

"Well, Emma, how did she react?" asked Tim.

"She was absolutely delighted for us. I put all the arguments that you had made to her. She just dismissed them and said that she knew we were in love – I think she knew it before we did. She sends her congratulations and is sure that Commandant de Bruin will be just as happy for us."

"That's a relief," said Tim, with a sigh. "I wasn't at all sure how they would react. I was afraid that they might think that I had taken advantage of the situation. Now, we have this wonderful future ahead of us – so much to look forward to."

"We'll be able to put this dreadful stuff behind us – start a new life to-gether. Everyone who matters to us are delighted for us. Monique said never let go of a love like ours, and that's my plan."

CHAPTER 44

THE LETTER

Muldoon and Alexander had just arrived in the door of Loughfarraig House, when they were approached by Gerald Moore, who looked as if he had been awaiting their arrival anxiously.

"Inspector Muldoon, Commandant de Bruin," he said, as he moved towards them, holding a large brown envelope.

"This fax arrived for you from Colombia. It must be something about Juan. We also received a phone call, we think from Garda Headquarters insisting that you deal with the matter urgently."

"Thank you, Mr. Moore," said Muldoon, as he took the envelope. "We'll certainly let you know if there are any developments. Could we order some coffee and scones please. We'll be in the small sitting room."

"Certainly, right away," said Gerald Moore, as he hurried in the direction of the kitchen.

Alexander and Muldoon sat at their usual table in the small sitting room. Muldoon quickly opened the envelope and removed all the pages. Muldoon read the first page to himself.

"It's from the Chief of Police in Bogota, Carlos Gonzales. He has enclosed a letter that Juan sent to his girlfriend Maria, dated 29th December. He states that it must have been lost in the post. Maria knew that it was important, so brought it to Bogota. We have the original in Spanish and the English translation. I'll read out the English version.

My beautiful Maria,

I miss you every day. I can't wait for you to come to Ireland to be with me. Christmas was so sad without you. I have very extraordinary news for you. News that means that I will be able to bring you here a lot faster. There is a very rich, powerful family staying in the hotel for Christmas. The head of the family is a man called Donal Hawke – he was a very powerful man – not a nice man. He was very rude to all of us. I was serving dinner on the 25th December. After my shift at about ten o'clock I went up to my room. I can see the lake from my bedroom window. I went to shut the curtains, but noticed two people down at the jetty. It was bright then, because there was a full moon. The powerful man, Donal Hawke was talking to one of the waitresses who is a good friend of mine, Emma. They were talking for a good while. He even hugged her. Then I saw someone else watching them from behind the bushes. I opened my window a little, so I could hear what was being said. I could only hear voices, but nothing distinctive. Suddenly the big man seemed to slip on the jetty, which is nearly always covered in slime and fell backwards into the lake. I heard a splash, Emma screamed and tried to catch him. Funny thing is she called out "Dad, are you OK?" The other person was still watching all this. Then the moon went in behind a cloud, and I could see very little for a minute or two, but I heard the big man shouting from the lake ."I'm OK, I'll get to shore. You go back into the hotel – we can't be seen together yet." The moon came back out again and I saw Emma running towards the hotel. The big man was wading out of the water a bit away from the jetty. Suddenly the other person came out from behind the bushes, picked up an oar that was lying beside the lake – drew it back and hit the big man on the head. The first time he kind of staggered in the water. Then he was hit again and fell back into the lake. The person threw the oar into the lake as well, then ran into the hotel by a side door. I watched for a while, but then the moon disappeared behind a cloud again – so I could see nothing. I froze – I didn't know what to do. I was afraid to interfere. The family is very powerful. I was a coward I suppose. The body was found the next day. There was a doctor staying here. I think he said that the blows to the head killed him – so I couldn't have helped him anyway. I thought and thought what to do. I had seen the murder. No one else had. I knew who the killer was. Then I thought to myself. Nothing will bring him back. The killer will probably give me money to keep quiet. So I wrote a note and placed it under the door, asking for £500 to be left under a plant in one of the rooms. I watched the room, and saw someone go in – very sneakily. I went in afterwards and the money was there. The funny thing is that it was someone else put the money there – so there were two people involved. Then Maria, I thought about it again – put another note under the door and asked for £2,000. This time I got a note put under my door saying that I would get the money, and no more, and they will tell me where to meet them. They must have seen me go into the room to get the money. So I'm going to get another £2,000. You'll be able to get here very quickly now. I'll have money for the tickets and get us a place to stay. You'll love it here. The police are here too, investigating, but there was a storm after the murder, so it's been difficult for them – so easy for me. I'm going to post this letter as soon as possible. When I get the money I'll write again. Everyone would be very surprised to know who murdered Donal Hawke."

Muldoon took a deep breath and looked across at Alexander who was awaiting the rest of the sentence with bated breath.

"Well, whom did he see killing Donal Hawke with the oar?" asked Alexander impatiently. Muldoon turned the pages towards his friend and pointed to the relevant words.

"There you are," he said.

"Well, Well, Well," said Alexander, "Quelle surprise!"

The two men sat back in their armchairs, holding their cups and saucers, sipping their coffee. Both gave a sigh of relief.

"It's a pity that this letter was lost in the post for so long," said Alexander. "There wouldn't have been the third murder nor the attempt on Emma's life. Of course we couldn't have saved Juan. He signed his own death warrant when he was seen retrieving the money and then asked for more. I suppose they thought that they would never get rid of him – that they would be paying him off for the rest of their lives. Poor naive, stupid Juan. What's the next move John?"

"I suppose, we'll ask the long suffering, patient, Gerald Moore if we can use his beautiful Loughfarraig House as a venue once more – to gather together everyone involved and make the arrests."

"We'll send a car to Ennis for Emma and Tim as we now know that they are no longer in danger."

CHAPTER 45

UNTANGLING
THE WEB

Gerald Moore allowed Muldoon and Alexander to use the billiard room once more to explain their findings to all the suspects and those affected by the three murders and the attempted murder.

A contingent of young gardai were put on duty around the house. Chairs were placed in semi-circles in the billiard room facing a top table where Muldoon and Alexander would sit.

Emma and Tim were the first to arrive at Loughfarraig House, having been driven the two and a half hour journey by Sergeant Michael Dunne. Alexander greeted them at the front entrance, and showed them to the billiard room. Tim was no longer wearing a sling on his arm. Emma was looking happy and radiant. The young couple were anticipating an end to this nightmare, and contemplating their future together.

Natalia arrived next, driven by her chauffeur. She alighted from the car wearing a white fur coat – no expense spared, or animals!

The next car that drove up was occupied by Jack, Ava and Winnie Hawke. Winnie was steady on her feet and was showing no signs of having consumed any alcohol. Ava was looking healthier, glowing in fact. Jack led the two ladies into the house, greeting Muldoon and Alexander curtly. Gerald Moore appeared in the foyer to show them to the assigned room.

Next, a jeep appeared on the avenue, driven by Francois. Joanne was in the passenger seat.

Francois parked the jeep in front of the house. Having jumped out of his side of the vehicle, he made his way to the passenger side to open the door for Joanne. They linked arms in a signal of affection as they strolled arrogantly past Muldoon and Alexander, just nodding as they passed.

"She's in for a hell of a surprise when she finds out who Francois actually is and what he has been up to, and with whom," whispered Muldoon.

"There are a number of shocks coming," replied Alexander.

Last, but not least, David and Emily arrived in their chauffeur driven Bentley. Emily too was clad in a long mink coat. David scowled at the two men and grunted some sort of greeting. Gerald Moore, once again, showed the two Hawkes to the billiard room.

"We'll give them a few minutes to get settled," said Muldoon, as both men looked out at the lake in front of Loughfarraig House. They could hear the ducks quacking, and they could see a pair of swans gliding gracefully across the still water.

"Time to bring this to a close," stated Muldoon.

Commandant de Bruin and Inspector Muldoon walked purposefully down the corridor until they reached the door leading into the billiard room.

As they entered, a hush descended upon the group. Muldoon and Alexander walked up to the top table, and took their seats. They noticed that Emma and Tim had taken their seats in the second row. Natalia was sitting on her own beside the window. Winnie was beside her son Jack, who had signs of jetlag following his trip from America, beside whom sat Ava, her two hands placed on her tummy.

Joanne and Francois were to the right, holding hands, sitting very closely together. David and Emily were centre stage, straight in front of Muldoon and Alexander. They looked like two people who still thought that they were in charge of the situation.

"Thank you all very much for coming here today," began John Muldoon. "As you can surmise, we have made progress in the case. We asked you all to attend because each one of you was affected by the events which began on Christmas Day. In case you are wondering why Tim McGrath is here, it was because Emma Jones wanted support from her fiance and we concluded that it was an acceptable request."

David Hawke glared in the direction of said fiance, as Tim nodded at everyone present.

"From the very beginning, this was a very complicated case. We were fortunate that Commandant de Bruin and his family were staying here with Colonel King and his family. They were able to take charge until the gardai arrived, which of course was delayed because of the storm. We were also lucky that a retired surgeon was holidaying at Loughfarraig, and could perform an initial examination of the body. As everyone knows, the gardai will always look for means, motive and opportunity. We realised very quickly that many people had motive to murder Donal Hawke. It wasn't just those present at Loughfarraig. The suspect pool was vast. Donal Hawke's business practices were underhand and dishonest. He left many victims in his wake."

Alexander and Muldoon watched the reaction of those present. Jack looked somewhat embarrassed. Ava beside him, sat stoically staring straight in front of her. Winnie fidgeted with her lace hanky, her eyes darting around the room.

David stretched his legs in front of him and crossed his arms defiantly. Emily had a look of utter disdain on her face. Francois put his arm around Joanne's shoulder as if to shield her from the words. Natalia sat as quiet as a mouse in her corner. Tim and Emma sat listening with interest.

"Quite a lot of information on these business practices were sourced from Donal Hawke himself, in the documents that he left behind. We also gleaned quite a bit from our American friend Bruce Gilbert who felt so strongly about the victims of Mustelus Developments, that he flew to Ireland with his evidence on hearing about the murder. More proof was forthcoming from our sources in England. Donal Hawke had destroyed many lives on his climb to the top – even to the point of a number of unexplained deaths. His association with gangsters in the East End produced more suspects. We had to consider a hit man, or a disgruntled gang member from his past. We even had to consider Joe Winters, the journalist, whose career he virtually destroyed because of a negative article he had written a number of years ago. He was ruled out fairly quickly. There were people in government, in councils and planners who received bribes – could any of these be a possibility? However, the murder itself did not have any of the hallmarks of a professional job. The murder weapon was not brought to the scene of the crime. It was an oar that was just at hand. If someone from his past had planned the murder, they would have brought a weapon with them – a knife, a gun, whatever. If it had been someone paid to do the job, we didn't believe that anything would be left to chance. There were so many more proficient ways of carrying out a hit, than hoping that Donal Hawke would wade out of the lake, that an oar would be conveniently lying on the shore. So, after much consideration we ruled out someone from his past seeking revenge for the wrongs that had been done to them. We also ruled out a hit, as it was not well planned, and then of course, the second murder of Juan, the waiter from Colombia, convinced us that it was someone closer to home."

Muldoon and Alexander once again examined their audience. They were glaring at each other wondering who in the room could be responsible. Emma and Tim were the most relaxed and taking the whole business in their stride.

"To continue," recommenced Muldoon, "we had to look next at the motives of all those present here. Donal Hawke's change of will gave his children a very strong motive. I know that you all deny having known about it before his death and that Jonathan Kelly, David Hawke's close friend and solicitor also denies passing on the information. However, we continue to have our suspicions about that."

The Hawke children and their wives moved restlessly in their seats, glancing at each other, looking decidedly guilty.

"None of you had a solid alibi for your father's murder except Francois Dupont, who never left the Long Room. We also ruled out Mrs. Winnie Hawke for obvious reasons.

Now we come to Emma Jones, the daughter that Donal Hawke never knew he had. They met by the lake where Mr. Hawke accidentally fell in. Emma came forward to tell us this story. Of course this was very suspicious, and most people would say unbelievable. Nevertheless, she was given the benefit of the doubt, and ruled out when Juan was murdered, as she wasn't anywhere near Loughfarraig when that occurred. Natalia Hawke claimed to have gone to bed early on the night of Donal Hawke's murder but there was no one to corroborate this.

The first murder, we believe was opportunistic – the murderer saw what had happened on the jetty and took advantage of the situation. They went down to the shore, saw the oar and hit Donal Hawke twice over the head. Unfortunately for them, they were seen by Juan from his window. Poor Juan was in need of money, so decided to blackmail the culprit. Of course this put him in immense danger. He made the mistake of asking for money twice. The murderer knew that they might never be rid of him. Juan met with his killer on the beach where he was stabbed to death. We immediately suspected blackmail as there was a piece of a £50 note found in his hand, and another note found in the crevice of a rock. The only person with a solid alibi for this murder was Natalia, as she was in hospital.

Frank Smith, the third victim was also stabbed – this time in his home in Galway. Everyone knew that Frank Smith was Donal Hawke's long time friend and "fixer". Smith informed us that Mr. Hawke had asked him to follow a member of the family. Even after his friend's death, he decided to complete his assignment. Commandant de Bruin and I had an appointment with him on the day of his murder. Whoever killed him had seen him following them and had acted, stabbing Frank Smith and stealing the evidence from his home. During the forensic examination of Smith's home, a key to some sort of locker or safe was found. Both Commandant de Bruin and I believed that a man like Frank Smith would keep copies of everything. So, we went in search of the safe or locker. As you recall, an appeal went out nationwide, asking for any witness who had seen Smith in the last six months. Two very important witnesses came forward."

The whole group was now very attentive, waiting for the next revelation. David Hawke was sitting forward in his chair, in anticipation. Natalia was sitting in the corner, wide eyed. Winnie had a frown on her face, obviously wishing that Muldoon would hurry up with the story.

"Get on with it man," said David impatiently.

"Oh, for heaven's sake, keep quiet, David," interjected Winnie.

David glared at his mother, but did as she had asked, and sat back into his chair.

"Once again, nobody had a solid alibi for the time of Frank Smith's murder. Joanne claimed that Francois was in France visiting a sick aunt. We checked out this alibi."

Francois suddenly became very white in the face. He looked shocked – his whole body tensed. Joanne could feel it and looked at him in confusion.

"It turns out," continued Muldoon, "that Francois does not have a sick aunt. He is estranged from his family. He has a police record and is known for duping wealthy women out of their money. It would appear that he was not in France at the time of Smith's murder."

Joanne stood up, pushed Francois away and shouted, "What's he talking about? Are you some sort of con artist? What about your business trips to Limerick? Did you make a complete fool of me?"

Joanne was staring down at Francois, who was sitting very still in his chair, staring at the floor.

"Answer me you shit," shouted Joanne in fury.

Francois remained silent.

"Please take a seat Ms. Hawke," said Alexander. "Unfortunately, there's more bad news to come."

Winnie Hawke stood up, went over to her daughter, took her by the arm and led her to a seat beside hers. They both sat down and looked up towards the top table.

"There are no business acquaintances in Limerick," continued Muldoon.

Everyone was staring at Francois who looked completely dejected. He looked as if he were about to get up and make a run for it.

"If you're thinking of leaving, there's nowhere for you to go. We have officers at every exit," stated Muldoon.

"But he couldn't have killed our father," said Jack Hawke. "As you said, he's the only one of us with an alibi."

"You're right," said Muldoon. "He didn't kill Donal Hawke."

Everyone looked up at Muldoon in bewilderment.

"So, who the hell did?" demanded Emily.

"Let him finish," said Winnie sharply.

"One of the witnesses who came forward regarding Frank Smith was a hotel owner in Limerick who had seen him several times on his premises. He also stated that a couple were staying at his hotel, each time that Smith was there. The description that he gave us of the male was very close to Francois' description. The female was harder to describe as she wore sunglasses and a scarf. It could have been any of you ladies."

"Well it wasn't me," said Joanne angrily.

"The second witness who came forward was the parish priest who had received substantial donations from Frank Smith towards his church renovations. Unbeknownst to the Father, Smith had installed a secret area behind the sacristy, where he hid quite an array of interesting objects and files including a dossier on the person whom he had been following on behalf of Donal Hawke. We asked ourselves why on earth would Frank Smith be employed to follow Francois Dupont? It made absolutely no sense. If he were being unfaithful to Joanne, why would it bother Donal Hawke – he disapproved of Joanne's boyfriends in any case. So, Commandant de Bruin and I wondered was it the woman that Smith was surveilling? Did Mr. Hawke suspect that one of his daughters-in-law was having an affair? When we read the dossier, it became apparent that Donal Hawke suspected his wife Natalia of being unfaithful."

There were several gasps from the group and everyone stared at Natalia, who looked like a rabbit caught in the headlights.

"But, I was in hospital when the waiter was killed," she shrieked.

"Yes, you were," agreed Muldoon. "You didn't kill Juan or Smith."

"But you said that all the murders were linked," snarled David.

"Yes, I did. But I didn't say that there was only one murderer," said Muldoon.

"Unfortunately, Juan had seen everything," said Alexander. "He decided to blackmail the murderer. He also wrote everything down in a letter to his girlfriend Maria, in Colombia. The letter got lost in the post and has only recently come to light. He described what happened at the lake. He told her who the killer was and also told her about his blackmail plans and who else was involved. In other words he had inadvertently named the second killer before his own death."

Everyone in the room went completely silent. Then Natalia began to sob. Francois rose from his chair, went over to her, sat beside her and put his arm around her. She laid her head on his shoulder.

"We fell in love," whispered Francois. "After all my years of not caring for any woman – just using them, Joanne introduced us and that was that. I've never loved anyone before. But we had no money of our own. Donal Hawke wouldn't give her a penny if she left him. If she was unfaithful, he'd leave her penniless as well. So, she was stuck with him – unless he died. Then she'd inherit a small fortune. We used to meet up in the hotel in Limerick. I'd tell Joanne that I had to meet my business partner or that I had to go to France."

"So, who killed our father?" asked Jack.

"I did," whispered Natalia. "It wasn't planned. I did go to my room early. I was fed up with you all. I thought Francois might meet me. I looked out my window and saw Donal with the waitress. I didn't know who she was. I was hoping he was having an affair, so I went down to watch and listen. I saw him fall into the lake. I was going over to confront him when I saw the oar. When he was getting out of the water I hit him twice. He fell back into the lake and that was that. I thought that no one had seen me. No one came forward. Everyone seemed to accept that I had gone to bed early."

"Then the note appeared under your door, demanding money," said Alexander.

"Yes," said Francois. "We decided to pay up but then he asked for more. So we knew that we would be paying him off forever."

"So you decided to kill him," stated Muldoon.

Francois nodded his head and stared at the floor.

"You then concocted an elaborate ruse," added Alexander. "Natalia pretended to be violently ill, so that she would be taken to hospital. You, Francois, had an airtight alibi for Donal Hawke's murder and Natalia would have an airtight alibi for Juan's murder."

Natalia began to weep, uncontrollably. Francois tightened his grip on her shoulder. The rest of the group were looking over at them in disbelief.

"That's why you were so upset when you heard that Donal was terminally ill," said Winnie, directing her comment towards Natalia. "I couldn't understand why that news had caused such a reaction. You realised that you needn't have killed him. He would have been dead in six months and you would have been free to do whatever you fancied. You would have inherited all that money."

There was distain in her voice, but also a hint of amusement. The older wife abandoned for the younger model – who murders the husband. Now the younger model is going to spend the rest of her life in jail. That was rather satisfying.

"How did you manage to kill Frank Smith – he was always very careful of whom he let into his flat?" asked Winnie.

"We had to kill him," said Francois coldly. "He had seen us together. If he passed the information on to you, Inspector Muldoon, you might have put two and two together. I telephoned his house. I found his details in Joanne's notepad. I asked to see him to discuss our predicament. He agreed, but I knew by his tone of voice that he was only playing games with me. I told him that I would pay him a lot to hand over the photos and documents to us. That was when I told Joanne that I had to go to France to visit my sick aunt. When I arrived at his flat, he showed me the photos and dossier with all the times and dates. I asked him if it was the only copy. Of course he said that it was. He was very arrogant. I knew that he wouldn't give them to me, so I stabbed him and took the evidence. I checked the whole place before I left. I thought I had the only copies."

"He must have become careless, in his old age," muttered David. "To be caught following you and then to let you into his flat wasn't a bit like him."

"You're correct," said Alexander. "Frank Smith had no intention of handing anything over to you Francois. He had an appointment with us on the day of his death. He intended to give us the files. Smith was probably just toying with you as you suspected. After all, you and Natalia had betrayed his best friend to whom he was completely loyal. He realised himself that he had been careless, that he wasn't as alert as in the past. It is baffling, however, that he allowed you to get close enough to stab him. I suppose we'll never know his thought process on this. Of course he also knew that we would eventually find his cache, hidden behind the sacristy of the parish church."

"Why did you try to kill me?" asked Emma suddenly.

"I knew that the police suspected that one of the Hawkes had killed Donal Hawke. They were looking very closely at them. They thought it was because of the will change. The police knew that they hated Emma Jones. I wanted the police to think that one of the Hawkes tried to kill Ms. Jones to get rid of her. I wanted to keep their attention away from Natalia and me. We had no motive to harm Ms. Jones but the Hawke children had."

"So you tried to kill Emma as a diversionary tactic," said Tim, angrily. "Have you no conscience?"

"What you didn't know," said Joanne with venom, "is that we no longer had a motive to harm her. If anything happens to Emma Jones, all the Hawke family will be worse off because of her new will."

"Nothing really worked out for you? Did it?" said Emily with a sneer. "You, Natalia, kill Donal Hawke when there's no need to, as he was going to be dead in six months anyway. You're seen by Juan who blackmails you. Francois kills him to silence him, but it's too late – he's already written the whole story in a letter to his girlfriend, which finally turns up in the post. My father in law has had Natalia followed because he suspects her of adultery. Francois kills Smith to get the evidence, but there's another copy which is found by Inspector Muldoon and Commandant de Bruin. It couldn't really have worked out worse for you two."

Both Francois and Natalia were glaring at Emily. They realised that everything that she had said was true. Francois put his hand into his breast pocket and removed a small item. He whispered into Natalia's ear. She looked up into his eyes. Francois placed something into his mouth, then kissed her.

Alexander de Bruin jumped up suddenly from his chair and ran towards the couple. When he realised what was happening, it was too late. Both Francois and Natalia had bitten down on the cyanide pills. When he reached them the effects were already in evidence. They both were writhing in pain, but holding onto each other. Within a couple of minutes they were dead.

Inspector Muldoon and Alexander stood over the bodies in shock. They had not expected this to happen. Emma Jones was crying, holding on to Tim for dear life. Jack led Ava out of the room as she was feeling ill. Everyone else looked over at the bodies of Natalia and Francois in disbelief.

"You can all leave the room," instructed John Muldoon. "We'll speak to you all later."

They all filed out of the room, leaving Muldoon and Alexander in situ.

"What the bloody hell happened?" asked Muldoon.

"Cyanide," answered Alexander. "He had the pills in his pocket. They must have planned this if they were caught. She took the pill, willingly from his mouth. I saw what was happening too late."

"Where could he have gotten the pills?" asked Muldoon, astounded by what he had just witnessed.

"God only knows," replied Alexander. "I doubt we will ever find out."

"This wasn't in the script, today," insisted Muldoon. "We were just meant to reveal the murderers. They were to be arrested, taken away and charged. How could this have happened?"

"No one could have foreseen this scenario, John. We weren't looking on them as Romeo and Juliet. This didn't fit their characters at all. What a dreadful end! – what a tragedy!"

Later that afternoon, Alexander rang his wife to tell her about the happenings of the day.

"Everything had fallen into place, Monique. The case was solved. We just had to make the arrests."

"I believe everyone underestimated the love and passion that they felt for each other," said Monique.

"No one could believe what they were witnessing," said Alexander.

"How is Emma?" asked Monique.

"She's in total shock. Tim is looking after her. It was all even too much for the Hawkes. Joanne, of course took it badly. She believed that Francois cared for her and that they had a future together. Instead she finds out that he is deeply, madly, passionately in love with Natalia. So much so, that he was willing to commit two murders and cause harm to Emma for no other reason than to throw suspicion back onto the Hawkes and away from him and Natalia."

"It's all a tragedy, Alexander, but one of their own making. There are innocent people who were very badly affected by their actions. Juan is dead and his family and fiancee will never recover. We must not loose sight of that. Natalia and Francois may have had a great love, but it caused such heartache. There are people dead because of it."

"I know you're right, Monique. It was like a Shakespearian tragedy. Muldoon thinks that we should have seen it coming. He's feeling very guilty."

"That's nonsense, and you know it. He's just in shock. This isn't something you would expect to happen nowadays. How could any of you have thought of cyanide pills – where would you get them?"

"That, we don't know," replied Alexander.

Gerald Moore and his wife awaited the arrival of the ambulance to remove the bodies from his billiard room. He was as white as a sheet and regretting ever having agreed to Inspector Muldoon's and Commandant de Bruin's request to conduct their meeting with all the suspects at his beloved Loughfarraig House. He had spent an hour trying to calm down the Hawkes, serving them tea and scones or something stronger, depending on the requests. Winnie Hawke ordered a large gin and tonic. She had temporarily dispensed with sobriety. Ava Hawke had been extremely ill in the ladies, overwhelmed by the sight of the death of Natalia and Francois. Her husband Jack was hoping that the shock would not affect the pregnancy.

The staff were very much on edge. There was talk of a curse amongst the more superstitious. Mrs. Moore spoke to them calmly, reassuring them that all would be well. She was also trying to convince herself that all would be well. She rued the day that she had ever laid eyes on the Hawke family. They had brought nothing but death and sorrow to her door.

That evening Muldoon and Alexander sat in the foyer, staring at the dancing flames of the turf fire. The two bodies had been removed discreetly, carried out the back door of the old house on stretchers by the paramedics and transported to Galway General Hospital. There would be a post mortem but everyone knew the cause of death. The Hawkes had left Loughfarraig as soon as permission had been granted, each returning to their own country residences in Mayo. Alexander noticed that they had lost some of their arrogance temporarily. Soon to return, he surmised. Tim and Emma had decided to have supper in their room. They yearned for some peace. So that only left Muldoon and Alexander to mull over the shocking events of the day. They had little appetite, so only ordered sandwiches and tea followed by large brandies, which they were now sipping in front of the fire. Alexander added two sods of turf. The flames jumped and sparkled. The turf smoke filled the air with an earthy aroma.

"How are you feeling, John?" asked Alexander as he swirled the brandy in the glass, cupped in his hand.

"Recovering," answered John Muldoon. "How about you?"

"It's been a dreadful day. I've never seen a death like that before. But we'll get there. Have you spoken to Garda Headquarters yet?"

"Yes, I had a brief conversation with the Commissioner. He was quite taken aback by the news, but lays no blame at our feet. He actually said that no one could have foreseen this."

"I've come to the conclusion that he's right. We had two people who were completely selfish all their lives – showed little empathy towards others. Natalia had married Donal Hawke for his money. Francois had used wealthy women to get what he wanted in life. They meet each other, fall madly in love – so much so that they decided to die rather than to be separated."

"If they had known that Donal Hawke was terminally ill, this would never have happened," said Muldoon.

"I presume that they had planned to kill him but that Natalia took advantage of the situation at the lake – that wasn't thought out."

"She was caught in a web and her only escape was to kill her husband," added Alexander.

"There were a lot of people caught in Hawke's web. He started spinning it years ago. Having killed the spider, Natalia started spinning her own web. Where did one end and the next begin?"

"I'm too tired for your philosophising," interrupted Muldoon with a wry smile.

"She could have just left him and run off with Francois."

"Yes, she could, but neither of them could live without money. They were used to the high life. Poverty wouldn't have suited them. We are now looking at their deaths as if it were a great tragedy but they were evil. They caused nothing but heartache."

Muldoon and Alexander sipped their drinks, and sat silently in the warmth of the glowing embers.

CHAPTER 46

PROTEUS

A year later there was a wedding reception at Loughfarraig House. The cobwebs of the past had been cleared away. Gerald Moore and his wife were attending to the needs of the wedding guests with great enthusiasm. The young married couple were glowing with happiness. The beautiful young bride was clad in a long lace wedding dress and wore a headpiece made of fresh flowers. The handsome groom wore his army dress uniform. There were other army uniforms in the crowd. The ladies were attired in their finest dresses, with hats of all colours on their heads. Laughter and clinking glasses echoed around the old house.

In front of the building, the lake shimmered under the rays of the sun. The ducks and swans floated on the water. Flowers were blooming in the gardens and the hedges were lush with new growth. In the distance the waves ebbed and flowed. The seagulls squawked and squealed diving into the water to catch their lunch. The shadows of the mountains were reflected in the greens and blues of the Atlantic Ocean.

Alexander and Monique stood on the seashore, holding hands looking out at the beautiful expanse of the water. The waves in the distance crashed against the jutting rocks sending white foam floating into the air.

As Alexander watched the sea constantly changing shape, making objects look different, the rocks seeming to sink as the waves appeared, he thought of Porteus, the shapeshifting Greek God, known as the old man of the sea with his powers to know all things, past, present and future.

Printed in Dunstable, United Kingdom